CAT IN THE LIMELIGHT

ALSO BY LOUISE CLARK

The Nine Lives Cozy Mystery Series

The Cat Came Back

The Cat's Paw

Cat Got Your Tongue

Let Sleeping Cats Lie

Cat Among The Fishes

Cat in the Limelight

Fleece the Cat

Forward in Time Series

Make Time For Love

Discover Time For Love

Hearts of Rebellion Series

Pretender's Game

Lover's Knot

Dangerous Desires

CAT IN THE LIMELIGHT

THE 9 LIVES COZY MYSTERY SERIES, BOOK SIX

LOUISE CLARK

ePublishingWorks!
love what you read.

CHAPTER 1

The fundraising gala in support of Point Grey College's At Risk Students Program was a sold-out success, the kind of event Vancouver's well-heeled liked to support. The dress was formal, the men in tuxes, the women in elegant gowns designed to proclaim status and position. The location was the stately McLagan House, built at the turn of the twentieth century in the desirable Shaughnessy district. The cause was worthy. The combination was unbeatable.

The pre-dinner meet and greet took place on the broad terrace that extended the mansion's full width and overlooked the extensive gardens. During the hour-long event, the terrace had been a tapestry of silk and lace. The vivid kaleidoscope of colors created an ever-changing design as participants shifted from group to group. Now all those guests were gathered around tables in the wood-paneled dining room, their attention focused on the college president as he spoke about his institution, the At Risk program, and the donors who made it possible.

Tall, good-looking, and dynamic, Craig Harding was currently thanking Christy Jamieson for arranging to have the Jamieson Foundation become a sponsor of the program. His enthusiasm was, to Christy's mind, over the top, and had her blushing with every praise-filled word. She hoped no one was noticing her embarrassment. She still wasn't used to being the face of the Jamiesons and at this fundraising gala she was very much on the job.

She had support, of course. Quinn Armstrong, her date for the evening, and the man she was falling in love with, was sitting beside her. At the next table were Ellen Jamieson, her aunt by marriage and current housemate, and Trevor McCullagh the third, Ellen's date for the evening. Roy Armstrong, renowned author and Quinn's free-spirit father, was also nearby, along with Rob McCullagh, better known as Sledge, the lead singer in the superstar band SledgeHammer. All of them had helped her through the schmooze and networking hour that preceded the dinner and would be there for her during the entertainment portion of the evening, after the dinner was over and the speeches wound up.

"The involvement of the Jamieson Foundation will ensure Point Grey College's At Risk Program can grow and benefit more young people trying to escape the hopelessness of life on the street." Craig Harding paused, scanned his audience for a moment, then smiled. "So please join me in thanking the Jamieson Foundation, and Christy Jamieson in particular, and to welcome them to the PGC family."

Enthusiastic clapping followed Harding's request and as Christy smiled acknowledgment she hoped she didn't look as uncomfortable as she felt. When the applause died down Karen Beaumont, seated on Christy's other side, tapped her on the wrist. She was the dean of the School of Entertainment Arts and the At Risk Program was part of her responsibilities. Unlike Christy, who was wearing a pretty, feminine gown in a quiet forest green with a bodice of figured lace and a flowing skirt, Beaumont was dressed in black, her gown a statement meant to make her stand out. It was floor-length, with a faux tuxedo bodice and a sassy satin sash knotted at her waist, the long ends falling almost to her knees. The deep V-neck was enhanced with traditional satin lapels, but she wasn't wearing a shirt underneath. The effect of the outfit was bold, commanding, a woman in control. From what Christy knew of Karen Beaumont, it suited her perfectly.

She had dominated conversation throughout dinner, talking about the School of Entertainment Arts and the talented students who graduated from the many courses. Mostly, though, she talked about the At Risk Program itself, because she'd been instrumental in its creation and implementation.

Christy didn't mind. She liked Karen's enthusiasm. Now the woman leaned close and whispered, "We must get together next week to discuss our expansion plans. I think you'll be pleased."

Since Harding had begun speaking again, Christy could only nod as she focused in on what he was saying.

"Tonight, you'll be treated to performances by our At Risk students. The first will be a scene from a new play written by a student in Creative Writing and performed by our Theater Arts students. Three years ago, Greta Amyotte, the young woman in the lead roll, was living on the streets. In April, she graduated from the Department of Theater Arts with a 3.7 GPA. In July, she auditioned for a part in a new television series being filmed at Burnaby Studios. She won that part and today she has a recurring role in the series and has been asked to audition for a part in a new movie, also being shot here in Vancouver."

While he was speaking, wait staff circled the room. As they placed Champagne flutes in front of every guest, Christy reflected that Greta Amyotte's story was the main reason she'd fast-tracked PGC's application. The result was the announcement of the Jamieson Foundation grant at the college's annual fundraising gala tonight.

"In a few minutes I'll ask all of you to move into the drawing room of this fine building to watch her performance," Harding said. "But first I want to celebrate another student, this time in the Musical

Theater program. Like Greta, Korby Usher was a troubled youth when he came to us. Now he is excelling at his studies, as you will see later this evening when we are treated to a scene from *West Side Story*. To round off the evening, we'll be entertained by Lightening Rod, a rock band made up of five of our most talented students. The lead singer, Anton Gormley, is another of our At Risk success stories."

A series of pops indicated Champagne bottles being opened and the wait staff wove through the tables, pouring the frothy beverage into the glasses.

When everyone had been served, Harding lifted his glass. "Before we proceed to the drawing room of this very beautiful old house to witness Greta's performance, I want to propose a toast to our students, and to their continued success."

Karen Beaumont immediately stood. She raised her glass and shouted, "Bravo!"

Christy shot a quick glance at Quinn, who returned it with an amused raise of his brow. They both stood, following Beaumont's lead, and raised their glasses, though neither shouted bravo as the dean had.

Around them, the occupants of the round dinner tables rose to their feet, some with enthusiasm, others simply because the majority were doing it. At the table to Christy's left she saw Ellen and Trevor standing with glasses raised. Ellen's expression said she thought all of this was beyond the bounds of good taste, but she was resigned to the imposition. Christy suspected she was standing because Christy had committed the Jamieson Foundation to sponsor the At Risk program, and she would do whatever was necessary to support Christy's first foray in public as the face of the Jamiesons.

With the audience still on their feet, the bravo cheers dying off, Harding said, "And now I invite you to join me in the drawing room for the first of tonight's performances." He smiled broadly and raised his arm in a sweeping gesture. Stepping away from the podium, he made his way through the tables, stopping to greet supporters as he went.

Already on their feet, the guests began to slowly navigate through the crowded tables. The rooms in the McLagan House were large and designed for entertaining. Spacious though it was, the dining room was packed with enough round tables to seat the nearly two hundred and fifty guests, so the space between them was narrow, making the exodus slow and leisurely.

Christy had a craven desire to slip through one of the French doors that led out to the terrace and wait out the crush. She was about to suggest the idea to Quinn when she was foiled by Karen Beaumont, who beamed at her.

"You will enjoy this play, Mrs. Jamieson. Greta is so incredibly talented. She's been rehearsing for this performance in whatever spare time she has from filming, because she knows how important tonight is for our continued success with the At Risk program."

"I look forward to it," Christy said, giving up on the idea of escape with a little internal sigh. Back on track, she smiled at Beaumont. Her smile was warm and quite genuine. After much soul searching, she'd concluded that the only way she would be able to cope with networking events like this one was if she immersed herself into the moment and truly believed in the value of what she was doing.

Beaumont nodded and appeared about to say something more, but she was caught by another guest and with an apologetic smile, paused to speak to her.

At the door to the room, Roy and Sledge caught up to them. At the meet and greet Sledge had been his usual relaxed affable self, but how his expression was uncharacteristically grim.

"What's up?" Quinn asked, by way of greeting.

"Sledge isn't happy," Roy said.

"No, I'm not." Sledge glowered at no one in particular.

Roy grinned. "The guy who runs the music department was giving him singing tips all through dinner."

Quinn cocked an eyebrow. "That must have been fun."

Sledge grunted.

Roy's grin turned wicked. "Apparently, with a few voice lessons—which the guy would be happy to supply!—Sledge has the potential to become a real star."

"A real star, eh?" Quinn said, his expression deadpan. "An opportunity you don't want to miss."

Sledge glared at him. "The guy's a complete idiot. He actually said SledgeHammer should lighten up, that we'd maxed out the hard rock audience and we needed to find a way to make ourselves more accessible to soft rock fans." He lifted his hands. "I ask you, who says things like that?"

"Samuel Moore, the third," Roy said. "He's from an old Vancouver family that has a huge fortune and not a lot of tact. When Sledge was pointedly ignoring him and schmoozing with Tamara, who was seated at the next table, Moore told me all about himself and the operatic career he could have had but didn't."

Tamara was Dr. Tamara Ahern, well known to Christy and not one of her favorite people, but Tamara and Sledge were friends, so it must have been a relief for him to have someone to turn to as he sought to escape Samuel Moore.

Quinn looked interested. "Why would family money stop him from pursuing a career in opera?"

Roy waggled his eyebrows in a mocking way. "Apparently, being an opera star conflicts with a family belief that their duty is to serve others, not to put themselves first, exactly what Moore would have to do to succeed in the opera world."

"That's a cover up. The truth is, he didn't have the chops to make the grade in the business." Sledge's voice was low and rough, the way it was when he sang during SledgeHammer's gritty, raw performances.

"Not for him long nights at seedy bars until you're offered the opportunity to go on tour as the front men for a second-rate band. Or releasing records no one buys, until one song hits it big and suddenly you're the one with the tour across North America and it's your name that has to sell the tickets and if you fail, that's it, no more career." He stopped, looked down at his hand, which had clenched into a fist, and drew a deep steadying breath.

When he looked up, he was once more Sledge of SledgeHammer, rock star, laid back and at ease in any situation. He smiled rather ruefully. "Sorry about that. The guy ticked me off with all his 'wanna be' talk."

"Definitely a pompous ass," Roy said cheerfully.

They wandered through the doorway into the foyer that divided the building into two halves. Across the wide hall, the door to the drawing room was already open and a steady stream of guests was flowing inside. Trevor, near the drawing room door and looking very dapper in his tux, caught sight of them and raised a hand. When they met up with each other, he said to Christy, "Ellen is inside, finding us seats. We thought you'd like to sit together as a group."

Since their seat placement at dinner had been arranged by the organizers of tonight's event, Christy smiled gratefully at him. "Thank you, Trevor, yes I would." She looked at the others. "Shall we go in?"

CHAPTER 2

After the theater production ended there was a moment of silence while the audience absorbed the performances, then applause, growing in enthusiasm, erupted. From her seat near the front of the stage, Karen Beaumont jumped to her feet and shouted, "Bravo," just as she had earlier. And, as earlier, polite members of the audience—or perhaps members of the PGC faculty and staff—stood as well. Gradually, the rest of the audience did too.

Christy thought Greta Amyotte's performance had done a great deal to make a lackluster piece of writing interesting, so she clapped and rose with the others. She didn't think it was worth a bravo, however.

Nor did Ellen, who was in the seat beside hers. "She actually is quite talented," she said into Christy's ear.

Christy nodded and thought with some amusement that from her expression, Ellen hadn't believed the pre-theater hype.

The clapping died down and Karen Beaumont mounted the stage to thank the students and to remind the audience to cross the foyer to the dining room, which had been reset for the musical theater production. There would be a short fifteen-minute interval between the two performances.

The audience began to shuffle from their seats into the aisles to exit. Seated in the middle of a row, Christy and the others waited for the congestion to clear. "So you enjoyed the play?" she asked.

Ellen raised her brows. "I didn't say that. The play was silly. That the actress was able to make it seem avant-garde is a testimony to her ability."

"The students put a lot of effort into the production," Trevor said mildly, from Ellen's other side.

She turned to him, nodding. "Yes, they did. Which was why I clapped. However—" She paused, her gaze on Karen Beaumont who was working her way through the crowd, the young actress in tow, introducing her to various movers and shakers in the audience. "I do think Ms. Beaumont's 'bravo' was more to do with enthusiasm than critical assessment."

"It's a good thing Beaumont is on the other side of the room," Quinn said in Christy's ear. "I have the impression she's the kind of woman who would take exception to a comment like that."

Christy choked back a giggle. "You're right about that. She doesn't strike me as the shy and retiring type." Then she did laugh. "I think Ellen is right. Ms. Beaumont is a cheerleader for her students."

The crowd had thinned, so they made their way from their seats to the foyer. Across the hall, the doors to the dining room were still closed. Gathered in the foyer, the crowd was closely packed together. People were chatting, moving between groups, while some climbed the grand staircase to the half-landing where there was a bench, and a few even spilled out the front door, which was open to the evening.

The buzz of conversation was loud in the confined space. Like the pre-dinner cocktail party, people were networking, only this time most of the conversation was on the entertainment they'd just seen. Ellen and Trevor stopped to talk to one of the partners in Trevor's law firm, while Sledge acquired a knot of fans that anchored him to a spot not far from the doors to the room they'd just exited. Roy spotted someone he knew, while Quinn and Christy were captured by Craig Harding, whose enthusiasm for the student production mirrored Karen Beaumont's.

"Hell," Quinn said, as Harding moved away. "Dad's been button-holed by Jackson Hargreaves."

"Who is Jackson Hargreaves?" Christy asked, looking in the direction Quinn was.

"He's a writer. His first book was a blockbuster and won the Booker Prize. Dad's known him for years. They're rivals—well, I'm not sure Dad sees him as a rival, but Jackson likes to take potshots at Dad because he publishes regularly. Jackson is one of those broody authors who spends years writing a book. He's never quite come out and said it, but he likes to hint that Dad's a commercial sellout. I'd better go rescue him before the idiot ruins Dad's evening."

Christy laughed and squeezed his hand. "Yes, go. The man sounds quite dreadful." Quinn nodded, and went on his way. Now on her own, Christy decided she'd head closer to the dining room doors so she could grab a block of seats when they opened.

The crowd shifted, providing Christy with a view across the foyer. She saw that Sledge was still on the far side, but his little group of fans had disappeared and he was talking to a dark-haired man who was waving a finger at him. As she watched, Sledge pivoted, turning his back on the man who still appeared to be talking. He strode over to the stairs that led down to the ballroom on the lower level without a backward look.

She was still wondering what that was all about, when the doors to the dining room opened. The crowd flowed into the room and the seats began to fill rapidly.

Christy searched for Quinn and found he'd reached his father and that they were standing at the base of the grand staircase with Jackson

Hargreaves and a woman who must be Mrs. Hargreaves. Hargreaves was clearly talking, gesturing with his hands, while the woman looked on, her expression bored. Roy's features were set in a careful, impassive mask, unusual for him. As she watched, Quinn smiled at the Hargreaves and said something that had Roy brightening. They moved away, back toward Christy. The two Armstrongs reconnected with Christy moments later and together they headed into the dinning room where Ellen and Trevor joined them.

After finding a group of seats, Trevor asked, "Anybody seen Sledge?"

Roy grunted. "Samuel Moore nabbed him while I was talking to Jackson Hargreaves. I heard him say something special, which Sledge was sure to like, would happen later in the evening. Then Jackson started to whine about his latest creation and I lost track of Sledge."

"Samuel Moore?" Ellen asked. She was frowning.

Roy turned to her with raised brows. "Yes. He's the chair of music at PGC, apparently. Do you know him?"

Ellen nodded, slowly. Her gaze slid to Christy then away. "I think so, yes. I know the family. Gerry Fisher was a great friend of the young man's father. The Moores wield a lot influence in the mining industry in the province."

Christy wondered about the careful way Ellen described the Jamieson family's relationship with Samuel Moore. She thought it was a topic she would have to delve deeper into, but not right now. "I saw Sledge go downstairs a few minutes ago. He appeared to be angered by whatever this Moore fellow was saying."

"No need to worry about Sledge," Trevor said. "The boy can take care of himself."

The lights dimmed and there was no time for more. Christy focused on the stage and frowned as she saw that one of the cast members was Samuel Moore, the professor who'd been causing Sledge so much grief.

"What's going on?" Ellen whispered to no one in particular. "I thought this was a student-focused production?"

Moore began to sing, obviously taking the lead roll. His voice was powerful, clearly professionally trained. He was good, Christy thought, but he was a professor at the college. He should be.

As their seats were toward the back of the room, she could observe most of the audience. She noticed Karen Beaumont off to one side, not far from one of the French doors that led out to the terrace. She was sitting straight and tense in her chair, as was Craig Harding, who was in the front row. Did that indicate they were upset, unaware that Moore would be performing?

The At Risk student who was the female lead was singing flawlessly, her soprano voice a fine counterpart to Moore's baritone. The performance was excellent and when it was over the applause was thunderous. The cast bowed and Moore brought his leading lady forward, gesturing toward her with a bow of his own, then he stepped back, leaving her center stage to receive the accolades.

It was an elegant gesture and the audience stood. Christy heard a few shouted *bravos* and wondered if one of them came from the enthusiastic Karen Beaumont.

With the performance over, Quinn suggested they head down to the ballroom to grab a drink and find a table before Lightening Rod, the live band that would provide entertainment for the remainder of the evening, started their performance. Christy nodded and linked her arm with his. He looked down at her, smiling, and missed seeing Tamara waving at him from the other side of the room.

Emerging from the dining room, Christy noticed Karen Beaumont and Samuel Moore huddled together at the end of the foyer, near the wide front door. Karen's back was toward her, but she saw that the dean had her head tilted back as she looked up at the much taller Moore. He was smiling, indicating that whatever Beaumont was saying, Moore liked it. Probably praising his superb voice, Christy thought, as she and Quinn turned toward the stairs that led down to the lower level.

The staircase opened into to a wide area furnished with big leather couches and assorted chairs, where people could lounge. A doorway on the left led into a large room where drinks were being sold. It was attractively decorated with small round tables for intimate conversation and a long walnut bar, complete with a mirror behind and shelves holding various bottles of liquor.

To the right of the staircase was a short hallway that led to the washrooms. The ballroom itself was accessed from the lounge area, through wide interior French doors. As there was already a line up at the bar, Christy and Quinn decided to find a table in the ballroom and get settled before organizing refreshments. As they passed through the French doors into the room, she saw the ballroom ran the entire width of the building. Tables were arranged at either end, with the stage and dance floor in the middle.

Quinn nudged Christy and pointed. "I think we've found Sledge."

She followed his finger and saw that Sledge was on the small stage with the band. He was holding a guitar and playing a song Christy didn't recognize, but from the expressions of delight on the young band members' faces, they did and they were having a great time jamming with their idol.

She chuckled. "We should have guessed this was where he'd slip off to."

The master of ceremonies for the night, a smiling, round-faced man who was one of the PGC professors, bustled in to check in with the band and make sure they were ready for their performance. Sledge put down his guitar, wished them the best, and came over to join Quinn and Christy at the table they'd found not far from the dance floor.

The ballroom filled. Quinn and Sledge went off to get drinks. When they returned, Quinn had wine for Christy and Scotch for himself, while Sledge carried a beer. Trevor and Ellen found them and sat at the table. A few minutes later, Christy caught sight of Roy. He was chatting with Tamara Ahern. Also with them was Olivia Waters, a computer security guru and Tamara's birth mother. To Christy's chagrin, when Roy joined them at their table, Olivia and Tamara did too. Sledge moved to slip into a seat beside Tamara, leaving Quinn between Christy and Ellen, to Christy's relief.

As Craig Harding had promised earlier in the evening, the band was good. Christy enjoyed herself immensely, dancing every number with one or other of the men.

The band had been on for almost forty-five minutes when Anton Gormley, the lead singer, announced, "For our last few numbers we're going to celebrate one of Canada's greatest bands, SledgeHammer!"

Sledge, sitting relaxed in his seat, lifted his eyebrows and raised his glass in acknowledgement. Gormley immediately launched into SledgeHammer's first big hit. The young singer's voice wasn't as strong as Sledge's and it didn't have that rough velvet edge Christy so loved, but what he lacked in technical abilities, he supplemented in his guitar work and performance. The next song was a fast rock classic too, then the tempo slowed with the beginning chords of a ballad, one of SledgeHammer's biggest hits.

There was a scuffle at the edge of the stage and suddenly Samuel Moore was standing beside Gormley. He was holding a microphone and had apparently arranged to activate it. As the song's intro chords turned into the melodic line, it was Moore's rich, melodious voice that sang the lyrics. The band faltered. Moore lowered the mic, flashed a dazzling smile at the audience, then said something to the young musicians that had them ease back into rhythm. The music continued with Moore as lead singer.

Across the table, Christy saw Sledge stiffen and when she looked back to the stage, Anton Gormley's face was a mask of fury. When the song ended, Anton stormed off the stage, while Moore thanked the band and suggested another song. There was some hesitation while the remaining band members glanced uncertainly at each other, then they bowed to the authority figure, and provided the background music as Moore's performance continued.

When he finished, he thanked the audience, promising that Lightening Rod would be back for another set.

"What a jerk," Quinn said to no one in particular as the audience began to clap.

Christy wasn't sure whether the applause was for the students or for Samuel Moore's superb voice. As she watched the students stash their instruments, she had an uneasy feeling that the most stressful part of the evening was about to begin.

CHAPTER 3

Samuel Moore was clearly pleased with himself as he jumped off the stage. Grinning widely, he strode forward. He acknowledged praise from people he passed with a regal nod, but it was evident he had a destination in mind. Christy had a horrible feeling it was Sledge.

Evidently, Quinn felt the same way. "Looks like there could be trouble if Moore comes over here." He was watching Sledge, who was now sitting stiffly, his usual casual posture nowhere in sight. His features were set in hard lines and he had both hands on the tabletop, flattened and still, as if it was the only way he could keep himself from lurching to his feet and launching himself at Moore.

He had to have met people like the horrible, encroaching Samuel Moore many times in his life, Christy thought, and she knew he was very aware of that whatever he did could—and would!—end up on social media in pictures and video uploaded by anyone with a cell phone.

Trevor shifted chairs to sit down beside him and he glanced at his father. His mouth curled in a small smile and he shook his head as their eyes met.

On the other side of Quinn, Ellen leaned forward as she turned toward Christy. "Trevor thinks this is going to be nasty." She sounded worried.

Tamara, who was sitting beside Sledge, and who had danced with him several times during the set, put her hand over his. He glanced her way, surprise on his face. She smiled at him supportively. Beside her, Olivia watched the interplay between her daughter and Sledge with a puzzled expression.

Roy, who was sitting on Christy's other side, stood up. He shot Trevor and Sledge a pointed look, then he sauntered toward Moore. They met a dozen feet away from the table. Somehow, Roy had managed to put himself between Moore and his destination.

He clamped a hand on Moore's shoulder. "Amazing voice, man."

Moore looked at the hand on his shoulder and frowned, but he managed to smile broadly at Roy as he said, "Thank you. Now, if you don't mind..."

"Really cool," Roy said, paying no attention to the man's obvious desire to move on. "You said at dinner you were classically trained."

It was a statement, but Moore nodded, his expression annoyed now.

Quinn whispered in Christy's ear, "Time for us to get involved." He pushed back his chair and offered her his hand.

She took it and stood, aware the people at the tables around them were focused on the interplay between Roy and Samuel Moore. She guessed many of them were aware of Sledge's tension and that they were waiting for a nasty scene to blow up. Jamieson manners, she thought. Time to defuse this situation.

She smiled at Quinn as if nothing at all was going on, and together, as a couple, they joined Roy.

Moore was saying, "Yes, but I only perform at private functions like this one. I'm not a professional singer."

Christy thrust out her hand and assumed a dazzling smile. "Mr. Moore, Samuel, isn't it? You're one of the administrators at Point Grey, right? Chair of the music department, I think?"

He nodded. His gaze shifted past her to Sledge. When it returned to Christy's face there was speculation in his eyes. "You're Frank Jamieson's wife, aren't you?"

The abrupt way he asked the question threw Christy for a moment, but she quickly regrouped and nodded. "That's right. I'm Christy Jamieson."

He glanced at Sledge again, then back. "And you're having an affair with Sledge—" He might have said more, but Quinn made a growling sound in his throat and he broke off.

Though Christy and Sledge had never been more than friends, speculation had raged in social media earlier that year when they'd been photographed kissing in front of a downtown hotel where Tamara Ahern was staying. The kiss had been part of a covert operation to help Tamara slip away from the hotel without being seen and was nothing but a diversion. However, Samuel Moore wouldn't know that.

Moore shot Quinn a blank look, then his eyes brightened with interest. "You're the reporter who wrote the book about Frank's disappearance and his supposed murder."

Quinn's in-depth book on the mystery of Frank Jamieson's disappearance was due to launch in a few weeks and there was already buzz from reviews of the advance copies.

Quinn raised his brows. "Supposed?"

Moore shrugged. "I thought his body wasn't found. No one can prove he's actually dead."

Christy knew her late husband was dead, so she simply raised her eyebrows. Moore was goading her, probably hoping she'd stomp off in a huff with Quinn following and he'd have a better chance of getting to Sledge. If that was his plan, too bad. She wasn't going anywhere and from his expression, neither was Quinn.

Roy, whose gaze had been drifting around the room, looking for allies, lifted a hand in greeting. "President Harding," he said. There was relief in his voice. "This is quite an interesting evening."

Craig Harding placed himself beside Moore. Between the four of them, they had the man surrounded. There was no way for him to get to Sledge now.

"It is, isn't it?" Harding said. "Samuel, if I could have a word with you in the lounge?"

Moore blinked. He glanced at Sledge again, his expression longing, then back to the president of the college, his ultimate boss. There was annoyance in his eyes. "Now?"

Brows raised and jaw set, Harding nodded. "Now."

"But I wanted to speak to Sledge," Moore said impatiently. He seemed unaware that he'd overstepped some boundary and was probably about to get told off. "His voice is perfect for the hard rock tunes he does, but it lacks the depth for ballads, like the ones I did tonight. I thought I'd give him a few tips on how to strengthen his vocal chords. With a bit of help, he might be able to take his voice to the next level."

Samuel Moore knew how to pitch his voice to an audience. Around them a hum of voices indicated the people in the nearby tables had heard every word he'd said. Now they fell silent as the audience waited to see who cracked first and backed down. Moore? The president? Sledge?

"Not tonight, Samuel," Harding said. "This isn't the time or place."

Though Moore's expression was guileless, Christy thought she saw a gleam of amusement in his eyes. She didn't like the man. She didn't like his style, or the way he was manipulating the situation. Channeling Ellen's snottiest Jamieson manner, she said, "The next level, Mr.

Moore? What would that be? The one you're on? As a professor at a college, perhaps?"

Beside her she heard Roy draw a deep breath, while Quinn choked back something that could have been a laugh, but she kept her gaze—as disapproving and haughty as she could make it—on Samuel Moore.

He flushed red and his eyes narrowed. "I chose not to become a professional, but the option was there."

"I'm sure it was," Christy said. Her tone was light, disbelieving. Moore flushed a deeper red and his dark eyes narrowed.

"Samuel. In the lounge. Now!" Harding said. The 'now' had an imperative ring to it that drew Moore's eyes to the president's face. Harding was tight-lipped. He raised his brows when Moore looked at him and gestured toward the exit. Moore glanced away, to Christy, then Sledge, and finally, back to his boss.

He shrugged, then allowed his gaze to skim over Roy and Quinn, before finally resting on Christy. Flashing a toothy smile that was far from pleasant, he said, "Nice meeting you, Christy."

Harding nodded to them, then he and Moore headed off to the lounge.

Very aware they still had an audience, Christy kept a smile on her face as she watched him go. She decided Samuel Moore was an egotistical idiot and she didn't like him at all.

Beside her Quinn said, "Would you like to go upstairs to the terrace with me and spend some time in the moonlight?"

She turned to him with considerable relief.

He smiled down at her. "There's an amazing view of downtown from there. I thought you'd enjoy seeing it."

Tension oozed out of her and the artificial smile eased into one that was almost teasing. "I would like that. Thank you, Quinn."

Roy looked at his watch. "It's early to end the evening, but I think we need to get Sledge away before Moore escapes from Harding and goes after him again."

They all looked at the table. Trevor and Sledge were standing and it was clear Sledge been prepared for whatever kind of battle Moore would bring his way. Now that the immediate crisis was over, Trevor was talking to him with an earnest expression on his face. Sledge was shaking his head. As she watched, Olivia tugged Tamara's arm and said something, but Tamara shook her head too. Olivia shrugged and moved away, perhaps to schmooze with other guests.

"It's worth a try, Dad," Quinn said.

Nodding decisively, Roy marched back to the table, apparently to add his support to Trevor.

Quinn nudged Christy. "Between them, Dad and Trevor will keep an eye on Sledge. Let's go upstairs."

She raised her brows and nodded. "Lead the way."

The terrace, which stretched across the back of the house, was accessed through tall French doors in both the drawing room and the dining room. The rooms were now still and empty, with no evidence that stages had recently been set up there. "The students have done a good job cleaning up," Christy murmured as she and Quinn walked through the dining room to the French doors. Their footsteps echoed in the vacant room.

"They'd already started as we were leaving the room after the performance ended. I noticed one of the PGC professors making sure the takedown was being handled correctly," Quinn said. They reached the French doors and he drew her to a stop by the simple procedure of slipping his arm around her waist and pulling her close to him.

She looked up, smiled, then raised her arms and wrapped them around his neck. "The students were probably being graded on their participation tonight."

His lips lifted in a half smile. "Teachers can be crafty that way."

He captured her mouth in a kiss that had Christy melting into him. When she came up for air, she couldn't contain a little gurgle of laughter. "I had no idea talking about school could be so sexy."

"Everything about you is sexy," he said, then he proved it by kissing her again.

When the kiss ended, she laid her head on his shoulder and leaned against him, enjoying the warmth of his body against her cheek and the scent of sandalwood and spice that was so much him.

The sound of a man and a woman arguing outside on the terrace broke into the quiet moment. As Quinn's body tensed, Christy raised her head and frowned. She looked at Quinn. He was staring at the doorway as he murmured, "We've got company."

Christy raised her brows. "Do we dare go outside?"

Quinn smiled that sexy half smile again. "Where's your sense of adventure? Of course we do."

She laughed. "If I agree to go out there, you'll have to promise to protect me."

"Consider it done," he murmured. He kissed her again, then they ambled through the doors onto the terrace.

The McLagan house had been designed to take advantage of the sloping terrain. The lower level where the ballroom was located jutted out from the main house and was capped by the wide terrace that overlooked the gardens. The result was a spectacular view of the Vancouver skyline and a ten-foot drop to the gardens below. An elegant stone balustrade about waist high ran the length of the terrace, allowing guests to safely enjoy the view of the gardens below and the cityscape beyond without fear of falling. At either end of the terrace, curving stone staircases swept down to the ballroom level where they met, joining into a single set of stairs that flowed down the hillside to the formal gardens below.

Round tables set with chairs, from the meet and greet earlier, were dotted around the terrace and were lit with candles in clear glass holders. At either end of the terrace, light spilled out through the French doors. The rest of the large space was in shadow.

As soon as they stepped out onto the terrace, Christy and Quinn saw the battling couple. They were standing near the curving staircase at the opposite end, in a pool of light from the drawing room.

Quinn said, "That's Jackson Hargreaves and his wife."

Christy sent him a sharp glance. "The novelist who was annoying your father earlier tonight?"

"One and the same. I wonder if they're arguing about the same things they were when I rescued Dad."

Christy raised her brows. "What was that?"

Quinn laughed softly. "Mrs. Hargreaves thinks Jackson needs to buckle down and turn out some pages. It's time he finishes his novel and gets it published.

"She doesn't sound very sympathetic."

Quinn nodded. "She said it was demeaning being married to a has-been. At that point they both lost interest in Dad and we were able to escape."

"Yikes," Christy said. She gazed across the shadowy space at the Hargreaves. They were standing close together. Mrs. Hargreaves' shoulders were hunched, her elbows tight to her waist and her hands clenched before her in fists. Hargreaves stood stiffly, detached, apart from his angry wife.

Suddenly, the woman shouted, "I've had enough, Jackson! Don't you understand?" She raised her hands on either side of her head in a classic gesture of dismissal.

"You should be on my side!" he shouted in reply. "I couldn't believe it when that bitch, Karen Beaumont, said she didn't think I was actually writing my damned book. I thought you'd defend me. But no, you just smiled and said nothing."

"What could I say? You haven't written anything new in a year!"

"Lies!" Hargreaves shouted. "You know perfectly well I come to my office in this very building every weekend and most evenings to write."

"I know you do." There was no release of tension in her body, though. She was a woman who had lost her trust in her partner and she wasn't even bothering to pretend it was still there. "Or at least you say you do."

There was a sneer in her voice and it goaded her husband into action. He leaned toward her, his face close to hers. "What is that supposed to mean?"

"It means you either sit in that office of yours and twiddle your thumbs, or you go somewhere else and do something else," she said, her finger stabbing out toward his chest. "But what you don't do is work on your novel!" She turned her back on him to stomp down the elegant curved staircase.

He hurried after her, still shouting. "You come back here. We haven't finished this!"

Christy and Quinn emerged from the shadows where they'd lingered while the couple quarreled.

"I'm glad they're gone," Christy said. They now had the terrace to themselves, but the Hargreaves' voices could still be heard below.

"Dad thinks Jackson Hargreaves is a pompous ass who talks a good story but never writes it down. I guess he's right." Quinn drew her toward him. "Now, where were we?"

She tilted her head as she looked up at him and rubbed her hands slowly up his chest, smoothing the fine material of the tux he was wearing. "I think you were going to show me the view of the city at night."

"Hmmm," he said, lowering his head to hers. "Later."

Christy chuckled, then their lips met in a kiss and she didn't bother worrying about the view from the terrace, at night or any other time. They were happily immersed in each other when the evening's quiet was broken by a scream, followed by shouts, then a babble of voices.

Quinn jerked his head up, looking toward the garden where the sounds had come from. "What the—" His concerned gaze met Christy's startled one and together they rushed to the balustrade where they looked over the edge and down into the garden.

Below, at the bottom of the single set of stairs, a woman lay face down. Her arms were flung outward as if she had tripped and fallen down the stone staircase and had tried to save herself, but to no avail. Her long black skirt had risen above her knees in the fall and one of her legs was bent at an odd angle, clearly broken. A little crowd hovered around her. Christy recognized Anton Gormley, the lead singer from Lightening Rod. A good-looking man in a tux, who was one of the professors, Christy thought, stood to one side, his hands in his pockets, his head bent.

The Hargreaves hovered on the landing at the bottom of the curving staircase they had used to depart the terrace, looking down the wide single staircase to the scene below. It was Mrs. Hargreaves who had screamed. Christy knew that for sure, because now she screamed again.

"Get a grip," Jackson Hargreaves said, without any sympathy at all, before he descended the wide stone staircase. Mrs. Hargreaves hiccupped, then she sniffed, but she didn't scream again. She remained standing on the landing, making no attempt to follow her husband.

The base of the stone staircase where the woman lay was a walkway paved in natural slate that led to a shadowed arbor from which other paths wended through the gardens. A figure appeared out of the shadowy arbor, then another followed. The indistinct figures solidified into a man and a woman. Christy gasped. "Quinn! Isn't that Sledge?"

Quinn nodded. "It sure is." He hesitated for a moment, then said, "Is that Tamara he's with?"

Christy's heart flipped, then started to hammer as she peered at the two figures. She swallowed a quick exclamation of guilty pleasure. If Tamara had been in that secluded arbor with Sledge, she was no longer interested in Quinn. "I think so." She sent him a quick, worried glance. "Looks like they decided to slip away for some quiet time, like we did."

"I have to admit, I didn't see that one coming." Quinn's tone was rueful. "I knew Tamara was interested in him, but I didn't think he reciprocated her feelings."

"Maybe it's a very Sledge way to avoid Samuel Moore and his singing lesson," Christy murmured, relieved Quinn wasn't upset.

Quinn snorted. "I wouldn't put it past him."

Christy chuckled, but quietly. Whatever had happened to the woman at the bottom of the stairs, it wasn't good, and levity seemed out of place.

Sledge and Tamara reached the injured woman about the same time Jackson Hargreaves did. Sledge gazed down at her, frowning, then looked at the others. "Has anyone called 9-1-1?"

Gormley shook his head. The prof in the tux shrugged.

Jackson Hargreaves snapped, "Of course not! I just got here."

"I'm a doctor," Tamara said, and crouched down beside the body. She lifted the woman's wrist, then touched her neck. Searching for a pulse, Christy thought, uneasy.

Tamara looked up at Sledge and shook her head. "There's nothing I can do. She's gone."

Sledge pulled out his phone and dialed the emergency number. His expression was grim. "I need to report a death."

CHAPTER 4

"S he can't be dead," Hargreaves said. "You must have made a mistake."

Sledge didn't comment. He simply raised his eyebrows and gave Hargreaves a hard stare. Tamara shook her head.

Hargreaves was apparently impervious to anything that didn't originate with him. He crouched down, his hand moving toward her body. "Karen, if you can, tell us where you're hurt."

"Honestly, Jackson," said his wife from her post at the top of the stairs. "You're such an idiot. Anyone can see she's gone."

Hargreaves stood without touching Karen Beaumont's body and rounded on his wife. "How can you tell if she's dead or not? You're ten steps up and at least fifteen feet away."

Mrs. Hargreaves waved her hand. "These steps are steep, and there is no railing to hang on to." She pointed to the body. "Look at Karen's shoes. They're gorgeous, but they're designed for appearance, not walking. They're held together with nothing but a few thin straps of faux leather and the heels are at least four inches high and needle thin. She probably tripped and fell down the stairs."

Everyone looked, including Christy and Quinn still up on the terrace.

"She's right," Christy murmured. "Not only are the stairs steep, but the stone edges are sharp. If she missed her footing and fell, then hit her head on one or more of the steps, she could have hurt herself badly."

"Or she might have broken her neck," Quinn said. "Poor woman."

Down below, the man in the tux said, "Karen always was a fool for fancy shoes. She had a whole bloody cupboard of them. Didn't matter what they cost, or if the money could be better used for more practical things. Oh, no. If she saw a pair she wanted, she grabbed them, like a crow stealing something shiny just because it glitters in the sunlight."

There was a moment of silence while the rest absorbed this bitter statement. It was Sledge who said, "That's a bit harsh."

Jackson Hargreaves snorted. "Declan has no cause to love Karen, not since she took his brother to the cleaners in their divorce."

"Shut up!" Declan, the man in the tux, said, glaring at Hargreaves. He had stiffened, and his hands were clenched in to fists at his sides.

"Heavens," Christy said. "They'll come to blows in a minute."

Again, Mrs. Hargreaves intervened. "Yes, do be quiet, Jackson. Karen Beaumont is dead. This is no time to be dredging up old animosities. Let the woman rest in peace."

"What was she doing out here?" Tamara asked.

Sledge looked at her curiously. "What do you mean?"

"She means, the dean should have been inside chewing out Professor Moore for taking over our set," said Anton, the lead singer. Anger colored his voice. "Instead, she's out here being useless."

"Would you listen to that," Hargreaves said. He was looking up at his wife and his expression was gleeful. "Makes my comment sound positively benign."

In the distance, the sound of sirens could be heard. "The cops should be here soon," Quinn murmured.

"Thank heavens," Christy said. "Should we go meet them and direct them to the scene?"

Quinn nodded. "I'm not sure how many people know there's been an accident, beyond us and the people with Beaumont's body." He looked down at the little group below. "Why don't you get the door? I'll stay here...just in case."

Christy nodded.

She half-ran across the terrace to the French windows, then walked quickly through the dining room to the foyer. Her shoes were not that different from the ones Karen Beaumont had been wearing and they were not designed for quick sprints across hardwood floors. She reached the large front door as the police cruiser pulled up.

A uniformed cop emerged from the vehicle. "Someone reported a death?"

Christy nodded. "In the gardens behind the house." She led the policeman through the foyer and dining room to the terrace, walking as quickly as she could. The cop followed her, his steady footsteps a strong counterpoint to the tap of her flimsy heels. On the terrace, she pointed to where Quinn was still standing. "You can see the victim from there."

The cop shot her a questioning look, even as he continued to the balustrade. "Victim? You think there's been foul play?"

"We think the lady is dead," Quinn said. "We don't know how she died."

The cop was frowning now, as he stood beside Quinn and stared down at Karen Beaumont's broken body. He looked around. Pointing to the curving staircase, he said, "Does that go down to the garden?"

"Yes," Christy said.

He nodded, then headed toward the steps, moving more quickly than he had when he followed Christy from the front door. Even as he started down the stairs, he was speaking into his walkie-talkie, requesting backup and providing more details of the accident scene.

"Anything happen while I was at the door?" Christy asked Quinn.

"More bickering, but not much else. Everyone shut up when the siren stopped."

The cop reached the bottom of the curving stairs. "Excuse me, ma'am," he said to Mrs. Hargreaves, who was standing squarely in the middle of the landing staring down the garden stairs. She stepped hastily to one side and he brushed past her. He started down the stairs, then paused, looking from where Mrs. Hargreaves stood to the bottom where Karen Beaumont lay. Then he nodded abruptly and continued down, passing Jackson Hargreaves on the way.

At the bottom, he checked the body and again spoke into his transmitter, confirming that Karen Beaumont was indeed dead. Then he asked the little group to move away from the scene. Sledge immediately stepped back. Tamara followed, standing beside him and watching the policeman uneasily. With one last look at Beaumont, Anton shrugged and moved away as well.

Declan turned his back on Karen's body and walked down the path toward the arbor where there was a rustic seat. He settled there, crossing his arms over his chest and stretching out his legs. Hargreaves retreated back up the stairs to where his wife still stood. The sound of more incoming sirens was loud in the night air.

"Let's leave them to it," Quinn said quietly.

Christy shot him a quick glance. "Go and answer the door again, you mean."

He nodded. "There's nothing more we can do here."

They didn't rush this time but walked together. Quinn held Christy's hand in a reassuring way, and they stood together as the second cruiser parked in front of the building. Quinn gave the officer, a woman this time, a quick description of the house and the location of the accident, and she headed off.

"We should probably go down to the ballroom and let President

Harding know that his dean is dead," Christy said, as she watched the cop disappear into the dining room.

"If he hasn't figured it out already," Quinn said.

"Good point," Christy said. There were doors at either end of the ballroom that led out onto the flagstone paths that wound through the gardens. By this time, someone must have wandered though them and noticed something was happening at the bottom of the stairs.

They were hovering in the foyer, not sure whether to go back to the terrace, or stay where they were, when another car pulled up. This time it was a man of medium height, with a thick neck, massive shoulders, and a broad chest. He was wearing a suit, with a white shirt and a tie. The tie knot was askew, indicating he'd tied it quickly and didn't care that it wasn't straight. He flipped credentials at Quinn and said, "Crime scene?"

Quinn sent him on his way with the same directions they'd given the female officer.

"Crime scene?" Christy echoed, watching the detective plod through the doorway into the dining room.

"We may as well sit down," Quinn said. "If the cops have designated this a suspicious death, there will be more arrivals."

They settled onto a bench with a view of the door and waited for more first responders to appear. The forensics crew and the EMTs had arrived and been given directions when they heard another car engine near, then stop as the vehicle was parked. They waited, prepared to send this new arrival the way of the others.

Firm footsteps, moving quickly, but not hastily, sounded on the flagstones of the front porch, then a woman strode through the open doorway. She was tall and lean, her long hair bound in a braid, then wound into a knot at her neck. Her face was a perfect oval, her eyes wide, her cheekbones defined, her nose straight. She might have been called beautiful, if not for the scar that ran down her cheek.

Christy smiled. "Detective Patterson."

Patterson stopped momentarily before she walked more slowly into the foyer. "Mrs. Jamieson. Mr. Armstrong." There was resignation in her voice. "Was it you who found the body?"

Christy shook her head. "No, Sledge."

One of Patterson's eyebrows rose, and her full, lush mouth twitched into something that might have been a smile. "Of course it was."

Quinn laughed, and Patterson said, "I'm told the body can be found through the dining room, then down the terrace stairs to the garden."

Christy nodded. "The dining room is through that door, over there."

Patterson nodded, her gaze following Christy's pointing finger. "Don't go away. I'll need to talk to you later." With that she strode off.

"Let's go back to the ballroom and join the others," Quinn said, as Patterson disappeared into the dining room.

"Good idea," Christy said. "I think it's going to be a long night."

CHAPTER 5

F our days after the eventful evening of the At Risk gala, Christy had shed her glamorous look as the head of the Jamiesons, and was back in her usual mom costume—jeans, a sweater, and a fall jacket—as she walked her daughter to school.

Noelle was dressed in much the same way as there were no fancy school uniforms at her local elementary. She plodded along the path that led from the townhouse development to the school. Her head was down, her shoulders hunched. Christy resisted the urge to sigh. The new school year was not going well and the reason was a simple one—when the classroom assignments were posted on the front door of the school the week before classes began, Noelle and her very best friend in the world, Mary Petrofsky, discovered they were in different classes. Noelle was in the full grade four class with Mrs. Weaver, while Mary was in a split three-four under Mrs. Vonk. Even worse, the classrooms weren't located side by side, but on either side of the inner corridor, which meant their outside doors were on different sides of the school.

To Christy it seemed a cruel punishment to separate the children this way, and she'd gone to the principal to ask for Noelle to be reassigned. She had no luck having her daughter moved, however. The principal kindly told her it was school policy to split best friends at the beginning of each year to discourage cliques and to help the children learn social skills, including mixing with others. Though Christy could see the woman's reasoning and even agree with it—in a logical, intellectual way—watching her daughter mourn the loss of her best friend ever as a classmate was hard to handle.

Rebecca Petrofsky was going through the same problem with Mary, so Rebecca and Christy got together to ensure that their daughters had as much together time as possible. They shared after-school visits and weekend sleepovers, which made the two girls' lives tolerable—just.

Today was Monday, so a long week of school and homework assignments beckoned, hence Noelle's gloomy mood. It was raining too, and not the big fat droplets Christy remembered from her youth in Eastern Canada, but Vancouver's light, misty drizzle that could seem endless as summer merged into fall on the West Coast. The overcast sky, the cooling temperatures, the gloom from the heavy tree cover, the damp from the rain, all came together to ensure a darkness of spirit.

Except, for Christy it didn't. She loved the misty rain and the moody lighting in the forest. She had a day to look forward to that would be filled with complications and challenges. There was a spring in her step that was noticeably different from her daughter's despondent trudge.

They reached the end of the path. The trees gave way to an open field where the students were allowed play at recess and where they had their gym classes on fine days. Beyond was the school. It was an unexciting building, low-rise and single story. Between the closed classroom doors, windows pierced the brick façade. Utilitarian, with no pretentions to architectural interest, it was what it was and got the job done.

An asphalt pad surrounded the school, paved so children could use skipping ropes, or draw hopscotch grids during recess and the lunch break. Backpacks were dumped against the school wall or beside parents who clustered in little groups while their kids played as everyone waited for the classroom doors to open.

Noelle and Christy reached the yard. Christy stopped near the edge of the pavement. Noelle stood beside her, her hands clinging to her backpack straps, her gaze on nothing in particular. The picture of despair.

A boy with black hair and a stocky build zoomed in on her, tapping her on the shoulder. "Tag, you're it!" he shouted as he danced out of range.

Noelle's head shot up. "Go away, Devon! I'm not playing."

His face fell. "Awe, come on!"

"No!" She resumed her head down, hunched posture. Devon shrugged and turned away.

"He was only trying to be sociable," Christy said.

Noelle lifted one shoulder in silent dismissal.

"He's in your class. You'll probably have projects with him sometime this year."

Noelle gave her a sideways glance. "I hope not. He's a boy. He's stupid."

Christy sighed. Noelle was usually a cheerful, happy child. She had been through so much change last year and had handled it in such an even-tempered way that Christy wasn't sure how best to help her daughter cope with this new and profound change. Fortunately, the classroom door opened and the kids, and sometimes their parents, straggled into the room.

At the door there was a bottleneck as moms said good-bye for the day and gave last-minute instructions of one sort or another. Last year,

Noelle and Mary Petrofsky would have been immersed in some kind of game or telling each other their deepest secrets at this point, and all Christy would be allowed was a quick peck on the cheek before they both danced into their room. Now, though, Noelle took her hand and dragged her into the classroom, as if she wanted to put off the beginning of the school day as long as possible.

She slipped her backpack off her shoulders and dropped it carelessly onto the floor, then shrugged off her jacket and hung it on the hook assigned to her. Both she and Christy had their backs to the classroom throughout this process, so it was a shock for Christy when she heard a well-remembered voice said, "Good morning, Mrs. Jamieson."

Christy resisted the urge to whirl about in an alarmed reaction. She looked down at her daughter, who looked back up at her. Noelle's eyes were wide and not a little frightened. Christy smiled reassuringly and kept that expression on her face as she turned. "Ms. Shively. This is unexpected."

Joan Shively, the child welfare worker unleashed on Christy the year before by the vengeful trustees who ran the Jamieson Trust at that time, smirked at her. Shively's clothing choices tended toward polyester pantsuits in monochrome colors, matched with faux silk shells. Her shoes were flat slip-ons and her hair was short and styled in something resembling a bowl cut. Though she might appear inoffensive and rather self-effacing, her sense of mission was rock solid. And it seemed to Christy that her mission was to save Noelle from Christy's inexpert parenting.

"It shouldn't be," Shively said, raising her eyebrows. "If the parent of one of my children appears on the national news, I take note. If she is in the news because she is involved in a murder, I will take action."

"Mom, who got killed this time?" Noelle asked, not helping the situation.

Christy looked down at her daughter. Abandoning her moody pout with the advent of the threat from Shively, Noelle had assumed her Jamieson manners. She was trying to be very adult and part of the conversation, but it wasn't working. Shively's brows had snapped together and in a moment she would burst out with some kind of accusation. Christy said hastily, "No one, honey. A poor lady tripped and fell down a flight of stairs at the gala I went to last week." She turned to Shively. "There were two hundred and fifty people at the event. The person who died was a stranger and I wasn't around when she fell."

"But you were at the party and the news report I saw said you were involved with the program she managed," Shively said briskly. "I have introduced myself to Noelle's teacher and I will be doing a home visit sometime during the next couple of weeks." She smiled at Noelle and said good-bye, then nodded curtly to Christy. "Mrs. Jamieson." She turned her back on them both and walked out of the classroom via the door that led to the internal corridor.

Mrs. Weaver called the class to order. "Children, to your desks, please."

Noelle whispered fiercely, "Mom, make her go away!"

"I'll try, kiddo. I'll try." She hugged her daughter. "Now, you've got to get to your desk and I've got to go."

Noelle's face puckered. "I don't want to."

"I know, but you have to." When Noelle's glum expression didn't change and she didn't move, Christy gave her another hug, followed by a gentle shove. Noelle gathered up her backpack and trudged despondently to her desk.

Christy sighed and left, closing the external classroom door behind her, as she was the last parent out. Her earlier good mood was gone. Now she was the one huddling in her jacket against the rain, feeling miserable.

Her destination was her townhouse, down at the bottom of the row of houses, but at the last minute, she turned up the Armstrongs' walk instead and rang the bell.

It was Roy who answered. "Christy! Come on in." He opened the door wide, providing access to the small landing from which stairs led both up to the main floor and down to basement level where Quinn had his office. "I was just filling Frank in on some of the details of the death Thursday night. He's upstairs. Quinn's on a video conference with a reviewer in Toronto. They're talking about the new book. He should be finished in a half an hour or so."

Frank was Frank Jamieson, Christy's late husband. After his brutal murder, his essence had taken up residence in Stormy, the Jamieson family cat. Christy assumed Frank would eventually move on, but more than a year after his death he was still co-habiting with Stormy. He was able to communicate with certain people using a kind of mental telepathy. Christy, Noelle, his aunt Ellen Jamieson, and Roy Armstrong, among others, could hear him. Quinn could not. Christy supposed that was to be expected because of her relationship with Quinn, but it might also be that Frank was still learning how to broadcast to a wider audience and not everybody could hear his thought-speak.

The new book Roy mentioned was Quinn's recounting of the search he and Christy had made to find out Frank's fate after his sudden disappearance last year. Quinn's editor predicted the book would be a bestseller during the important fall publishing season, and the publisher had organized a series of interviews and signings to publicize it.

Christy stepped inside. Roy shut the door and said, "Come upstairs and have a coffee."

"Okay. Thanks." Christy shrugged off her damp coat, hung it in the cupboard, then followed Roy up the stairs, through the living room, then into the kitchen beyond. She knew the way. The layout was exactly the same at her house.

Stormy the Cat had been curled up on the couch in the living room, and as Christy passed he hopped down to twine around her ankles, doing his best to trip her up, but Christy was an expert at keeping her footing and she made it to the kitchen table without incident. There she sat down, while the cat hopped up onto the tabletop so he could be part of the action. He sat in his usual tidy way, with his tail curled around his paws, and let Christy pat him from head to tail in long, slow strokes.

The tabletop was surprisingly bare. Roy's laptop was usually open on it when he was working on a book, but for now the computer was closed and stashed on the window seat behind the table.

After he'd finished making the coffee, Roy brought the mug over to the table and put it in front of her. Then he sat down in a nearby chair and said, "What's up?"

She wrapped her hands around the mug and stared at him through troubled eyes. "Shively's back. She heard about the death at the gala and she thinks it's a murder and that I'm involved because I was at the gala. I'm tainted by association," she said bitterly.

It was a murder? The cat turned accusing green eyes on Roy. *You told me she tripped and fell down some stairs. That's an accident.*

They all knew that at best Shively was a pest, at worst a danger, but Roy was frowning for other reasons. "What made her think the poor woman was murdered?"

"I have no idea. I told her it was an accident. She didn't pay any attention. Now she's advising the teacher that I'm a bad mom and she's going to start doing home visits again."

The cat stood up and butted her hand with his head. *Shively's a moron. We'll deal with her.*

Christy sighed as she turned her hand to scratch Stormy under the chin. "Thanks, Frank. The problem is that she's got authority behind her and because I'm involved in another death, I'm vulnerable." She turned the scratch into a pat. "Noelle isn't helping things. She's so bummed about her new classroom assignment that she's moody and clearly unhappy. It will be easy for Shively to interpret that as problems at home, rather than at school."

I'll talk to Noelle.

"Please do. Maybe you can make her understand that not being in the same class as Mary Petrofsky isn't the end of the world."

While Christy and Frank talked, Roy set up his laptop and did an Internet search. Now he said, "The cops upgraded Beaumont's death yesterday, from suspicious to murder. It made the national news last night."

Christy stopped patting the cat to stare at Roy. This time when Stormy butted her hand, it wasn't a gesture of sympathy from Frank, but Stormy himself wanting attention. She started patting him again as she said, "The national broadcast? But why? Surely the death of a college dean is just a local matter. And why did Patterson decide it was a murder? From their questions on Thursday night, it sounded like the cops thought the fall was an accident, caused by too much wine and inappropriate heels."

Roy clicked a link to the recorded broadcast and brought it up. He found the segment, then turned the laptop so they could all watch.

When she died, Karen Beaumont was Dean of Entertainment Arts at Point Grey College, but before that she'd been the producer of a number of high-profile Canadian television shows. She'd also been the driving force behind the development of the At Risk program and had been widely praised for the work she'd done on it. Moreover, she was apparently one of those people who knew how to network. During her television career, she'd worked with Canada's artistic community throughout the country, and she used those relationships to support her work at PGC. Famous faces, looking bereft, spoke sadly of what a loss she was to the arts community, to Vancouver, to Canada as a whole.

After Beaumont's background had been thoroughly described, the scene switched to a live feed from in front of the mansion where the gala had taken place. "Initial investigations led police to believe Ms. Beaumont's death was accidental, and that she lost her footing on the stone steps in the garden of MacLagan House behind me. She had been seen drinking throughout the event and she was wearing evening sandals with very high heels. However, autopsy results now confirm that her injuries indicate that her fall was not natural."

The host back in the studio said breathlessly, "She was pushed?"

The reporter nodded. "Yes, exactly. The police do not have a suspect in custody as yet, and the investigation continues."

"Ms. Beaumont's death occurred at the Point Grey College At Risk Gala, didn't it?" the host said.

The reported nodded. "Yes, it did. And some of Vancouver's most famous—and infamous!—personalities were there." As the reporter reeled off names the screen split, showing photos of the individuals.

Roy's picture flashed up early, along with Jackson Hargreaves and Harold Wilkinson, who was one of the chairs at PGC and the author of graphic novels, then the names began to hit home. "Mitchell Crosier, a prominent record executive, and his wife Kim were great friends of Ms. Beaumont. Eugene Sawatzky, the president of Sawatzky Restoration and Renewal and his wife are big supporters of Point Grey College. Ms. Beaumont's death must have been devastating for them. Their daughter was found murdered at a SledgeHammer concert earlier this year. Incidentally, Sledge, the lead singer of SledgeHammer, was the one who found Ms. Beaumont's body. Olivia Waters and her daughter, Dr. Tamara Ahern, were also in attendance. You'll remember that Dr. Ahern was recently suspected of the death of her natural father, provincial minister, Frederick Jarvis."

Christy groaned. The final image turned her groan into a whispered, "Oh, no."

It was the infamous photograph of her in what she thought of as her bimbo stage. Her hair was long, curling seductively over her shoulders, and died a brassy blond. She was holding a wine glass, her hand raised in a toast, and the drink was clearly not her first of the night. The picture had been taken after she'd suffered a miscarriage early in her marriage to Frank. She'd been grieving, fighting demons, and partying too hard. She'd taken a lot of flack for that picture, then, and again when Frank disappeared last year.

The reporter said, "Also attending was Christy Jamieson. Her husband Frank, heir to the Jamieson Ice Cream empire, disappeared last year and Christy was accused of embezzling the Jamieson fortune. She is reputed to be in a relationship with Quinn Armstrong. His new book is an exposé of Frank Jamieson, written with the help of Christy Jamieson."

A still image of Quinn standing before the devastation at the medical outpost where Tamara had worked in sub-Saharan Africa replaced Christy's image. "Mr. Armstrong is also reputed to have been in a relationship with Dr. Ahern."

"So the police have plenty of suspects to work with," the host said. Christy could almost imagine him rubbing his hands together with glee as he scented scandal.

The reporter nodded. "I'll be following this story and there will be more to come. I'll keep you updated."

The host thanked the reporter and the segment ended with a commercial break. Roy cut the feed and started to type.

She implied you killed me so you could hang out with Armstrong!

Christy nodded. She felt sick. "No wonder Shively came after me this morning. I would have too, if I were in her place."

A woosh sound from Roy's computer indicated he'd been writing an e-mail. "I sent Three the link to the broadcast and asked him to call. We need to get on top of this." Three was Roy's nickname for his old friend Trevor McCullagh.

You think?

Frank's sarcastic comment had Roy glaring at the cat. "Obviously."

The sound of footsteps interrupted them before the argument could develop further. Quinn smiled as he entered the kitchen. "Christy! I didn't expect to see you this morning." The smile faded as he examined her face. "You look upset. What's wrong?"

She filled him in, her voice shaking as she came to the last part of the news report. "They targeted you, too, Quinn. The reporter implied you were in a relationship with me so you could get info for your book, and that you were two-timing Tamara."

By the time she was finished he was at the table and she stood so she could move into his open arms for a hug. The cat jumped off the table and slunk underneath, where he hunched, clearly uncomfortable.

"It's okay," Quinn murmured, rubbing her back comfortingly. "We'll sort this out."

Roy said thoughtfully, "I wonder how the cops could tell she'd been pushed."

That had Christy lifting her head and staring. "What do you mean?"

Roy shrugged. "She was found at the bottom of a flight of stairs, obviously having tumbled down them. How can you tell if she tripped or someone helped her fall?"

Christy shivered. "Not enough booze in her stomach for her to be drunk? A bruise on her wrist because someone twisted her arm? Does it matter? The cops have decided she was murdered. It's their call."

The cat peaked out from beneath the table, his head angled, looking up, eyes wide. *You're a suspect. Looks like we need to investigate.*

Christy pulled out of Quinn's hug. "No! We're not investigating another murder, because I'm not a suspect. None of us are. If we were, Patterson would have been here asking more questions before the announcement to the press ever went out. That was just a reporter looking for ways to add interest to a police statement that said nothing except that Karen Beaumont's death was not natural."

What about Shively?

"What about her? The damage has already been done. Patterson will find the culprit and make an arrest. It won't be me, but that won't matter to Shively."

Unblinking green eyes stared up at her. *You'll be under suspicion until the killer is caught.*

"I will not! Solving murders isn't a game, Frank." She drew a deep breath to help herself calm down. "This isn't our fight."

"I take it the cat is talking again?" Quinn asked. He smiled at Christy as she nodded. "If it means anything, I'm with you. No amateur detective stuff."

Christy let out a breath she didn't realize she'd been holding and smiled back at him. "Thank you."

Roy cleared his throat. The cat glared.

Wuss. This will not end well for Christy. And it will be up to me to protect her!

CHAPTER 6

Noelle plodded down the path, her head bowed, and her shoulders slumped as she and Christy made their way to school. It was Wednesday, two days after Shively's visit to Noelle's classroom.

Christy kept up a stream of cheerful talk, to which Noelle returned a gloomy grunt or a one-syllable answer. Christy didn't really expect anything more. She was talking to cover the grim silence more than anything else.

As they reached the point where the path turned into the school field, Noelle straightened. She shifted her shoulders, rearranged her expression into one of polite interest, and lifted her head high.

Christy stared at her in astonishment. After a moment she said, "Did Daddy talk to you about school?"

Noelle nodded.

"What did he say?"

"School is stupid and the principal is mean." Noelle stared straight ahead. Her expression didn't change.

Well, that was helpful. Not. Okay, maybe a little helpful if it got their daughter out of the dumps. "Anything else?"

"He told me I had to use Jamieson manners in class or people would think I wasn't happy." She paused to shoot Christy a mutinous glance. "And I'm not." Another pause. "Except I am. I'm happy at home. I'm happy when I'm with Mary Petrofsky after school. I just hate school."

No surprise there, Christy thought.

"Daddy said people wouldn't understand. That they judge other people, even when they don't have the full story."

"That happens," Christy said, when Noelle paused.

Her daughter nodded. "So that's why he says I should use Jamieson manners and not confuse people. 'What they don't know, won't hurt them,'" she concluded, apparently quoting her father.

Christy suspected Frank had used Jamieson manners to get through his rocky childhood. By the time she'd met him they were second nature and it had taken months for her to peel them away to reveal the man beneath. When they'd come back to Vancouver, he'd donned them again, like armor against the emotional blows from his trustees, and the man she'd fallen in love with in Kingston had disappeared. He never did return, no matter how hard she tried to bring him back.

She said carefully, "Jamieson manners are important, but sometimes you just have to be yourself. You use Jamieson manners to get you through tough situations and with difficult people, but you need to be yourself with people you trust and care for."

Noelle nodded seriously. "That's what Daddy said."

Christy stared at her. "He did?"

Noelle nodded again. "He said friends are important and they deserve to know you for yourself."

They were nearing the asphalt skirt that surrounded the school. Dozens of children were already there, mingling in little groups as they waited for the classroom doors to open. "So use Jamieson manners to get you through these gloomy days, but be open to the other kids in your class." She looked down, deliberately catching her daughter's gaze. "Okay?"

Noelle nodded and produced a smile. "Okay, Mom."

Jamieson manners at work, Christy thought with a pang. Not exactly what she had in mind.

The little boy who had tried to coax Noelle into a game of tag on Monday, zoomed toward her and came to an abrupt stop a foot or two away. "Erin and Lindsay have a long jump rope. We'll all take turns at the ends if you want to skip with us."

Noelle glanced at the two girls who had staked out a section of the asphalt and were lazily turning a long plastic skipping rope. One of them waved. Christy wasn't sure if it was Lindsay or Erin, but it didn't matter. Noelle was being invited to join in and Christy knew her daughter loved to skip.

The boy, whose name was Devon, danced away. "Come on, Noelle!"

Noelle stared for a decision-making moment, then she looked up at her mother and shrugged. "Jamieson manners," she said as she pulled off her backpack and handed it to Christy. She followed Devon at a walk rather than a run, but when she reached the skipping rope, she jumped right in.

Christy resisted the urge to laugh, but it was a rueful laugh. If Jamieson manners helped Noelle through this bad patch, great. She'd make sure her daughter understood they were a tool, not a barrier to hide behind.

The skipping lasted until the classroom door opened. Energy was burned off and there were even very natural shrieks and giggles as the children tumbled through the door to begin their day. Christy set off home in a better mood than the one she'd started with.

Her mood brightened even more when she saw Quinn at the junction where the path to the school met the main trail through the woods. He was wearing jeans that hugged his slim hips and a leather jacket. The misty rain that had plagued them all week had added a gleam to his dark hair. She thought he looked great. She almost wished she was wearing the sophisticated skirt suit she planned to change into before she went into the Jamieson Trust offices this morning. Almost, but not quite. She knew he was fond of seeing her in snug fitting jeans and a sweater. "Hello," she called. "I didn't expect to see you here."

He held up his phone. "I come bearing gifts."

She frowned at that, but then he reached her and for a while she was busy responding to his kiss. Well, kisses, because both of them were enjoying themselves so much one wasn't enough.

"Um," she said at last, when he drew away. "That was nice."

"It was, wasn't it?" He smiled at her as he waggled his phone back and forth. "I think you'll be happy about this, too."

She looked at him curiously. "What is it?"

He handed her the phone, open to a news report about the murder at MacLagan House. It didn't take her long to absorb the information. According to the article, the culprit was Anton Gormley, one of the students who made up the band, Lightening Rod.

Her eyes wide, Christy said, "It was a student who killed her?"

Quinn nodded. "That's what the cops think."

Gormley had been the one who found Karen Beaumont's body, Christy remembered, though it had been Sledge who phoned 9-1-1.

"So it's over," she said. She sighed as she handed the phone back to Quinn.

He pocketed it, then put his arm around her waist and they began to stroll toward home. "Apparently, he has a history of violence and he was a street kid before he joined the At Risk program."

"He certainly became very angry when that horrible music professor took over the band so he could sing Sledge's songs in an operatic way." She chuckled. "I don't think he quite understood why Sledge wasn't enthusiastic."

"Guys like him figure they're showing their appreciation by outdoing the original. Sledge coped well."

"Yeah." They ambled along in comfortable silence for a couple of minutes, then a thought struck Christy. "The article didn't say why the kid decided to kill Karen Beaumont. She a dean, not one of his professors. He probably hardly ever saw her."

Quinn stopped. When she looked up at him, a question in her eyes, he put his finger over her lips. "Not our case, remember? Patterson is in charge. She'll make sure all the questions are answered and the right person is charged."

Christy laughed. "You're right. I'll stop speculating."

They started walking again. They'd almost come to the end of the path, where it met the top of their street, when a sudden realization hit her. "Oh no!"

Quinn looked down at her, his brows raised. "What's the matter?"

"The At Risk program. Anton Gormley was one of its success stories. What will his arrest do to the program's reputation?"

He considered that. "I expect PGC will take a hit in the short-term. Having a senior administrator killed by a student doesn't look good and Karen Beaumont had a lot of supporters who are grieving and angry. Gormley's motive will be important. If her death was simply a senseless act of violence, the program will suffer. If there was a deeper cause, a personal one that isn't college related, it could be nothing more than a blip."

They turned onto the road. "The At Risk program is the first program The Jamieson Foundation has invested in. What will this arrest do to our credibility?" She sighed. "I was going down to the Trust's offices this morning anyway. I just didn't plan to spend my day trying to figure out if I made a big mistake on my first initiative."

Quinn hugged her. "You didn't. Talk to the president at PGC—

what was his name? Harding, that's it—and get his input. It's his college. He's probably already deep into redirect mode. If he can validate his program, there shouldn't be any problem with your foundation being involved."

She drew a deep breath. "Good point. I'll call him as soon as I get in."

They reached her house. Quinn lowered his head to give her another kiss. "Why don't I take you out to dinner tonight and you can tell me what he said?"

She beamed at him. "Good idea." She slipped her arms around his neck and kissed him back.

The restaurant Quinn chose for their dinner out was small, quiet, and crowded. Located in the Metrotown area in central Burnaby, it had the reputation of serving the best Thai cuisine in the greater Vancouver area. Though she'd heard about it, this was Christy's first time eating here.

She reviewed the menu with considerable interest, but quickly realized this meal would truly be one of experimentation, because the descriptions beneath the names of the items explained the ingredients, but not the flavor palate.

Quinn had been to the restaurant before and warned her that when the menu showed a banana pepper icon beside an item, the dish would not only be spicy, but hot. She decided to take a risk and chose a dish that included shrimp, eggplant, and Thai chili peppers in a black bean sauce. Quinn went for barbeque duck in a red curry sauce. Their meals chosen, they settled in to exchange news.

"Were you able to talk to President Harding?" Quinn asked, sipping red wine.

Christy looked at her own glass, though she didn't drink. She'd shed her Jamieson CEO power suit and was dressed in a pair of black wool slacks and a plum colored silk blouse that dipped into a vee in the front. She was more relaxed than she'd been at the office, but she was still conflicted about the conversation she'd had that afternoon. "He was difficult to get hold of, but we eventually connected. I expect he was dealing with a lot of people like me who were skittish about the At Risk program because of Anton's arrest."

Quinn leaned back in his chair, moving the glass and swirling the wine inside lazily. "Or he was avoiding the tough conversations."

"He may have been." Christy sighed. "Quinn, he doesn't think the kid did it. He said Anton had turned himself around, that he was getting treatment for his violent tendencies."

"How does he know that?"

"Part of the At Risk curriculum is self-knowledge and counseling. Apparently, Anton Gormley accepted he has a temper that is quick to ignite and he's learned coping strategies to keep it under control. According to Harding, the professor he's working with and his counselor are both shocked he's been accused of harming Karen Beaumont. They say he's too aware of his weaknesses to allow it to happen."

Quinn sent her a long, level look. "And reformed alcoholics never go back to the bottle."

"I know! That's it exactly." She leaned forward, intense and frustrated. "Just because Gormley has been doing well, doesn't mean he didn't revert. Harding's reaction worries me. Does he believe in his students so intensely that he has no objectivity? Or is he trying to cover his ass?"

The appetizer they were sharing arrived. The server, a pretty young woman dressed in a traditional long skirt, placed the platter of Satay Chicken brochettes on the table and quietly moved away. Quinn took a skewer and stripped the chicken pieces onto his plate, then he picked up a slice with his chopsticks and dipped it into the thick peanut sauce before he popped it into his mouth.

Christy watched him with some amusement. Her manipulation of chopsticks was hopeless, so she'd opted for a knife and fork. She followed his lead, stripping the meat from the skewer, then dipping the chicken breast into the peanut sauce before she ate. Flavor burst onto her tongue. "Oh, my. This is delicious."

Quinn chuckled. "I thought you'd like it." He toyed with another piece of chicken, though he didn't raise it to his mouth. "I checked out Craig Harding this afternoon."

She swallowed her morsel. "What did you find out?"

"He's got a good reputation as an academic and in the three years since he became president of Point Grey, the college has developed new courses like the At Risk program that are designed to make education more relevant to young people on the fringe, like Anton Gormley."

Christy cocked her head. "Sounds impressive, but from your tone, I sense a 'but.'"

He nodded. "There was a murder at Point Grey not long before Harding became president. A chef and the vice president of a college in Victoria were killed by an individual who worked for PGC."

Christy thought back, then nodded slowly. "I think I remember it. Things weren't good between Frank and me then, and Noelle was only six, so I didn't pay much attention, though. But how are these murders relevant if they were before he became president?"

"It all happened around a cooking competition Harding organized that took place at PGC's Yaletown campus. He was vice president academic at the time."

Quinn dipped his slice of chicken into the peanut sauce while Christy stared at him. "That's a bit close to home, isn't it? Another murder related to the institution where Harding works." Then she shook her head and laughed. "Who am I to talk? Since I set out to discover what happened to Frank, you and I have been involved in five murders. And that's in a year. At least President Harding has had a few years between his."

Quinn looked at her with a smile in his eyes. "That's a very pragmatic attitude."

Christy grinned as she shrugged. "Has to be. Facts are facts." She drew a breath. "Back to the present and my problem. A dean at Point Grey College was murdered. The police have arrested Anton Gormley, a student in one of her programs. Though the president of the college doesn't dispute that Dean Beaumont was murdered, he refuses to acknowledge that the police have the correct person. Is that going to cause problems for my foundation?"

"In what way?"

She dipped some chicken in the sauce, then it chewed thoughtfully. "Say Anton is guilty and he admits to killing Beaumont for some obscure reason in a rush of temper. What does that say about the At Risk program and their curriculum?"

"That it's a good curriculum for most of the people who are in it? That nothing is perfect and no size fits all?"

"Okay. But what about the professor's absolute faith in Gormley? Or Harding's uncritical acceptance of that professor's opinion? I mean, the woman who was killed was a senior member of Harding's management team. Doesn't he have any loyalty to her?"

Quinn drank some wine. "I'd say his choices are few. The cops are in control of the investigation, so there's not much he can do for Karen Beaumont. If he honestly believes Anton Gormley isn't guilty, then he may feel he has to do all he can to support the kid."

Christy finished her chicken. "Especially if it helps his program at the same time." Quinn raised his eyebrows and she added, "Okay, cynical viewpoint, but..." She sipped some wine, then put her glass down as she sighed. "He asked me not to pull my funding from the At

Risk program and I..." She shrugged. "I agreed. I'm not sure if I was right or not."

Quinn leaned forward and reached across the table to take her hand. "Then take counsel. We'll get everyone together tomorrow night for dinner at my place. Tell them your concerns and ask them what they think. You'll get lots of opinions and most of them will be good." He stopped, made a face, and added, "Except maybe the cat's."

Christy laughed, as she guessed he expected her to. "I like your idea. Noelle is already scheduled to do an overnight at Mary Petrofsky's, so I'm free for the evening. I don't know Ellen's plans, but I'll see if she can come."

"Good. I'll talk to Dad when we get home. Now, let's forget about murders and talk about something much more fun."

Christy tilted her head and gave him a small smile. "What's that?"

"Us."

CHAPTER 7

On Friday afternoon Christy arrived home twenty minutes before she had to pick up Noelle from school, just enough time to change from the fashionable heels and business suit she'd worn to the Jamieson Trust offices into jeans, a sweater, and runners. Pretty as her fashionable shoes were, they weren't designed for a brisk walk along an unpaved woodland path.

After collecting Noelle from her classroom, they circled the school to reach Mary Petrofsky's room on the other side of the building. Mary was waiting in the doorway. She gave a little skip when she caught sight of Noelle and Christy, then raced toward them. Noelle ran to meet her and the two collided not far from the doorway.

Mrs. Vonk, Mary's teacher, was standing just inside the classroom watching the last of her charges depart. She had already seen this behavior in action a number of times, and she shook her head. "We all thought being in separate classes would help these two to be open to new friendships. I expected that to have happened by now."

Christy resisted the urge to remark that no one had paid much attention to the desires of the girls themselves. More diplomatically, she said, "I'm glad Noelle's best friend is such a thoroughly nice little girl. Have a good weekend, Mrs. Vonk. Come on, you two, let's get you home."

Mary spent the afternoon with Noelle in Christy's basement. They had created a whole world down there for their dolls and were happy to spend hours building complex stories around the dolls' lives.

When Rebecca Petrofsky returned home from work a little after five, she came over to pick up her daughter and Noelle for the planned sleepover. She and Christy chatted while some important element in the dolls' most recent story problem was played out, then the two Petrofskys and Noelle headed up the street, leaving Christy to organize the salad she'd agreed to bring to the dinner at the Armstrongs' that evening.

Shortly before six Christy was ringing the Armstrongs' bell. Quinn opened the door. She paused a moment to admire the way the royal blue sweater he wore enhanced his eyes and skin—not to mention the way it showed off his strong chest—before they both headed up the stairs to the main level, but Quinn had other ideas. He removed the bowl of salad and the bottle of wine from her hands so he could take her in his arms and kiss her, which suited Christy just fine.

She found Sledge sprawled on the sofa in the living room when she finally climbed the stairs. He was dressed in jeans and a front button shirt with the tails untucked. One ankle was propped over the other knee and he had a bottle of beer in front of him. Bowls of chips in a variety of flavors were set on the coffee table.

Christy raised her brows when she saw him. "Hello. Are you the first to arrive?"

Sledge grinned as he pulled what looked like a barbeque chip from one of the bowls. "The Cat's here. He's in the kitchen watching Roy make rice to go with the stew he cooked."

Christy shot an amused glance at Quinn, who hadn't mentioned that Frank had arrived along with Sledge. Quinn settled down on the couch where a beer was waiting, while Sledge crunched chips and Christy took the salad and wine into the kitchen. There she helped Roy; setting the table, opening a bottle of white and one of red wine, so both could breathe. They chatted about an idea Roy had for his next mystery. Christy wasn't surprised when she learned it revolved around the murder of a prominent politician. She wondered how closely it would mirror the actual events that occurred when they investigated the death of Tamara Ahern's birth father a few months earlier.

Ellen and Trevor arrived not long after, bringing more wine and dessert, a cheesecake, which Christy had learned was Trevor's favorite. They all settled down to enjoy the stew, including the cat, whose portion included meat, the gravy, and a selection of vegetables that made a more balanced meal than Frank would have consumed when he was alive. As they ate, they discussed the death of Karen Beaumont and the arrest of Anton Gormley.

"The Jamieson Foundation is brand new," Christy said, helping herself to rice as the bowl was passed around the table. "I want it to make a difference and I'm afraid people will be wary if they find out that the Foundation is funding a program with poor, or even just dubious, decision-making."

"The At Risk Students program began three years ago," Trevor said. "It's a two-year diploma for students in the Entertainment Arts." He frowned a little. "Twelve students participated in the first year, enrolled in various specialties. They all passed their first year and returned for their second. Last year another twelve were enrolled. Five dropped out, but seven remained, including Anton Gormley, and returned for their second year. Twelve more began the program this September."

"Since Gormley is one of the group that already had problems with maintaining their enrollment, maybe the selection process was flawed," Christy said.

"Could be, though all twelve students from the first intake graduated and most have found jobs in the industry." Trevor added stew to his plate and passed the serving dish to Ellen. "The only way to tell if there's a systemic problem is if this year's class starts to drop out."

Sledge already had both rice and stew on his plate. His fork half way to his mouth, he paused. "What's the matter with Gormley? I thought the kid was pretty talented."

His father looked at him, puzzled. "Anton Gormley was arrested for Karen Beaumont's murder. Didn't you know?"

Sledge's fork clattered onto the plate. "No! I was down in LA for some meetings. I only got home last night. When did they arrest him?"

"Wednesday," Quinn said.

Having finished his meal, the cat hopped up into Christy's lap so he could watch the action. Quinn took note and his jaw hardened, but he didn't say anything.

"So the kid has been in jail for two days for a crime he didn't commit?" Sledge asked. He sounded indignant.

"He didn't kill Beaumont?" Roy looked over his wine glass at Sledge. "How do you know?"

The cat put a paw up on the table and sniffed Christy's stew. She eased the paw away and made him sit again.

Sledge said, "Because I was there! After that idiot professor turned my ballad into an opera aria, I hooked up with Tamara, remember?"

"We were going to take you home," Trevor said. Christy couldn't be sure if he disapproved of his son slipping away with Tamara, or not.

"Yeah, well, I didn't want to slink away and give the jerk the satisfaction of thinking he'd bested me. So Tamara and I went into the garden. She wanted some fresh air, or at least that's what she told me. It didn't quite work out that way, but..."

"It didn't?"

Christy thought she heard amusement in Quinn's voice, but his

62

CAT IN THE LIMELIGHT

expression was politely enquiring.

Sledge shot him wary look. "No, it didn't. The path led to a covered arbor and we, er, got distracted."

Distracted? Oh, please!

Sledge glared at the cat. "The thing is, we didn't see Gormley, either when we were on the path or later when we were in the arbor."

"The path that begins at the bottom of the stairs leads down to the arbor," Christy said.

"It does, and you can see the top half dozen stairs from the arbor. You can't see the last couple, though, or where they meet the path. Anyway, we were, ah, involved in each other—"

"Involved in each other?" said Trevor, sending his son an incredulous look.

"Okay, we were kissing. It doesn't matter, though, because that's when we heard footsteps and a gasp, then a voice swore, and said, 'Dean Beaumont? Are you okay? Are you hurt?' At that point Tamara said, 'Sounds like she needs help' and then she dragged me out of the arbor. The thing was, in the arbor we couldn't see Beaumont's body, but we could see Gormley. It wasn't until we got closer that I saw her stretched out on the path."

"Mr. Gormley could have killed her earlier," Ellen said.

"When?" Sledge asked. "Not when Tamara and I were in the arbor. We would have seen them both at the top of the stairs and we'd have witnessed him pushing her down them. But we didn't. Gormley isn't the killer."

"There must have been a reason the police concluded Gormley murdered her," Trevor said. He frowned at his son. "Did you tell Detective Patterson what you just told us?"

Sledge shook his head. "Patterson didn't talk to me. I gave my statement to the guy built like a sparkplug, the detective who arrived before Patterson. He wanted to know where I was and who was around the body when I called 9-1-1. He wasn't interested in what I'd seen or what I thought. He said he'd contact me if he needed to clarify my statement. He didn't."

"The cops talked to everyone," Roy said. "They must have a lot more information than we do."

Or maybe they simply got it wrong.

"Exactly," Sledge said. "They don't have my information."

"If they questioned Tamara, surely she would have told them what you just told us?" Christy said.

"They might not have asked the right questions." Roy shrugged. "They didn't go into any depth with Sledge."

Trevor's expression was thoughtful. "I'll call Patterson in the morning. She should hear your story."

"This puts the murder in a different light," Christy said. "If Gormley isn't the one who killed Karen Beaumont, then the quality of the At Risk program isn't in question. I think I can continue the Foundation's involvement, at least until we find out if Sledge is correct or not."

"Since three of the trustees are in this room, why don't we take a vote," Ellen said. The shake up that made Christy the face of the Jamiesons also saw new trustees appointed to manage the Jamieson Trust. Ellen had agreed to stay on, with Trevor, Roy, and Harry Endicott, the forensic accountant who unraveled the embezzlement of the Jamieson Trust and arranged for its return, in the new positions. Harry preferred to focus on ensuring the financial aspects of the Trust were in good order. He left the social and family issues to the other three.

"Is it agreed that the Jamieson Foundation continue to support the At Risk program at Point Grey College?" Ellen asked. "Who votes yes?" Trevor and Roy raised their hands, and a moment later she did as well. "Then we are agreed. Christy, contact PGC and confirm our participation."

"I'll do it first thing Monday morning," she said. "Thanks, Ellen."

CHAPTER 8

B illie Patterson, her long, gorgeous, dark hair loose around her shoulders in a style that was highly unprofessional, said, "It's Saturday, my day off, at ten o'clock in the morning. Whatever it is you want to tell me, Mr. McCullagh, it better be good."

Patterson, Sledge, and Trevor were sitting in the bare-bones coffee shop near the station where Patterson worked. The location was Sledge's idea. He had serious stuff to talk about and he didn't want to be interrupted by an excited fan. He trusted the cops who frequented this café to respect his privacy. He hadn't expected Patterson to show up wearing a soft, gauzy blouse and tight-fitting jeans that when combined with the loose curling hair made her look all woman, with the cop nowhere in sight.

Except for the brisk tone and the authoritative demand.

He raised his eyebrows. "Mr. McCullagh, Detective? Surely, we're beyond that kind of formality by now." He added a note of sardonic amusement to the facial expression. He hoped one or the other, or both together, would push her off balance, because in his experience people thrust out of their comfort zones were more likely to act in the way he wanted them to, not the way they would if they were able to let their own agendas play out.

And he was pretty sure Patterson wasn't going to be happy about what he had to say. She had her perpetrator in a jail cell, safely locked up because the poor sod was unable to post bail. She'd probably been planning to enjoy her weekend, secure in the knowledge that her most recent case could be filed in the solved drawer. She wouldn't want to start looking for a new culprit and that was what he was about to ask her to do.

Not at all intimidated by his attempt to manipulate her, Patterson leaned across the Formica tabletop and said in a very cold voice, "Nice try, Mr. McCullagh." She straightened, then lounged against the back of the booth, keeping her eyes locked with his.

Sledge blinked at her. Well, so much for raised eyebrows and rock star cool. Patterson was a tough nut who was not going to crack just because he referenced their shared camping trip a couple of months ago. So what if he and the others had saved her damned brother-in-law? Evidently, Patterson wasn't going to let a little thing like an obligation influence her attitude.

He thought about meeting intimidation with intimidation, leaning forward and shooting his own crack back at her, but that would be stupid, probably what she'd expect. She was a detective, after all. She was used to dealing with hard cases who were themselves expert at keeping secrets. His goal was to get Anton Gormley out of jail as fast as possible. He needed Patterson on his side.

So he assumed a serious expression, the one he used when he was talking to interviewers or influencers who were cultural know-it-alls whose critical reviews could make or break a career. He knew how to play the influence game pretty well himself. Clasping his hands together, he leaned his elbows on the tabletop and said earnestly, "I think it's important information, Detective. I hope you will too. It concerns what I saw at the gala last week."

"The Beaumont murder. Your father said as much when he called me this morning. At seven-thirty. Waking me from a sound sleep."

This statement did not sound promising and it was all his fault—again. Last night, after dinner wound down, his father had made some phone calls and discovered that Patterson had the weekend off. He'd then told the assembled group he'd make an appointment with her on Monday. At the time Sledge had agreed, but reluctantly. It wasn't until he was home that he started to wonder if he should have pushed for an earlier meeting. He spent the night tossing and turning, brooding, and coming to the conclusion that Anton Gormley's incarceration was his fault, because he'd let the male detective who took his statement choose what information he gathered. If Sledge had insisted on making the man listen to his interpretation of what he'd seen, would Gormley have been arrested? Probably not.

His mistake. His to fix. Sooner rather than later.

Being awake most of the night wasn't unusual for him, so when he rose at six in the morning it was simply another hour in the day. He'd thought about calling Patterson, but he didn't have her cell number. His father did, so Trevor got the six AM call, not Patterson. Which was probably a good thing, thinking about it now.

"I'm sorry about that, but Anton Gormley isn't guilty of Karen Beaumont's murder. He shouldn't be locked up."

To his surprise, Patterson sighed. This time when she leaned forward there was no aggression in the move. She looked from him to his father and back. "Sledge, Mr. McCullagh, you and Mrs. Jamieson and the Armstrongs have helped me out in the past, and I appreciate it. But the evidence in the Beaumont murder is conclusive. The case is closed."

"She wasn't at the top of the stairs. Nor was Gormley. He couldn't have pushed her down. Neither of them were where they had to be for him to be her killer."

That caught Patterson's attention. Frowning, she said, "Take a step back. What exactly do you mean, they weren't where they had to be?"

Encouraged by her interest, Sledge described the way the ground dipped, hiding the bottom of the stairs from his viewpoint in the arbor, but giving anyone standing there a clear view of the terrace, the curving staircases that ran down from either end to meet above the garden stairs and the top of the garden stairs themselves. How he and Tamara had seen Anton standing at the base of the garden staircase, swearing, then the arrival of one of the profs, who appeared from the shadows near the house, and had apparently come to see what was happening. He was followed by Jackson and Mrs. Hargreaves, arguing loudly as they came down the curving stairs from the terrace. Then Mrs. Hargreaves screamed, and Tamara had rushed out of the arbor to provide assistance to the injured woman.

"And that didn't do my ego any good, I can tell you," he added.

His father sighed. "Stick to the facts, Rob."

When his father called him by his proper name, Sledge knew he was serious. He resisted the urge to snap out a cocky, 'yes sir!' and nodded instead. "Right. So, I didn't see Gormley arrive at the body— Tamara and I were, er, busy—but I heard his footsteps walking along one of the other paths."

"The steps you heard could have been him walking down the stairs after he pushed Ms. Beaumont," Patterson said.

Could have been but weren't. Sledge drew a deep breath. "Then why didn't she scream as she fell? Why didn't Tamara and I hear her arguing with Gormley?"

"Maybe she was standing at the top of the stairs, looking out at the garden and he came up behind her, then pushed her. She wouldn't have known he was there. They didn't have to argue."

This sounded highly unlikely to Sledge. "Wouldn't she have screamed as she fell?"

"Not necessarily."

He studied Patterson, trying to figure out if she really believed what she'd said, or if she was brainstorming possibilities. He hoped she was just trying to be thorough. "Okay, so she didn't have to scream, but there would be sound as her body fell, right?"

Reluctantly, Patterson nodded.

"I heard nothing."

She opened her mouth to say something and he waved her quiet.

"Listen, you know me, Detective. I live a public life. I have to be aware of what I'm doing, of what people see me doing. Cell phone cameras are everywhere. People video me doing anything. Everything! Every stupid little thing, because I'm a celebrity. That night I was in the trees making out with a woman who has good reason to be camera shy. Did I want what we were doing caught on someone's cell phone? No way. Yeah, we were kissing. Yeah, I was involved. But part of me was aware of what was going on around me. Those footsteps? I was pulling out of the kiss the moment I heard them. If a body had fallen down those stairs? I'd have been three feet away from Tamara before it hit bottom."

He stopped to draw a deep breath. "Karen Beaumont didn't fall when Tamara and I were in that arbor, or when Anton Gormley walked into the area. She was dead before then."

Patterson studied him. He knew his tension showed in his body, as well as in his face and voice. After a moment she said, "And you'd be prepared testify to that."

"I'd prefer not to, but—"

"Rob will do his duty," his father said.

He didn't have to interrupt. The 'but' was coming before a promise to stand by his words. After shooting an annoyed glance at his father, he said, "I only have to testify if Gormley goes to trial, am I correct?"

His father cleared his throat. Patterson smiled. It wasn't a particularly nice smile, Sledge thought, more smug than friendly.

"Perhaps, perhaps not. We have yet to determine the exact time of

Ms. Beaumont's death. You can attest that it didn't happen in the few minutes before Gormley found her body, but we knew that."

Sledge thought back. "Tamara said she'd been dead for awhile."

"We already had Dr. Ahern's testimony, which yours now supports. We didn't arrest Gormley because he showed up on the scene shortly before you and the others. We arrested him because he stormed out of the ballroom before the end of the set. He had plenty of time to find Ms. Beaumont and kill her before her body was found."

Trevor said reluctantly, "Inside the ballroom the music was loud enough to cover the sound of screams."

Patterson nodded.

"Why would he kill her? What's his motive?" Sledge asked. He didn't believe the kid murdered Karen Beaumont. Patterson was going to have to go a long way to prove it to him.

She watched him as she said, "Anton Gormley wasn't the only member of the band we interviewed. Jesica Kushnir, their drummer, is a big fan of SledgeHammer. Did you know that?"

He nodded. "All the members of Lightening Rod are."

Patterson gave him a little nod. "Kushnir is a graphic design student in the At Risk program. When she was helping make the place cards for the gala, she discovered you would be one of the guests. She immediately told her band mates in Lightening Rod and together they cooked up a tribute to be included in their first set."

Sledge thought he should be cocky, rock-star cool, and say something like, 'I'm not surprised. It happens all the time.' But he couldn't. He was touched that these kids who had so many strikes against them cared enough about him and his band to want to celebrate them during a performance that must have meant everything to them. So he said gruffly, "I didn't know. I thought they came up with the idea when I came down to the ballroom and jammed with them."

Shaking her head, Patterson said, "It was definitely pre-planned. Jesica said she and the others wanted to launch it as a surprise at the gala, but Gormley insisted they should run it by the dean. He had an interview with her two days before the gala. According to him, Beaumont loved the idea."

"That was why he was so angry when that opera jerk took over the stage," Sledge said.

Patterson laughed. "Opera jerk? You mean Samuel Moore?"

Sledge nodded.

Patterson's amusement died. Her expression was grim as she said, "Mr. Gormley believed Ms. Beaumont should have stopped Moore from singing and in his own words he went off to find her to see why she'd screwed him over."

"What did she say when he talked to her?"

"He claims he couldn't find her."

"Well?" Sledge said. "Then he didn't kill her."

Patterson raised her eyebrows. "We think he did find her. That he demanded she step in and stop Moore. When she refused, the anger he was already feeling boiled over. There were hot words and he got physical. He pushed her, she lost her balance, and tumbled down the stairs. Realizing what he'd done, he took off, but he couldn't stay away, so later he came back to see if she was still alive. That's when you and the others saw him."

Sledge was incredulous. "Are you saying he didn't try to find out if she was alive or dead after her fall?"

Patterson shrugged. "He might have, but I doubt it. Look, he's a violent guy with a history of assault."

Trevor cleared his throat. "He's one of the At Risk students at PGC. The program includes counseling and self-awareness training. President Harding claims Gormley had cleaned himself up."

Patterson shrugged. "For Gormley, Moore's action was an immediate and public humiliation. It would take a lot more inner fortitude than what he'd learned from a couple of college courses to keep him from backsliding. His temper played out and he went rogue. When

Beaumont wouldn't help him, she became the target instead of Moore."

Sledge grappled with that—and found the flaw. "The stairs are steep, but not so steep that you'd expect someone to die if she fell down them."

Patterson stared at him, expressionless. "Your point?"

"You're describing a man consumed by anger. Anger is energy. If he pushed Beaumont the anger would be used up, the energy lost as he watched her fall down the stairs. He'd go down to check on her. He would have been the one to call 9-1-1, not me."

Her gaze steady on him, Patterson said, "Murder is a crime with a lot of incarceration time attached to it. When a person realizes he's committed a crime, he'll look for ways to keep from being caught. Murderers do not easily admit what they've done. Anton Gormley is scared of doing time. He's angry circumstances forced him into an action he knows is wrong, and he feels guilty. He's not going to admit that he pushed a woman down the stairs in a fit of unbridled rage."

"He's pleading innocent?" Trevor asked.

Patterson nodded.

"Your evidence is circumstantial. Has he retained counsel?"

His father was looking interested, Sledge thought, and he saw Trevor perk up further when Patterson nodded.

"He's been assigned a public defender."

"Busy people, public defenders," Trevor said, sounding thoughtful. "In my experience, they never turn down a little freely given assistance."

Sledge almost laughed at the artificially innocent expression on his father's face. In that moment, Anton Gormley's future looked a little less grim.

Patterson stared at Trevor for a long moment, then she said, "All right, Mr. McCullagh. You've made your point. I'll look a little deeper into the case, but I don't expect to find a different outcome. Anton

Gormley killed Karen Beaumont because she refused to intercede with one of her instructors on his behalf."

"Thanks," Sledge said. He didn't like that Patterson sounded pretty sure nothing would change, but he trusted her to be thorough and he knew she was honest. If she discovered proof Gormley didn't do it, she'd cut him loose and start again.

She slid to the edge of the booth and stood up. Looking down at them, she said, "You know you've ruined my weekend, don't you?" Before either he or his father could respond she turned and walked away.

CHAPTER 9

"Thank you for agreeing to meet with me, Mrs. Jamieson." Craig Harding stood as Christy was shown to his table.

It was Tuesday afternoon and she and Harding were meeting at that most neutral of locations, the coffee shop of a high-end hotel, where a patron could sit over coffee, choose a snack, or order a full meal. In this case, the restaurant was decorated in a modern, minimalist style, all glass, pale wood, and bright lighting. It was elegant, not tacky, and, to Christy's mind, the perfect venue for a discussion between the representatives of a funding organization and a progressive, modern college.

They both looked the part, she thought with some amusement. She was wearing a cream-colored, tailored suit, with a pencil skirt and her heels had been handmade in Italy. Her jewelry was subdued, and her purse was a small clutch that matched her shoes. Harding's suit was well cut, the fabric expensive, his white shirt was fine cloth and his royal blue tie was silk. His appearance was impeccable, but then he had the kind of body that wore clothes well and he was a man firmly in control of himself and the situation around him.

He waited until she was settled before he resumed his seat, showing her he had excellent manners. Ellen would approve. Christy approved, too, though she promised herself she would never be as obsessive about proper behavior as Frank's aunt was. "I was surprised when you called this morning and asked me to meet you here," she said. She knew he would want to confirm that the Jamieson Foundation would continue to fund the PGC At Risk program. She hadn't expected a face-to-face to discuss the future.

The server put a menu in front of her, but she waved it away. "Just coffee for me, please."

Craig ordered the same. After the woman gathered the menus and moved off, he said, "I've had news regarding the investigation into Karen Beaumont's death."

So that was what this was all about. "I heard the young man from Lightening Rod had been arrested for her murder."

Craig nodded. "I'm not surprised. It was all over the news last week. Unfortunately, the press hasn't publicized his subsequent release."

In her mind, Christy cheered. So Sledge's intervention had worked. "I see."

"You can imagine how relieved we all are that Anton has been exonerated."

"He has an alibi for the time of the murder, then?" Christy asked. The waitress reappeared with mugs of coffee in tall, pristine white cone shaped cups. She set bowls with creamers and sugar packets down, followed by a carafe in the same vivid white, and asked if they needed anything else. When they each said they were fine, she nodded, then slipped away, quietly efficient.

Craig doctored his coffee and stirred it slowly. "Apparently, the pathologist concluded Karen had been dead for at least a half an hour before she was found and could have died as much as several hours earlier."

Christy had assumed the autopsy report had been delivered before Gormley was arrested. She wondered if Sledge's information had caused Patterson to intervene and ask for more details from the pathologist. Or perhaps they looked at the report more carefully once their obvious suspect was cleared.

"The police are trying to pinpoint when she was last seen to help narrow down the time of death." Harding hesitated, then said apologetically, "I've been told to make my staff available for further questioning, so I expect you and your family should be prepared for a visit from the police as well."

At that, Christy laughed. She couldn't help it. "That doesn't worry me, President Harding—"

"Please, call me Craig." He smiled ruefully. "President Harding still sounds like someone else."

Christy smiled. "Of course. And you must call me Christy." That formality concluded, she said, "I've known Detective Patterson for some time. She's a good cop, fair and honest. I'm not worried about being questioned by her."

He frowned a little. "That's right. Last year you helped her prove that your husband was murdered."

She was sipping her coffee—black—from her elegant mug when he spoke, so she was able to wait a moment to formulate her answer before she replied. "Quinn Armstrong and I did, yes. We've worked with her a couple of times since, so you could say we've gotten to know each other."

"I hope Anton's release will make it easier for you to continue to fund At Risk Students." Craig spent a few moments outlining the benefits of the program and its value to the community.

Christy listened without interrupting. She'd planned to reassure him that her foundation would not pull out of the program, but after Sledge's revelations on Friday night she decided to wait until Patterson had completed her deliberations. Still, holding back her decision,

CAT IN THE LIMELIGHT

giving Harding the opportunity to convince her, created an illusion of cautious decision-making. Asking questions would help too. "I'm glad for the young man's sake that he has been released. I thought he was quite talented when he performed at the gala." She smiled faintly. "Sledge thought so too. He was rather upset when your professor took over the SledgeHammer tribute songs."

Craig grimaced. "Samuel likes the limelight. I've spoken to him about that evening. I don't think it will happen again."

Since Moore had also shoved himself into the musical theater performance, she hoped Harding had given the man a tongue-lashing he wouldn't soon forget. Holding her cup between her hands, she studied Craig Harding. "Did the police tell you why they zeroed in on Anton Gormley? Was it because he was an At Risk student?"

Craig nodded. "As a teenager, he was arrested for assault and served time in juvenile detention for it. Before he joined the program, he was living on the street and had a reputation for having a violent temper. I'm sure that influenced them, particularly as he was so agitated when he stormed off the stage. He appeared to be a young man out for blood."

Christy put her cup on the table. She raised her brows and looked carefully at Craig. "Although the At Risk program may benefit from Gormley's release, I'm sure you must realize that Point Grey College is even more deeply involved now."

From the grim expression on his face he was aware and had hoped she wasn't. Still, he said cautiously, "What do you mean?"

She moved the cup on the table for a minute, following it with her eyes, before she sighed and looked up at him. "Whoever killed Karen Beaumont did it for a reason. From anger, jealousy, greed, self-advancement. He or she knew her, perhaps personally or as a colleague at PGC. Since most of the people at the gala were there because they were involved with PGC somehow, it was probably someone related to the At Risk program."

Craig's face was an expressionless mask, but Christy wasn't fooled. He didn't want to talk about this with an outsider, particularly one who, like her, was providing financial support for one of his initiatives. She was digging deep, exposing a murky bottom beneath the clear, clean waters of his educational institution and he didn't like it.

She sighed and said, "You mentioned you'd heard I helped Detective Patterson expose my husband's murderer."

His gaze sharpened. "I understand Quinn Armstrong is releasing a book on your...quest. He's scheduled to talk to our publishing students later this week."

Christy nodded. "Yes, I believe he's quite looking forward to it." She refilled her cup from the carafe the server had left them. "My husband Frank was the victim of a vicious conspiracy to embezzle his fortune and blacken his name. He disappeared in the spring, along with most of the family trust, and for a very long time everyone, including the press, thought he was in Mexico living the high life on the embezzled funds with the sweet young thing who was his mistress. I didn't believe it, but that didn't matter. In fact, there were also suggestions that I was the one who did the embezzling."

She paused to sip her coffee, then put her cup down and looked directly at Harding. "I tell you this because I want you to understand I have experience dealing with the damage that unfounded suspicions and gossip can do to a reputation, to a life, to every action you make."

"You're telling me I need to be prepared for serious scrutiny."

"Not serious, but malicious, uninformed, and repetitive. Mob mentality. An influencer says this is the truth and people react as if it is, even if it's not. Karen Beaumont was murdered. Someone wanted her dead. Why? We don't know and not knowing is what causes the problem. People will speculate and act as if the speculation is fact. They will create a motive that means something to them and believe it's the truth. But it's not. Until the real culprit is found, the situation will get very ugly, Craig."

He fiddled with the handle of his cup. After a moment, his expression impassive, he said, "I have no idea why Karen was killed. She was an excellent administrator, tough, but fair. She was the one who came up with the At Risk idea and that was only one example of the innovations she made. I can't imagine any of her people being angry enough at something that happened at work to kill her. Yes, they might go to the union and make a grievance against her, or if they weren't part of the union, they might go to the Vice President Academic to protest some decision she'd made. But to push her down a flight of stairs? That implies passion and I just can't see it."

"So you think it was personal?"

He grimaced. "Point Grey is not just an educational institution, it's also a community. Many of our employees are related or are involved with another employee in some way. My assistant's father is a professor in the culinary department. My wife is the events manager for the college."

Christy raised her eyebrows as she smiled. "I remember. She had to rush off to deal with a crisis just after you introduced us at the gala."

Craig grinned at her. "Yeah, that happens. My point is that there are a lot of personal relationships, but as long as one person in the relationship doesn't report to the other, we don't have any problem with it. Karen was no exception. Her former brother-in-law, Declan West, works in the Theater Arts department. He's Professor of Physical Acting."

"Former brother-in-law?"

Craig nodded. "She divorced his brother the not long after she became dean. It was quite a nasty split at the time, but that was five years ago. I can't see Declan as the murderer." He stopped, shook his head. "I can't see anyone as the murderer! This is a damnable situation."

"It is," Christy said with a nod. She paused, then said, "Patterson will take statements, dig into timelines, build a case that will stand up in court. She's good at her job and she gets it done. But...If you have insights, she's willing to listen to them."

"You're suggesting I should investigate the murder myself."

"I'm suggesting that everyone needs help, including the cops." Christy smiled as she glanced at her watch. "I must be on my way if I'm to get back to Burnaby to pick my daughter up from school. It has been a pleasure talking to you, Craig." She gathered her purse and stood up.

He stood as well and held out his hand. "Thank you for meeting with me, Christy."

She smiled and nodded. After a moment of hesitation, she said, "If I can help in any way, please, call me."

He smiled in response, but she wasn't sure if it was one of those empty, it's-never-going-to-happen smiles, or surprise at an unexpected offer.

She wasn't sure which one she really wanted it to be.

CHAPTER 10

Q uinn shut his front door behind him and thought with rueful amusement that he was being an idiot. He didn't have to invite Christy to his reading at PGC tomorrow afternoon—she was already coming. He wondered if having her there was the reason he was so stupidly nervous about the speaking engagement. It wasn't as if he wasn't used to talking to an audience. He'd spent years in front of the camera, reporting from hot spots around the world to millions of viewers.

Millions he couldn't see, of course. Maybe that was part of his problem. He knew the audience existed, but he never had to look into their faces. Tomorrow he would. He'd feel their emotions as they listened, be aware of their response, know they were judging him— and his work. Maybe that intimate, personal effect was what had his stomach in knots even now.

Idiot.

"Hi, Quinn. Mom's in the house." Noelle's yell brought him out of his funk. She was standing stork-like on one leg in the middle of the hopscotch board she and her dear friend Mary Petrofsky had chalked onto the pavement midway between their two houses. As Noelle spoke, Mary Petrofsky, waiting at the end of the board for her turn, shot him a cheerful smile and waved.

Quinn waved back as he ran lightly down his stairs. "Thanks," he said feeling the nerves leave him. The kid had a way of grounding him. Or maybe it was her connection to Christy that was making him feel that whatever happened tomorrow, he could handle it. When he turned at the end of his walk for Christy's house, there was a spring in his step.

He slowed as he started up Christy's walk and saw the cat crouched on the porch, in front of the door. The creature eyed him balefully, as only a disapproving cat can. Quinn suspected, though, it wasn't the cat who was glaring at him, but Frank Jamieson. He resisted the urge to glare back and instead said pleasantly, "Keeping an eye on Noelle and Mary, are you?"

The cat stood and arched his back in a sinuous stretch, before settling on his haunches. He then shot out one back leg and proceeded to industriously clean himself. Incredulously, Quinn decided he'd just been given the cat equivalent of the finger. Shaking his head, he ran up the stairs, stepped over the cat—who hissed at him—then entered the house through the door that was ajar to allow entry for cat and children. "Christy, are you around?"

"In the kitchen," she called back.

She met him in the archway between the living room and the kitchen. "Ellen and I are having a cup of coffee before we start diner. Would you like to join us?"

"Sure." He followed her into the kitchen without doing what he would have liked to—draw her aside for a quick, but thorough, kiss. With Ellen in the kitchen, though, that wasn't going to happen. She might have unwound a lot in the past year, but she still believed there were certain ways a Jamieson behaved and acts of affection played out in front of others weren't among them.

Christy inserted a pod into the coffeemaker and set the machine going. "Ellen and I were discussing Karen Beaumont's death. Now that the student has been released, Patterson has to find the real culprit."

Quinn hadn't come over to talk about the murder, but speculating on who the actual killer was, was fine with him. He settled at the table. "Any ideas?"

Ellen had her leather binder open in front of her. It was filled with her personal letterhead and she'd arranged three fountain pens beside it. Each would be filled with a different color ink, Quinn knew. Ellen was prepared to make a list and start organizing suspects.

"I believe her death was personal," Ellen said. "The murder was committed in a public space, with two hundred or more people in close proximity. It was risky. For someone to take the chance he or she might be observed, the motive would have to be a strong one. The most powerful reasons to cause harm are always personal."

"Money and fear are also good motivators," Quinn said.

The coffeemaker hissed and chugged, then fell silent. Christy brought the mug over to the table for Quinn, then sat down between him and Ellen. "The problem with personal is the venue. Her death happened at a party, a well-publicized gala filled with colleagues and donors and industry professionals. Surely, if her death was a personal relationship gone wrong, that individual would have chosen a different venue to kill her."

"Perhaps that's why she was killed at the gala," Ellen said. "So that suspicion would be cast on many and the real culprit ignored."

"Could be," Christy said. "But if that was the reason, then the murderer was probably the professor Craig Harding mentioned, Declan West. He's the only one who seems to have had a personal grudge against her."

The cat hopped up on the remaining chair. When he sat down, all Quinn could see was the top of his head, ears perked, and green eyes staring balefully at him over the top of the table.

"He works at PGC," Christy said. "I thought you were watching Noelle and Mary."

'He works at PGC.' The cat must have asked who Declan West was. Quinn resigned himself to a tiring conversation where he had to guess half of what was being said.

Christy's frown cleared as she stared at the cat, who must have told her why he was here in the kitchen and not outside doing his job.

"Frank said Rebecca Petrofsky is home and the girls went to help her carry in her grocery bags," she said, filling Quinn in. "From what Craig Harding told me, Declan West has good reason to be resentful of Karen Beaumont. She was married to his brother, but they divorced about five years ago. Apparently, the divorce was a nasty one, which I suppose is as good a reason as any to be angry at someone, but he also said it was several years ago and they've worked together since then with no evidence of a problem."

"So, it's the length of time between the issue and the action that you don't buy," Quinn said.

She nodded. "I think the motive must come from inside the college, from the decisions she made or the way she interacted with her colleagues."

"I suppose it could be something like that," Ellen said. It was a grudging agreement as she wrote Christy's observation on her elegant paper.

The ink color she used, Quinn noted, was green. She'd written Declan West's name, and notes about him, in red. Red for violence, green for jealousy? Well, why not? "There's another possibility." One Ellen would probably note down in blue ink. "Beaumont was deeply involved in the film production industry here in Vancouver before she moved on to academia. She could have old enemies with scores to settle from that part of her life."

"I'm not sure," Ellen said, "but I spoke to Mitch Crosier and his wife, Kim, at one point in the evening."

The cat must have asked who was at the gala who had links to the film industry. Though Crosier was more influential in the music world, he'd been involved in the production of music videos and wanted to branch out into other fields as well.

"I like Kim too," Christy said. "And no, I agree. I don't think she's a killer."

"I saw Gillian Stankov, the CEO of the Arts Association," Quinn said, ignoring the comment about Kim Crosier, which must have come from the cat. "She looked pained. I noticed her with Beaumont earlier. Perhaps they'd been arguing." The Arts Association was a professional organization that provided artists of all kinds a voice in the competitive industry.

Ellen made a note of Stankov's name—in blue ink—then carefully capped her pen. "We have reached a state of complete speculation. We don't know enough about the murdered woman or her life to really make a difference." She sounded frustrated.

Her comment dovetailed nicely with his excuse for coming by this afternoon. "I'm giving a talk on my writing process at PGC tomorrow at four in the afternoon." And to promote his book on Frank Jamieson's murder, though he wasn't about to add that detail with the cat staring unblinking at him across the table. "There's a reception afterward and a possibility that some of the faculty and staff will be there. Christy agreed to come as my guest, but you're more than welcome to join us, Ellen. Dad has already decided he'll be there. He wants to do some sleuthing."

Ellen looked pleased by the invitation, though it was hard to tell from the precise way she answered. "Thank you, Quinn, but I have a committee meeting tomorrow afternoon I cannot miss."

Quinn nodded, then turned to Christy. "Will you be driving down with Dad and me?"

"Absolutely," she said, smiling.

Until she frowned. The cat must have said something rude.

"Great," he said, pretending not to notice. "We can do dinner after." He stood. "I'll see you tomorrow."

She nodded, then stood and deliberately leaned over to kiss him.

He made his way home floating on air.

~

The traffic along Broadway was heavy, even at three-thirty in the afternoon, which was a good thing because it meant he had something more to focus on than his nerves. They'd come back this morning with a vengeance while he'd put the final polish on his notes for the talk this afternoon. No matter how many times he told himself he could handle it, the butterflies in the pit of his stomach just wouldn't go away.

It was ridiculous. He'd spent seven years of his life standing in front of a cameraman reporting on dangerous situations throughout the world. He assembled facts in advance, decided which were important, then spoke without notes, confidently, without hesitation. Why, then, was he dreading this speaking engagement at Point Grey College?

Was it because his audience would be mainly students in the college's publishing program? Critical young people used to assessing everything as they sought out flaws and imperfections? Or was it that he'd lost his edge in the three years since he'd left his post as a foreign correspondent with the country's premier network and gone freelance?

He didn't like the idea that he'd lost his edge. He might not want to be on camera anymore, or to go to those regions where upheaval was an everyday fact of life, but he still saw himself as a journalist who looked for the story underlying the careful cover overtop. In the year since he'd convinced Christy Jamieson that he could help her find her missing husband, he'd been involved in five murders and helped solve

CAT IN THE LIMELIGHT

each of them. Those cases had resulted in articles in the press, and interviews on the national news shows. The book he was promoting at today's talk was only the first of a series of true crime exposés under contract with his publisher.

He was busy and, according to the publicist his publisher had assigned him, about to become even more well-known that he'd been when he'd reported for the nightly news broadcasts. The publisher was convinced the book would be a bestseller before Christmas and by the new year they'd be looking at movie deals.

So why was he sweating this talk to a bunch of students?

Maybe it was for the same reason he hadn't wanted to define the reason for the talk yesterday at Christy's house. The book laid bare the sordid and tragic end to Frank Jamieson's life and it exposed private parts of Christy's life that were painful to her. After she'd discovered and confronted Frank's killer, she'd given Quinn permission to write about what they'd learned through their investigations, but that was in theory. Once the book was out a few short weeks from now, the reality would be renewed media interest in Frank's death and Christy's life with him.

And this damned murder at the gala, with both his and Christy's involvement, was only going to make matters worse.

Too soon he was pulling into the parking lot behind the red brick building that housed the college. He could hear the car engine slowly ticking as it cooled. And, damn it, he still couldn't shake his ridiculous case of nerves.

The sound of a car door slamming behind him snapped him out of his introspection. His father, who had been the back-seat passenger in their commute from Burnaby to Point Grey College, was out of the car and stretching.

Christy put her hand on his and said, "I don't care what the students think, I'm looking forward to your talk."

How did she do that? How did she know just what he needed to hear at exactly the right moment? He turned to her. "Are you sure? I'll be referencing the investigation and I know it won't be easy for you to hear it all again." That was why his father had decided to come. He was there to support Christy if she needed it.

She put her finger over his lips, effectively silencing him. "Hush. I wouldn't be here if I had problems with it." She smiled. "Let's head into the college and find the room you're giving the talk in."

He smiled back at her, then lifted his hand to catch her head and draw her close for a quick kiss. She responded with a tenderness that shook him and after he drew out of the kiss, he took a moment to caress her cheek with his thumb before letting her go.

Outside the car, he discovered that his father had done some scouting while he was making his peace with himself and Christy.

"The entrance is over there," Roy said, pointing to a glass door on one side of the structure. "There's a woman hovering in the doorway, waiting for us, I think." He glanced at his watch. "We're not late, but she seems pretty antsy."

Quinn drew a deep breath, ran his fingers through his hair, and nodded. Show time. "Okay, let's go."

The woman turned out to be Celene Warden, the associate dean of Entertainment Arts. She was small, with dark hair cut in a businesslike bob, more nose than her small face should have, big blue eyes, and a bright, excited smile. "Mr. Armstrong, it's a pleasure meeting you," she said after introducing herself.

"It's Quinn, please," he said, then introduced Christy and his father.

Her eyes widened. "Roy Armstrong, the novelist? Oh, this is a wonderful surprise. I'm such a fan. My first job after I graduated from university was as an editorial assistant at your publishing house, but I never got the chance to meet you." She went on to explain she'd worked in publishing for several years before joining the publishing program at PGC.

"Nice to meet you, too, Ms. Warden," Roy said. "But this is my son's show this afternoon. I'm just here to watch and listen."

"As am I," Christy said.

Eyes wide, Celene nodded. "Of course." They all set off for the lecture theater where the talk was to take place. "You will all stay for the reception afterward, I hope?"

Quinn let them talk while he practiced deep breathing as he focused his thoughts on the points he wanted to make and how he wanted to make them. By the time they reached the venue, he was in the zone and after Celene Warden had introduced him, he let old habits take over and simply talked. The audience became his ally instead of his adversary, and he realized he was enjoying himself.

Judging from the applause that erupted after he'd finished, he'd been a hit. Celene opened the floor to questions and, after a slow start, the students inundated him with sharp, in-depth queries about the story, his writing process, and his career as a journalist. He had more fun than he'd imagined possible and was disappointed when she finally called a halt.

The audience filed out of the room, the students no doubt on their way to the reception, which included food. Only Celene Warden, Christy, and his dad remained. He relaxed and realized he was tired and riding a high at the same time.

"That was wonderful," Celene said. She seemed to be one of those people who were enthusiastic no matter what the situation. Though he supposed this event could be considered a success by anyone's standards.

"It was," Christy said, coming up and smiling at him.

He soared a little higher from sheer relief.

"I wish Karen Beaumont was here," Celene said, her bright smile dimming. "She booked the event, you know. She was tremendously excited about having you speak to us."

That was interesting. Beaumont hadn't mentioned it when they'd been introduced at the gala last week.

"With her death, there must be some confusion in your organization," Christy said in a sympathetic way.

Celene smiled again, her sadness pushed aside by that unending positive thinking. "Not at all. Karen was tremendously organized. I have stepped in as Acting Dean until the college can strike a hiring committee to find a permanent replacement. We worked closely together, so I feel comfortable implementing her ideas and the initiatives she had in place before her death."

Roy raised his brows. "Initiatives? She was making changes?"

Celene nodded. "Some. She wanted the faculty to reach out more to industry. She used the publishing program I taught in as an example. All of our professors are industry professionals who are either currently active in the field, or who have kept their industry contacts fresh even while they teach in the program."

"Ah, that's why she was pestering Jackson Hargreaves to get off his duff and write his long promised third opus," Roy said cheerfully.

His comment flustered Celene. "Well, I wouldn't describe it as 'pestering.' Rather, I'd say she was encouraging Jackson to do his best work."

"I suppose there are a lot of people here at the college who will be competing for the position of dean," Christy said.

Celene accepted the change of subject gratefully. "Oh, I'm sure of it. Several of our chairs and coordinators have mentioned they intend to apply. People like Monique McGrath, who was chair of music for three terms, and Samuel Moore, the current chair of music, for example. I expect Gibson Jessop, the chair of Theater Arts and Paige Moran, coordinator of Music Composition to apply too, though neither has spoken to me. There will be others from PGC, I'm sure, as well as some from the outside."

"You're not applying, Celene?" Christy asked.

She shook her head. "I was hoping to work with Karen for a few more years before I moved on to a position at her level. I learned so much from her and there was more I wanted to learn! I feel I don't yet have the experience I need to become dean." She laughed and added, "Then too, my kids are still in grade school and I want to be able to spend time with them."

Christy asked about her children, and Celene chattered happily about her family as they slowly progressed down the aisle toward the door, and from there on to the large room where the reception was being held.

Quinn thought the conversation revealed a great deal. Not only had Celene Warden not been at the gala, but she seemed to have absolutely no reason to want her boss dead. If she was right, though, there were a number of people at PGC who coveted Karen Beaumont's job. Was that enough motive to kill her?

CHAPTER 11

The moment Quinn walked into the reception he was mobbed by students who wanted a personal moment with the speaker. He responded in a good-natured way and was soon deep in conversation. Roy looked past the scrum to see who else might be attending.

He spotted Samuel Moore, the chair of music, looking natty in a leather jacket, round-necked sweater, and tight black pants. His dark hair, which had been styled by an expert, was long enough to hint at his artistic pretentions, but like the rest of his outfit, it was more part of his costume than what he truly was.

He was talking to Craig Harding, smiling broadly, and looking animated, as if he was having the best time in the world chatting with his ultimate boss. Celene Warden was headed their way, probably to find out what Moore was up to, or maybe to do her own bit of schmoozing, Roy thought cynically.

His gaze drifted further, past several faces he didn't know, to one he did—except he couldn't place it. Today, the man was dressed in an open-necked shirt and chinos, but he had been at the gala, dressed in a tux, of course, and he'd done something memorable. What was it? Oh, yeah, he'd been the MC for the evening. He'd introduced each of the theater performances and the band as well. What was the fellow's name? Didn't matter. It would come to him later, when he didn't need to remember it.

Beside him, Christy said, "Looks like Quinn is going to be busy for a while."

There was amusement in her voice and something else. What? Ah, pride. She was pleased Quinn's talk had been so successful.

"I notice several people from the gala are here today," she said. "Do you want to split up and see what we can find out?"

She must have been scoping out the room as he was. He nodded. "Good idea." He pointed to the man whose face he remembered, but whose name he did not. "Do you know who that is?"

Christy studied him for a minute. "He was the MC."

"Yes, but what was his name?" Now that he wanted to know it and couldn't remember, it was bugging him.

Christy frowned. "Jessup, maybe? I think he's the chair of Theater Arts. Do you want to talk to him?"

"He won't know anything," Roy said. "After he introduced the band, he sat at the table with Harding the whole time. I was just curious."

Christy nodded, apparently finding nothing surprising in this. "Do you see anyone else who was at the gala?"

"Apart from Samuel Moore, you mean?"

Christy grimaced. "Yes. Horrible man. He was on stage while Karen Beaumont was killed, so he's not a suspect, and he's so absorbed in himself I doubt he'd notice anything not related to his own interests."

Roy acknowledged this was a smile and an absentminded chuckle. His roving gaze had caught on two other people who were there that night and he knew he would have to be the one to question them.

With an inner sigh, he said, "Jackson Hargreaves and Hal Wilkinson are over by the bar. I'll go talk to them."

"Hargreaves is the author Beaumont was harassing, but who is Hal Wilkinson? Another professor?"

"He writes graphic novels and used to teach a course on the subject, but he's a chair now, I think. I know both of them a little. Well, Hargreaves too much, in fact, but anyway, I'll see what I can get out of them."

"Okay," Christy said. "I'll tackle Jessup. He might have noticed something useful. We'll meet back here once Quinn is free of his mob of fans."

"Can't happen too soon," Roy muttered as he headed off toward the bar. There, he ordered a glass of red wine and pretended to notice Jackson Hargreaves. Like Samuel Moore, Jackson Hargreaves was wearing a jacket, round-necked sweater, and slacks, but the jacket was tweed and the slacks were baggy at the knees and too tight in the waist, exposing the beginnings of a middle-aged belly. Hal Wilkinson was dressed in a dark suit, a white shirt, and a striped tie, probably to emphasize his position as an administrator, not a professor.

"Hello, Jackson, Hal," Roy said, nodding to the two men. "Strange old world, isn't it? I don't see you for months, then it's twice in a couple of a weeks."

Hargreaves glowered at him. "Strange, indeed."

"Your son was the speaker today, wasn't he?" Hal asked. He was drinking beer, and he guzzled half the glass in one go.

Roy blinked as he nodded.

"Talented kid. I used to watch him on the national news. He had a way of bringing you into the action of whatever he was reporting on." He drank some more beer, then added in a rush, "I pre-ordered his book from the campus bookstore. I wish the copies were already available. I'd ask him to sign mine before he left."

"Honestly, Hal, you sound like a fan boy," Hargreaves said, his tone as disparaging as his words.

Hal looked chagrinned and Roy rose to his defense. "If you get your copy to me, I'll make sure Quinn signs it with a personal note."

Hal brightened and stammered out a thanks.

Hargreaves snorted.

Twerp. A list of what he didn't know about selling books would be longer than his next ponderous novel.

Hal downed the last of his beer and offered to buy another round. Hargreaves accepted without a moment's hesitation. Roy looked at his half-full glass, then at Hal's hopeful expression, and nodded. While Hal was off at the bar, Roy drank his wine far too quickly, then said to Jackson Hargreaves, "I guess you're relieved Karen Beaumont is dead."

Hargreaves tipped his glass and consumed the last of his white wine. "A crude way of putting it, but yes, the woman was a horror. I'm not sorry she's no longer running the School of Entertainment Arts."

Hal caught the end of that comment as he returned with their refills. He handed Hargreaves his white wine and took his empty glass. "Karen was a lifer," he said. He gave Roy a full red wine, accepting his now empty glass in trade.

"What do you mean by that?" Roy asked, surprised. But Hal had wandered off to return the empties and pick up his own refill.

It was Jackson who answered. "It's what we at the college call someone who has hit their top position. Karen Beaumont liked being dean and she didn't have any plans to either apply for a more senior position or to move to another college. She was dean of Entertainment Arts at PGC for the rest of her career. A lifer."

Hal was back by that point and he was nodding. "If the person in the job is good, everyone is happy. But someone like Karen? She was a reformer." He made a gesture indicating double quotes as he said the word reformer, except he was only able to use one hand as the other was busy with the beer glass, so it looked odd. "Her mission was to clean up Entertainment Arts."

"You don't think she needed to?"

"Hell, no," said Hal. "Students might not like every course in the curriculum, but they need to experience the pure arts, even if they don't know they should."

There had to be a reason behind that particular gripe, but Roy couldn't fathom it.

Hargreaves nodded, then gestured to the group around Quinn with his free hand. "At least five of those students are in my basic English seminar. I have to teach them the difference between the possessive 'their' and the directional 'there'." He shuddered. "Basic sentence structure. Paragraphing. What an adverb is. The list goes on and on."

"Tough job," Roy said, not meaning it. He wasn't a teacher, but he thought that taking a mind that wanted to learn but had no idea what it needed to know to succeed would be an exciting challenge.

Hargreaves was nodding, apparently in the belief that Roy agreed with him. "It is indeed, and Karen Beaumont forced me into doing it."

Now that was interesting. "How?"

Hargreaves drew a deep breath and puffed out his chest. "She said it was my purgatory until I completed my third novel. She said teaching someone to write might help me learn how to do it myself."

Roy resisted the urge to give the late Karen Beaumont a cheer.

Hal was shaking his head. "I went to bat for Jackson. Told her he had all skills he needed and that his Elements of Literary Fiction course proved he knew what he was doing, but she wouldn't listen." He gestured with his beer glass. "Know what she told me?"

Fascinated, Roy shook his head.

"She said his course was under-subscribed!"

"I always have at least six students in my class," Jackson said. "That's more than enough."

Six students didn't sound like a lot to Roy, but then, he wasn't a professor.

Hal rambled on. "Students, she said, want to learn from the best in their field. Not enough students know who Jackson is because he hasn't had a novel out in so long. Jackson Hargreaves! I ask you, was the woman deluded or what?"

Not deluded, Roy thought, but right on the mark. Fame faded fast in the publishing world.

Hal had paused to swig down the beer that remained in his glass, but he wasn't done yet. "I saw her, you know, at the gala. Chatting up potential donors like that music guy with the hot wife."

It took Roy a moment to realize that Hal was talking about Mitch and Kim Crosier. He wondered what Kim, who might look like a blond bimbo, but who was smarter than her empire-building husband, thought of Hal Wilkinson, comic book creator.

"All Karen cared about was the bottom line. Increasing student retention, eliminating courses with tremendous value but that were under-enrolled."

"She was out to get your graphic novel course," Hargreaves said with a nod.

Roy wasn't sure if that was a dig or an expression of sympathy and support. Either way, it was interesting. "I thought you were chair of the creative writing department, Hal. Do you have to teach as well as administer?"

Hal shook his head. "No, the chairs have full administrative release, but my term as chair is almost up. If I'm not re-elected, I go back to faculty and teach again."

"Is that likely to happen?"

Hal shrugged.

Hargreaves said, "You never know. Monique McGrath was chair of music for three terms and was running for a fourth when Samuel

Moore threw his name in. Suddenly, all the work she'd done for her department didn't matter and Samuel was the new chair."

"I like to teach about graphic novels," Hal said. His glass was empty again and he was looking a little owlish. "But I don't want to be stuck in Basic English Skills with Jackson here."

"Thanks a lot," said Hargreaves bitterly.

"Karen liked change in the chair positions," Hal said, peering into his glass as if it held the answer to all life's questions. "I saw her schmoozing with Samuel at the gala after he'd taken over the staring roll in the musical. If any of us had done what he did, she'd have been chewing us out, but not Sammy boy. He was new blood. He was special. Did you see his face? His smile was so huge she must have told him he should have been on Broadway."

"Not that his ego needs it," Hargreaves said.

"No indeedy, it doesn't." Hal shrugged. "But Karen? She wouldn't know that."

"Or maybe she wouldn't care."

"That too," Hal said, nodding at Hargreaves' comment. "After fueling his ego, she went off to stroke a few donors, I expect, though I didn't see her at it. That's what she was good at. Pulling in the cash and cutting the courses." He lifted his empty glass. "Who's for another round?"

Hargreaves immediately downed the wine that remained in his glass and held it up. Hal looked at Roy. "How about you, Armstrong?"

Roy looked at his half-full glass and shook his head. "Thanks, but no." At Hal's somewhat sodden look of reproach, he said, "I'm driving."

"Ah," said Hal, nodding acceptance. He went off to secure drinks for himself and Hargreaves. Roy took the opportunity to move on. He figured he'd found out about all he was going to get from Jackson Hargreaves and Hal Wilkinson.

CHAPTER 12

As Roy marched off to intercept his two colleagues, his expression was determined, as if he was about to take an unpleasant medicine he knew was good for him but tasted awful.

Christy chuckled and looked about for Professor Jessup. She sighted him some distance away, deep in conversation with a person she didn't recognize. Deciding she'd wait a minute before seeking him out, she fell into conversation with an enthusiastic student who identified herself as a journalism major and was interested in Christy's pursuit of justice for Frank as she was in Quinn's talk today.

They were deep in conversation when a resonant voice said, "Is this student bothering you, Christy, my dear?"

Christy, my dear? What the heck? Frowning, she turned to find that the voice belonged to Samuel Moore. She should have known.

The girl blushed fiery red. "I'm sorry, Mrs. Jamieson, I didn't mean to offend you."

Christy shot an annoyed look at Moore and said, "You didn't." She resisted the urge to say it was Moore who had offended her with his smarmy comment. 'Christy, my dear,' indeed.

Still blushing furiously, the girl said, "It has been good talking to you, Mrs. Jamieson." She gave Christy a little nod, then hurried away.

Christy turned back to Samuel Moore. "I'm surprised to see you at an event directed toward the journalism and publishing students, Mr. Moore. I thought music and theater was more your style."

He showed his teeth in a smile that was neither friendly nor amused. "Publishing is part of the School of Entertainment Arts, Christy. I think it's important to support all of the special events associated with the School, even if the department is not my own."

"I see," she said, and thought perhaps she did. With Karen Beaumont dead, her position as dean would have to be filled. It looked like Moore was doing the groundwork to brand himself as the ideal candidate for the job.

He nodded. The toothy smile had given way to a more somber expression. "Craig was mentioning your foundation's participation has given the At Risk Students program a tremendous boost. I hope you are not concerned about the recent sad event. Anton's arrest was a blow to the At Risk program, but I believe his release indicates the program can help even the most unpromising cases."

The man had an interesting way of describing things. Christy gave him a serious look and said, "You don't think Anton Gromley is an asset to the program?"

Moore glanced over her shoulder, scanning the room. He was looking for someone, she thought, wondering who it was.

Returning his attention to her, he shrugged. "Anton is an example of a subset of students who register in the music department. Our mandate is to encourage excellence in musicality in our students, whether it's in the use of an instrument or the human voice. Our graduates have worked in symphony orchestras all over the country and are members of some of the best choral groups. However, we do get students like Anton who want a career in popular music and who have no interest in the classical repertoire. Sadly, that number is increasing every semester."

While he was speaking, Christy did her own inspection of the room. At first, she thought he'd been looking for someone more interesting to chat with, but he'd sought her out so she wondered if there could be another reason. She noticed that Craig Harding was a little distance away, in conversation with a student. Was Moore being cautious, fearful he'd be overheard by his boss? He'd made sure Craig was too far to hear his disparaging remarks before he'd spoken.

If he was worried about Craig overhearing his comment, why make it in at all? Was he concerned that popular music was the direction the college was officially moving toward and it made him so angry he couldn't keep silent? Or was Craig Harding's support for the At Risk program so profound that he wouldn't listen to criticism and Samuel Moore's negativity would be frowned upon?

Time to find out. "Was a focus on pop music part of Dean Beaumont's initiatives?"

Moore's eyes flashed and his mouth tightened, but just for a moment. Then he smiled. "I will be honest with you. Karen was a fan of SledgeHammer and groups of that sort. She thought including a pop music stream would draw damaged young people to the At Risk program. And she was right." He spread his hands, suddenly serious. "Almost all of the music students in the At Risk program have opted to take courses that will lead them into the popular music business. However, our chosen students, the ones who must apply and fulfill rigorous entry requirements, tend to focus on traditional musical choices."

According to Trevor, only thirty-six students had been admitted to the At Risk program and not all of them had chosen music as their major. Craig Harding had told her that with the Jamieson Foundation support they planned to double enrollment to twenty-four per year.

As with the earlier intakes, not all of these students would choose the music faculty. "Karen Beaumont created a pop music section just for the At Risk students? Were there enough students to fill the classes?"

Moore stared at her blankly for a moment, then he smiled broadly. "Oh, no, you misunderstand, Christy. I'm so sorry, my dear, I didn't mean to confuse you. No, there has always been a pop music stream at the college. Karen just thought it would be of more interest to the At Risk students than a traditional symphonic stream would be."

"I see," Christy said, though she didn't really see at all. Moore seemed to be telling her two different truths. "So Karen Beaumont understood the music program as well as the At Risk students."

"Karen was..." He paused to shoot another furtive look around the room. Apparently satisfied, he said confidentially, "Karen was never a very collegial dean. She had her ideas and she acted on them, even if the majority of the faculty and the departmental chair didn't agree. She created anxiety with the appointments she approved and the decisions she made."

Christy's parents both worked for a university so she knew that a dean who had poor organizing skills, or whose focus was narrow and one-sided, could be difficult to work with. But creating anxiety seemed to be an extreme description. "What kind of appointments?"

Again that careful look around before he refocused on Christy. "Well, Celene Warden as her associate dean for one."

"Oh? I only met Celene this afternoon, but I thought she seemed quite capable."

"She is very friendly and presents herself well, but she is so focused on creating harmony that she doesn't really lead."

"Creating harmony?" Christy shot him an amused look. "To clean up Karen Beaumont's uncollegial behavior, I presume."

"Exactly! Celene will never be capable of running the division on her own, of course, but as a second, tasked with mopping up problems, she is terrific."

"It sounds to me like Celene Warden's appointment was a benefit to the division. How did it create anxiety?"

Moore leaned in and said in a low voice, "Many people felt slighted when they were not chosen for the position."

Christy couldn't help it, she said, "Including you, Mr. Moore?"

He reared back, a startled expression on his face. "No, of course not. I only recently became chair of the music department. I owe my faculty my complete attention for the duration of my appointment."

"But there were others who felt differently?"

Another quick glance before he replied. "Many. People like my predecessor Monique McGrath, for instance. And Hal Wilkinson in creative writing and Gibson Jessup, who is the chair of theater arts." He shook his head. "Karen didn't intend to do it, of course, but she destabilized the school when she created the associate dean position and staffed it with someone from publishing."

"You are very specific. What's wrong with the publishing department?"

"Nothing, I suppose. It's a new initiative that Karen spearheaded. Her pet project, you might say. Choosing her associate dean from amongst her handpicked staff caused resentment in those who had worked at the college longer."

Karen Beaumont didn't sound like a particularly capable dean, Christy thought. "You did mention the decisions she made caused strife. I suppose choosing the wrong person for an important appointment was one of them."

Moore nodded as she spoke, his expression approving. "Yes, exactly. She had been involved in movie and TV production before she became dean here, and she tended to be blunt and rather abrupt in her way of handling things. Take Jackson Hargreaves, for instance. I talked to him not long after he found her body and he was quite pragmatic about her death."

Christy raised her brows, hoping she looked disapproving. The expression must have worked, because Moore nodded emphatically. "I know! Not very nice of him, but you must understand. Karen was horrible to Jackson. She actually told him he had to produce a new book and soon. The poor man was devastated. It's not as if he wasn't trying." Moore looked around the room again, then moved a little closer. His voice lowered, he said, "Jackson has the reputation of being a great author, you know, but he suffers from writer's block. He simply cannot write a coherent page of prose. Karen knew that, but she pushed him anyway. Cruel, but that was Karen. She didn't care about the creative spirit, only measurable results."

Christy thought about Roy's work schedule. There were times where he wrote in marathon binges that could happen at the oddest parts of the day and lasted for hours, but he also did a lot of solid day-in-day-out plodding. "Perhaps Karen thought that by making Jackson sit down and work on his book, he'd get over his writer's block."

Moore stared at her for a minute. Was it disdain she saw in his eyes? But why? Because she was taking the dead dean's side? Or was his expression more calculating?

"Karen was not trying to help Jackson. In fact, she wanted to get rid of him."

"She was going to fire him?"

Moore nodded. "She needed an excuse, though, so she went after his professional credentials."

That struck a chord with Christy, who knew publication was an important part of an academic's life. If Jackson Hargreaves was under threat of losing his job because he couldn't finish his novel, he would certainly not be one of Karen Beaumont's supporters. Was that a strong enough motive to murder her, though?

"Will you excuse me, Christy?" Moore said. His gaze had wandered again, this time settling on the little crowd of students around Quinn. "President Harding asked me to keep an eye on Quinn to make sure the students didn't pester him. I think he looks a little beleaguered at the moment. I'll wander that way and move some of the students along."

Christy turned to check out Quinn. The crowd that swarmed around him when he first entered the room had thinned, but there were still enough students so that he was surrounded. That didn't seem to be bothering him, though. In fact, he looked like he was enjoying himself. He was smiling warmly and as Christy watched he laughed at something one of the students had said.

"It's been a pleasure talking to you this afternoon," Samuel said with a nod. He bustled toward Quinn.

"And you," Christy said to his retreating back. Samuel Moore seemed to like being the center of attention, but then that shouldn't surprise her. Entertainment Arts was full of creative people who lived life in their own individual style. Being self-absorbed was probably fairly normal behavior. Keeping this group working effectively must have been a difficult task. She found she had a lot of sympathy for Karen Beaumont.

Christy was mulling over the woman's management challenges when a large, balding man bustled up to her. He was smiling broadly, his round face cheerful and his dark eyes bright. "Mrs. Jamieson, isn't it?" he said, thrusting out his hand.

Christy recognized him from the gala evening, so she smiled as she shook his hand. "Yes, Mr. Jessup, I'm Christy Jamieson. I thought you did a wonderful job as the MC at the gala."

If possible, his smile broadened. "Thank you. I was an actor before I began teaching and I always preferred appearing in a stage production to doing film work. It's the audience, you know. The immediate response you get from every word spoken."

Gibson Jessup was a much more positive person than Samuel Moore was, which made him an easier conversationalist than the other man. Christy relaxed a little. "I think teaching itself is like being on stage in some ways. You have to engage the students—your audience—or you lose control of your classroom."

"How correct you are," Jessup said, nodding. "Have you taught, Mrs. Jamieson?"

She laughed. "No, but I grew up in an academic family. I learned about the joys and problems of managing a room full of young adults over the dinner table."

"Ah, so you understand." He nodded again, and his cheerful expression turned wistful. "Sometimes I miss the classroom."

"You're the chair of theater arts, aren't you?"

He sighed. "Yes." Then he brightened again. "Directing faculty members doesn't have immediate feedback you get from a stage production or a classroom, but it does have rewards."

Christy smiled. "Lots of difficult people."

He tilted his head and pursed his lips in a thoughtful way. "But all people are difficult, don't you think? You assume they're going to do one thing, then they do another. Entertainment Arts is full of people who are, perhaps, more challenging than faculty in other schools, so you have to be flexible and ready for change, but I don't think we have a lot of problem people."

Christy raised her brows. "And yet I heard Karen Beaumont had a hard time keeping the school running smoothly."

Jessup wrinkled his nose as he frowned. "Karen loved the School of Entertainment Arts. She cared about the day-to-day management, but she was focused on its future success. That's why she created the publishing department and why she was always aware of student registration numbers. How can a program be successful if students don't enroll in it?"

That was a good point. "What did she do if a program or a course had small enrollment?"

"Karen had a set of criteria of what made a course or program viable." He ticked the list off on his fingers. "Enrollment, of course, but also value to the student and the community. She also considered opportunities for the student, both for their personal growth and for their career aspirations. If a program had a steady enrollment and the students were able to find jobs in the field, Karen kept it going, even if the numbers were low. It was those outliers that no longer provided strong benefits for the students that she considered canceling."

"Were there a lot of those?"

"No, not at all," he said, shaking his head. "More often she would tweak the details, refocus direction, add new course content. For instance, the instrumental program in the music department has been facing declining enrollment for several semesters. Karen's solution was to change the focus from a classical orientation to a modern one. There were only a few courses she considered cancelling outright, like Comics and Graphic Novels in the creative writing department."

"I heard she was very hard on Jackson Hargreaves. Did she ever consider canceling his course?"

Jessup laughed at that. "Jackson was one of her refocus projects. Not that she wanted to rewrite his course. It was Jackson she intended to change."

"Seems presumptuous. What did she know about writing a novel?"

"Nothing at all, but she did know about reading them. She loved Jackson's work. She wasn't trying to get him back to writing again to punish him, but to help him. That was Karen. Her goal was to provide everyone with the tools they needed to perform at their peak. She cared about Entertainment Arts. She'd do whatever it took to make it great."

"You sound as if you miss her," Christy said.

"I do. Celene is trying her best, but she's not ready to manage our motley crew. I don't know how long it will take to post the dean's job, but I expect it will be a couple of months at least before the interviewing is finished. I hope someone from outside wins the competition, because I don't think anyone here at PGC is ready for the position."

CHAPTER 13

S urprised, Christy said, "You don't intend to apply, Mr. Jessup?"

"Heavens, no. I have a small part in an ongoing TV production filmed here in town. It keeps my skills up and the pay is ridiculous for what I do. If I had to put in the hours Karen used to, I'd never have time for my acting."

Christy must have looked shocked because Jessup said earnestly, "Karen knew all about my second job. In fact, she supported it. She considered it professional development, in the same way Jackson completing and publishing his novel would be."

Roy joined them at that moment, so Christy introduced the two men. As they exchanged polite conversation, she looked around. Celene Warden was nowhere to be seen and only a sprinkling of the other professors remained. The last of the students around Quinn had wandered away to sample the refreshment table, leaving Quinn talking to Samuel Moore and Craig Harding. He was facing Harding, with Moore standing to one side between them and as Christy watched, she saw Moore say something, then look earnestly from Quinn to Harding.

"I think I'll go join Quinn," Christy said when there was a break in the conversation. "It's nice to see you, Mr. Jessup."

Roy glanced at his watch. "Later than I thought," he said, sounding surprised. "Nice talking to you, Jessup."

As they moved across the room, Christy said, "Did you find out anything interesting?"

"Lots," Roy said happily. "How about you?"

"Karen Beaumont appears to have been a woman with many different sides."

"Plenty to talk about then. We'll do it over dinner so Quinn can join in."

"Any preferences for restaurant?" Christy asked.

Roy pulled out his phone. "I'm not sure what's in this area. Let me check."

As they neared Quinn, Christy heard Moore say, "Karen Beaumont was an excellent administrator. The division will miss her vision and her careful handling of all of the faculty and staff."

She frowned and put a hand on Roy's arm. She leaned over and pretended to be examining his screen as she whispered, "Let's stay here a minute. I want to hear a bit more of what Samuel Moore is saying."

Roy frowned at her in surprise, but he nodded, saying nothing. He found a website aggregating local restaurants and began to scroll through the list. Christy studied the little group around Quinn while pretending to watch what Roy was doing.

Samuel Moore was still speaking. Moreover, he was now staring earnestly at Craig Harding and pretty much ignoring Quinn. "The college will have to choose carefully to ensure that Karen's many initiatives are properly appreciated by the incoming dean. Her legacy will be an important aspect of the School of Entertainments Arts as it moves into the future."

That was interesting, Christy thought. A half an hour before

Samuel Moore had been completely negative about Karen Beaumont. Now he was spouting a different story to his boss. She wondered again if he was positioning himself for the woman's job, because right now it sounded like he was doing his best to convince Craig Harding he should be Karen Beaumont's successor.

"Karen was my mentor, you know." Moore continued, achieving a soulful look as he droned on, allowing neither Quinn nor Harding to get a word in. "She was the one who convinced me to run for the post of chair of music. She told me it would be an excellent stepping-stone for the Dean's position."

Christy saw Craig Harding raise his brows. He looked surprised by the statement. She wondered if he was buying what Moore had on offer.

Though he appeared to be engrossed on what was on his screen, Roy had apparently been listening to the conversation just as Christy was. He said with some indignation, "We have to rescue Quinn. This crazy singer guy isn't talking to him, he's sucking up to his boss and hoping he'll get appointed Dean of Entertainment Arts, rather than have to apply for the job."

Christy nodded. "Let's do it." She now had a pretty clear idea of the kind of person Samuel Moore was. Listening to more of his glib lies would add little to their knowledge of what was behind Karen Beaumont's murder.

When they joined the men, she linked her arm with Quinn's. "You've lost your horde of admirers."

He looked down at her and gave her his special smile. "Yeah. The need for food got them."

Samuel Moore didn't look too pleased at being interrupted, particularly when Craig Harding reached out to shake Quinn's hand and thank him for speaking to the students.

A few more minutes of polite conversation and they were on their way, with one of the few remaining students happily guiding them through the maze of corridors to the parking lot exit.

At the car Quinn said to Christy and Roy, "Thanks for coming with me today. I hope you weren't bored."

"I enjoyed it," Christy said, smiling at him.

As he climbed into the backseat, Roy said, "I talked to Jackson Hargreaves and Hal Wilkinson for a half an hour. I need a drink and food in that order."

In the driver's seat, Quinn looked at his father through the rear-view mirror. "Was Hargreaves needling you again?"

"Doesn't he always try? He never succeeds though. Let's eat and I'll tell you about it."

"Works for me. Where to?"

Roy's troll through the Internet resulted in a list that included an Italian, French, and sushi restaurant. Eventually, French won, because the restaurant's website advertised both steak with fries and French onion soup. Roy liked the idea of the soup, Quinn wanted the steak, and Christy was certain she could find something on the menu that would suit her.

The restaurant was a small, chic bistro located in a storefront on West Broadway. The walls were white, the tables had butcher-block tops on metal frames and the chairs were simple blond wood. The combination made the most of the light in the long narrow space.

They began with a bottle of wine while they perused the menu. With their choices made, they settled down to analyze what they'd learned.

"Jackson Hargreaves hated Karen Beaumont," Roy said. He savored the wine, which was a pinot noir recommended by the waiter. "This is so much better than the stuff they were serving at the reception."

"A bit harsh, don't you think, Dad?" Quinn was drinking the wine too, but he wasn't savoring it.

CAT IN THE LIMELIGHT

Roy opened his eyes wide. "You don't like this wine? I think it's pretty good."

"I didn't mean the wine," Quinn said impatiently. "I was talking about Jackson Hargreaves and Karen Beaumont."

Roy shook his head. "You didn't hear him. According to Jackson, she made his life miserable and was torturing him because he wouldn't produce a novel on her timeline."

"Samuel Moore agrees with Jackson," Christy said. "He thinks Beaumont wanted to fire Jackson and was using his lack of writing productivity as an excuse. Gibson Jessup, on the other hand, said she was pushing Jackson to complete his novel because she wanted him to be the best he could be."

"That fits with what Celene Warden told us after my talk." Quinn drank more wine, then said, "So who was Karen Beaumont? One group of people is telling us that she had impossible expectations and was willing to sacrifice anyone who couldn't meet them. The other group seems to think her actions were caring and benevolent."

"She was probably both," Roy said. "People are rarely one-sided. Jackson Hargreaves was failing at the task she'd set him. Hal Wilkinson was afraid she was going to cancel his pet project, a course on writing graphic novels. She was a threat to each of them and I think they were both afraid of her. So they saw her as having cruel and ridiculously demanding expectations."

"How interesting. Gibson Jessup told me he has a part in a TV show that's filmed locally which Karen saw as part of his ongoing professional development. Since he's an actor, and is the chair of the theater arts department, being on a TV show fits into her structure perfectly."

Roy nodded. "So they got along and he wasn't threatened. He sees her standards as being reasonable, because he was able to meet them."

"Unfortunately, we know Jackson Hargreaves didn't kill Beaumont.

Do we know where Hal Wilkinson was when she was killed?" Quinn asked.

Roy drank more wine, then said gloomily, "He was in the foyer before we all went down to the ballroom. I followed him down the stairs and saw him go into the ballroom. After that, I didn't notice him leave. I'm pretty sure he was in the ballroom the whole time."

"Pity," Quinn said.

Their appetizers came, French onion soup all around. Their discussion halted while the waiter served them. When he was gone, Christy said, "Despite what he was saying to Craig Harding before we left, I don't think Samuel Moore liked Karen Beaumont much. He told me she wasn't a good manager and that she created more problems than she solved. He seemed to think that Celene Warden's appointment as associate dean caused friction among the other chairs and coordinators because they all wanted the job and were overlooked."

"That is possible," Quinn said. He dug into the soup, which was thick with cheese and bread. "Celene admits she isn't ready to be dean. Maybe people thought she wasn't ready to be associate dean either."

"Wouldn't that show a lack of management skills on Beaumont's part?" Christy asked.

Quinn nodded and Roy said, "So we could be looking at every person in an administrative role as a suspect?"

His mouth full of chewy melted cheese, Quinn nodded.

Roy shook his head as he dipped his spoon into his soup. "Patterson has her work cut out for her."

"There must be some way to narrow down the list," Christy said.

Roy paused in his consumption of the soup to take a sip of wine. "There could be a way. Beaumont's job was recently posted, right?"

The others nodded.

"Well, Patterson can narrow the list to those who applied. If they didn't, it indicates that person didn't want her job and so probably didn't kill her."

"That would work for Gibson Jessup, but not for Samuel Moore," Christy said. She'd consumed all of her bread and cheese and was now sipping the tasty broth.

"What do you mean?" Roy asked.

"Do you remember what we overheard when I asked you to stop for a minute before we picked up Quinn?"

Roy nodded.

"Moore sounded as if he was trying to convince Craig Harding he should get Karen's job. Yet, when Moore and I were talking earlier, he told me he wasn't applying for the dean's position."

Quinn shot her a sharp, questioning glance. "Could be he's the kind of guy who likes to be in the limelight. He may even say whatever he thinks will make him attractive to the person he's talking to." He pushed his empty soup bowl aside. "I was still chatting with a few of the students when he came over. It took him about three minutes to chase them away so I'd be focused on no one but him. When Harding joined us, Moore refocused on him and started talking about the School of Entertainment Arts and Karen Beaumont's legacy. It was like he forgot I was there."

"So does he want Beaumont's job? Or was he making sure someone from inside the college got the job, but not necessarily him?" Roy asked.

Christy shook her head. "No, this doesn't make sense. Why would he be praising Karen Beaumont and talking about her legacy when he was one of the people who said she was a poor manager? What kind of legacy is that?"

Roy rubbed his chin. "Good point. It's a pity we have to rule him out, too, like Hargreaves and Wilkinson."

Quinn shrugged. "So it's someone other than those three. What else do we know?"

"Jackson and Hal both said that she wasn't the kind who climbed the academic ladder. They called her a 'lifer,' which apparently means she was happy where she was and didn't intend to move up or on," Roy said.

"So anyone with ambition was stuck. They'd have to leave the college or switch to another faculty to get a raise in position. That's a possible motive for the chairs and coordinators. Anything else?" Quinn said.

"Hal thought she should have chastised that guy Moore for taking over the lead roll in the scene from *West Side Story*."

"Again, management skills," Christy said. "There were probably other people who felt the same way."

"But we don't know who they are," Roy said with a sigh. He brightened. "There is one thing, though. Hal said he saw her talking to Mitch and Kim Crosier before everyone went down to the ballroom. Maybe one of them can shed some light on what she was thinking."

Quinn shot his father an incredulous look. "You want to talk to Mitch Crosier again? The last time you did, he pestered you for weeks trying get you to sign a deal with his company."

Roy rubbed his chin. "True enough, but Kim Crosier is a smart woman and she can talk to Frank. Might be worthwhile chatting with her."

"Go for it," Quinn said.

"I'd hoped someone else might consider taking on the job," Roy said, staring innocently at his son.

"Right now, all we know about Crosier's involvement is that he and Kim were there and that they talked to Beaumont sometime before she was killed. I don't think either of them are suspects and I can't see a lot of valuable information coming from them."

Roy sighed and Christy laughed. Then she sobered. "We have no clear main suspect and a lot of weak possibilities based on really thin motives. I mean, how many people will go to the effort of killing someone so they can get a new job?"

"Probably not a lot," Quinn said.

The waiter came to clear away their soup bowls. When he was gone, Christy sighed. "I hope Patterson is further ahead than we are."

CHAPTER 14

"Detective Patterson may want to speak to you as well," Christy said as Ellen descended from the living room to the landing and the front door.

"Then she will be disappointed," Ellen said. She drew a light fall coat from the cupboard. The garment was new, a study in luxury from the fashionable wide lapels to the excellence of the merino wool cloth. Last year's equally expensive coat had been sent to a charity. She slipped the coat over the dark blue dress—also exclusive and just as beautifully designed—she was wearing. "Miss Kippen has found an apartment she believes is perfect for me and we have arranged to visit it this afternoon."

Miss Kippen was the dogged real estate agent Ellen had been working with for nearly a year now, ever since a young woman's body was found in Ellen's West End apartment. The apartments Miss Kippen found were never suitable and Christy believed that secretly Ellen didn't want to commit to a new residence. "Where is it this time?"

"In Shaughnessy. One of the old mansions has been divided into flats, which Miss Kippen claims have been beautifully done." Her hand on the doorknob, Ellen paused. "I have to admit the Shaughnessy location intrigues me. Such a lovely area. So many memories."

Yes, many memories for both of them. Shaughnessy was where the Jamieson mansion was located. Ellen had grown up there and Christy had lived the ten years of her marriage to Frank in the same building. It was also the house Frank had disappeared from and where Christy had been accused of embezzling his fortune. When you added in that MacLagan House, the site of the At Risk Gala and Karen Beaumont's murder, was a prominent landmark in Shaughnessy, Christy thought that over all, Ellen probably had better memories of the area than she did. "Good luck, then. I hope you like this apartment."

Ellen drew the door wider. It was already open since Stormy was outside. "Thank you, Christy. Ah, here is Trevor. He's agreed to go with me today and he promised to pick me up. We'll meet Miss Kippen there."

Christy came down the stairs to wave hello to Trevor as Ellen descended from the porch and went down the front walk to where Trevor's car idled. She stood on the porch and watched the car drive away, then she sat down on the front steps for a minute to see if Stormy was in the area.

He was. As soon as the sound of the car engine died off, the cat poked his head out of the bushes that hid the foundation of the house on the other side of the road. Seeing Christy, his body followed his head out of the greenery, and he trotted across the pavement to where she sat.

Where was Aunt Ellen going?

"Apartment hunting."

Again?

"Yup. Listen, Frank, I need to let you know that Patterson is visiting this afternoon. You're welcome to come and listen to what she has to say."

The cat sat in his neat and tidy way, his tail curled around his front paws, his back straight. He stared at her with unblinking green eyes. *I'd like that.*

"I thought you might." She stood. "I'm going in now. I've got some cookies in the oven and I don't want them to burn."

Cookies. There was a wistful sound to the word but demand too.

The cat gazed at her in what Christy thought of as a hopeful way. "Cookies aren't good for cats. I'll give you some salmon cat treats instead."

It's not the same.

The cat turned and headed back across the road to his watching post in the bushes. Evidently, he intended to wait outside until Patterson arrived. Christy left the door ajar when she went inside.

Half an hour later she had the cookies neatly arranged on a plate, and along with a cream jug and sugar bowl, it was already on the coffee table in the living room. The coffee was brewed and just had to be decanted into an elegant urn, and she had two bone china mugs to match. She'd changed from her jeans into a nice pair of slacks and a pretty sweater to go with them. She didn't entertain afternoon guests much these days, so she was making an effort.

Even though it was, well, Patterson, the cop, and this was not a social call, as the detective was coming here on police business. That thought made Christy smile at herself, as she set the china mugs along side the cream and sugar.

A few minutes later she heard the sound of a car engine coming down the street and when she looked out the kitchen window, she saw the dark sedan Patterson drove park in front of her driveway. Technically, according to the complex's bylaws, parking there was illegal, but Patterson was a cop and so, Christy supposed, immune to such rules. She poured the coffee into the urn and was putting it on the coffee table with the rest when the doorbell rang.

Christy went to the stairs as Patterson called, "Mrs. Jamieson? Christy?"

"Come on up," Christy called from the top of the stairs.

Patterson moved cautiously into the house. "Your front door was ajar. Is everything okay?"

"It's fine. I had it open for the—"

Stormy bolted through the open door, past Patterson's feet and up the stairs where he halted at the top. He rubbed Christy's ankles, then sat to stare down the steps at Patterson.

"For the cat, who likes to come and go," Christy finished off. "He's in now, so why don't you close the door, Detective?"

Patterson looked from Christy to the cat, then she turned to shut the door before coming up the stairs.

Christy indicated Patterson should sit on the sofa while she made herself comfortable on the chair beside. She lifted the coffee pot, ready to pour. "Detective?"

"Sure," Patterson said. She accepted the delicate china mug with the hint of a smile.

Stormy hopped up onto the sofa and settled at the other end. *Where are the cat's treats?*

Christy ignored him. "Cookie, Detective?" She held out the plate.

"These look homemade," Patterson said, taking one.

They are.

"Fresh today," Christy said, taking one herself and putting the plate back on to the table.

The cat stood up and sniffed before taking a tentative step toward Patterson, who was biting into her cookie and not paying any attention to him. Patterson chewed, then the rest of the cookie disappeared into her mouth. The cat took another cautious step closer.

"Wow," Patterson said. "That was delicious. You made them?"

Christy nodded and held out the plate so the detective could take another. "Our chef taught me the recipe when Noelle was little. She figured every mom, even rich ones, should know how to make cookies for their kid."

"Lucky kid," Patterson said. She looked over, suddenly aware the cat was now mere inches away from her. She raised her brows and looked at Christy.

"He's blackmailing you. Cookies aren't good for cats, so I have salmon treats for him. He knows they're around and he's hoping you'll get the message and give him some. Stormy," she said using her authoritative mom voice.

The cat sat and stared at her.

"The treats are in your bowl in the kitchen."

You're making me go into the kitchen instead of having them here with you?

Christy didn't reply. The cat glared at her for a moment longer, then hopped down and headed for his bowl, tail high.

Patterson finished her second cookie then picked up her coffee mug. She stared down into the dark liquid as if to marshal her thoughts. When she looked up at Christy she said, "I asked the pathologist to take a closer look at Karen Beaumont's body. He determined that she did not die from her fall down the staircase."

Christy frowned. "Then how did she die? She was found at the bottom of the staircase and she certainly looked as though she lost her balance on the stairs."

"The pathologist believes she did die from a fall, but she didn't trip on the stairs. She fell from the terrace. It's a drop of ten or more feet to the top of the lower staircase. Depending on her trajectory, she would have hit the top of the garden stairs and continued to tumble down them until she came to a stop at the base."

"How horrible," Christy said.

Patterson nodded.

Christy frowned a little as she envisioned the scene. "There's a stone balustrade that runs along the edge of the terrace. It's only about waist high, but it would be difficult for someone to go over the edge accidentally."

"Her death wasn't accidental."

Christy met Patterson's level gaze. "Someone pushed her off the terrace, and then what?"

"If it wasn't premeditated, he or she may have checked on her to see if she was injured and needed medical assistance. When the killer discovered she was dead, he or she may have pretended nothing had happened and joined the rest of the guests." Patterson hesitated, then said, "This new evidence also pushes back the time of death. It is very likely the assault occurred much earlier than we previously assumed. Can you give me an idea of the timing during the evening?"

"Of course." Christy thought back. "I saw Beaumont in the foyer after the second performance, the musical theater one. The next section of the evening was a concert by the rock band, Lightening Rod, so this was an interval of sorts before we all trooped down to the ballroom. The stairs to the lower level were at the far end of the foyer, behind the grand staircase to the second floor. The bar was down on the ballroom level, so there was a steady stream of people going down. There were lots of people in the foyer, milling around and chatting, but Quinn and I didn't linger. We went down to the ballroom where we claimed a table and bought drinks."

"But you did see her before you went down to the ballroom?"

"Oh, yes. She was wearing a spectacular gown, designed to look like a man's tuxedo. The skirt had a slit up the side and it molded her form. She stood out."

"Did you see her talking to anyone?"

"One of the PGC administrators, Samuel Moore. He's the chair of music."

"That fits," Patterson said. "I have statements from several people to that effect."

The cat came in from the kitchen and hopped onto the sofa where he made a show of cleaning his whiskers. *What did I miss?*

"What happened when you were in the ballroom?"

"As I mentioned, we found a table and Quinn went to get drinks. Sledge was already there, and he was jamming with the band. As the room began to fill, he left them to prep for their set and came over to our table. Gibson Jessup, the PGC prof who was the MC for the evening, went over to the stage to discuss something with Anton Gormley. People talked and the other tables filled. Jessup introduced the band. They played for about forty-five minutes, then they started a tribute session for SledgeHammer and midway through that idiot Samuel Moore took over the mic. That's when Anton Gormley stormed off the stage and disappeared."

"Did you see Karen Beaumont after you—" Patterson broke off as the doorbell rang.

Christy frowned. She didn't get a lot of drop by callers. "Excuse me a minute. I'd better see who that is."

She went down the stairs, aware that the cat had hopped off the couch and followed her. When she opened the front door she wanted to swear. Joan Shively, the children's services worker, had come to do a house check. "This is not a good time," she said.

"Then it's perfect for me," Shively retorted, pushing past her into the house. She marched up the stairs, shoulders back, head jutting forward, expecting problems. Unfortunately, she wasn't watching where she put her feet and almost tripped over Stormy, now positioned in the middle of the last stair before the top. "Stupid animal," she muttered as she stumbled up the last step. There she stopped. She pointed at Patterson. "Are you the person who drives the car parked outside this residence?"

Patterson stood slowly. "Yes, the vehicle is mine."

"There is a bylaw that requires all visitors to park at the top of the hill. That is where I parked. You should be fined and your car towed."

Christy had followed Shively up and now gently urged her deeper into the room. "This is Detective Patterson. Detective, Joan Shively of Children's Services."

Shively drew a deep, indignant breath. "Detective! You should know better!"

"Why are you here, Ms. Shively? Mrs. Jamieson and I are having a conversation." Patterson's expression was impassive, her voice calm, her tone neutral.

Shively's eyes opened wide. "The murder," she said. "The boy was released. Karen Beaumont's death is now an active case again." She turned on Christy, excitement gleaming in her eyes. "You're a suspect. I'll be removing your daughter immediately!"

Christy stared at her horrified. This was worse than the last time Joan Shively had decided she was guilty of criminal behavior. "No! You can't."

"I can."

The cat butted Shively's leg, then sat on her foot. *But you won't.*

"Mrs. Jamieson is not a suspect. I'm here because she is one of the few people in the case I know is not guilty and who can give me good, clear, information on the whereabouts of some of my suspects at the time of the victim's death."

Shively cautiously tried to remove her foot from underneath the cat. She'd had run-ins with Stormy before and knew he wouldn't hesitate to use his claws. As she tried to shake him off, the cat lifted his front paws to one pant leg and clung.

When Shively squeaked, Christy thought his claws had probably gone through the polyester fabric and reached skin. She bent and picked up the cat. "Leave Ms. Shively alone, Stormy."

Why? She's threatening you and my kid.

Christy patted the cat's head and didn't reply.

Shively drew a notebook and pen from her purse. "I need to see your credentials, Detective, so I can make a note of your particulars."

Narrow-eyed, Patterson withdrew an ID folder from a pocket in the jacket she was wearing and showed it to Shively, who did indeed note down the details. "You are a senior detective," she said, sounding incredulous.

"Yes," said Patterson, "and you are hindering my investigation. If you are really here to do a home visit, then please do so quickly and don't interfere in my discussion with Mrs. Jamieson."

By this time Shively must have noticed the plate of cookies and the coffee service on the coffee table, which were hardly indicative of a hostile interview between a detective and a suspect. She tapped her pen on her notebook, then finally nodded. Turning away, she made for the stairs to the bedroom level.

Patterson and Christy sat down again. "She's probably under the gun," Patterson said.

"Under the gun? What do you mean?"

"During the summer, while we were all on holiday, camping at ClanRanald, there was a scandal at Children's Services. A child was being abused by his father and the case worker didn't catch it. The kid committed suicide. The minister of Children's Services has ordered a review of all open cases. I expect Shively is being ultra-cautious. If she causes you any trouble, let me know. I'll vouch for you."

"Thanks. I will," Christy said. She had a dreadful fear she was going to have to take Patterson at her word.

CHAPTER 15

Patterson stuck around until Shively finished her house visit. They talked about nothing in particular since Christy was keyed up listening to the sound of Shively moving around her house, pulling open drawers, slamming cupboard doors.

Shively inspected the whole house, but there was nothing untoward for her to find. Christy had taught Noelle to keep her room and the basement playroom tidy, and she and Ellen kept up the rest of the house.

Shively's final stop was the kitchen, where Christy's baking utensils had been put in the dishwasher, leaving the counters clean, the table clear. That didn't stop her from sniffing in a disdainful way as she emerged into the living room and saying, "I suppose you have servants who keep this house so spotless." It was a parting shot, not meant to open a conversation, for she didn't even pause on her way to the staircase down to the front door landing.

She doesn't have servants, but she deserves them! Stormy stood, tail bushed, back arched and fur standing on end.

Christy picked up the cat before he charged Shively and dug in his claws. At the bottom of the stairs there was the sound of the door opening, then closing again as Shively took her departure.

"Wow," said Patterson. She looked dumbfounded at the woman's overt hostility.

"She'll probably put something about servants into a report," Christy said, rather sadly. "She'll make it into a problem and I'll have to defend myself again." She put Stormy back onto the sofa. "This has not been a good day."

"I'm sorry," Patterson said. "I should have suggested we meet somewhere else."

Yeah, you should have.

Christy shook her head as she smiled, glad that Patterson was one of those people who couldn't hear Frank. "This is my house and I can meet with anyone I choose to in it. Shively can make up whatever conspiracy theory she wants, but I'll fight her on it. And it won't stick, because I have friends who will support me."

"All the same," Patterson said with a shake of her head. "Next time I'll figure out somewhere else. I'd better get going."

Christy followed her down the stairs and after she had gone, left the front door open for Stormy, although the cat showed no interest in going outside. She returned to the main level and retrieved her iPad from the side table in the living room where she'd last used it. Grabbing a sturdy mug from the kitchen, she poured herself another cup of coffee, then took both the cup and the iPad out to the front porch. There she settled, enjoying the last warm sunny weather before the fall rains set in.

The cat followed her outside. *We have to do something about Shively.*

"What do you suggest?" She opened her browser and typed in a query about the child services scandal Patterson had alluded to.

The cat could scratch her eyes out.

"That would be effective." The query turned up a series of articles from both the newspapers and the television news broadcasts. Christy quickly realized there had been two incidents, both linked to a case worker not meeting expected standards, resulting in harm to the child under supervision.

No need to be sarcastic.

Christy sighed. "Frank, I know you're angry and you're frustrated. I can understand that and I sympathize, but Shively doesn't know you're Noelle's father. She thinks you're my cat. If Stormy attacked her, she could demand he be put down and neither of us wants that."

The cat sat down beside her. *What do you suggest?*

Christy gestured to the articles on her iPad. "Patterson was right. Shively is under pressure. The agency she works for is being examined by the ministry that funds it."

So?

"Her job is on the line. She has to prove herself and that means she has to be seen to be doing everything she can for every child in her caseload. What we have to do is make sure that when she talks to Noelle she finds a happy, well-adjusted young girl. And when she looks at Noelle's home life, she has to see a clean, comfortable home and a happy family focused on providing the best for the child." She scratched Stormy behind the ears. "And that includes a well-mannered cat, not one that turns manic at a moment's notice."

Stormy arched and rubbed against Christy's leg. *Stormy can do that. He loves Noelle. I can do that, too. I guess.*

"I know you can." She turned back to the iPad and scanned a few more articles. There was more of the same—outrage that a child had been failed by the very service that was supposed to keep him safe, references to the agency wide review, the agency itself issuing apologies and self-serving explanations. All of the articles were clustered together in a two-week period during the time they'd been away, disappearing when a new crisis had arisen to take its place.

Still, while there might not be any more media attention, the agency review was on-going and Christy guessed no one at child services wanted to see the organization back in the public spotlight. Shively would do whatever it took to ensure she followed every protocol to the letter. That meant she'd be on Christy's case for the next few weeks or months.

That was unfortunate. When she'd been unable to find anything negative in Christy's care of Noelle last year, she'd eased up on school and home visits, and after a quiet summer, Christy had been optimistic she would close Noelle's case.

No hope of that now.

She sat and considered what she should do, her elbows on her knees, her chin on her hands, staring out at nothing in particular. Stormy ambled off to check out some action across the street, leaving her alone with her thoughts.

She was still there when Trevor drove up and parked in front of her driveway, just as Patterson had. Ellen got out, smoothing her dress, and Trevor followed.

"You look pensive," Ellen said. "Was the interview with Patterson that difficult?"

Christy sighed and straitened. "It wasn't Patterson. Shively did a house call in the middle of the meeting."

"Ugh," Ellen said. "Loathsome woman."

"Any problems?" Trevor asked.

"She decided Patterson was here to arrest me."

"Good heavens! What made her imagine such a thing?" Ellen looked as dumbfounded as Patterson had been earlier.

Christy shrugged. "Patterson is a cop. The media have been throwing my name around in regard to Karen Beaumont's murder. Shively added one and one and got seven."

"Do you want me to have a word?" Trevor asked.

Christy thought about that. "No. Not yet, anyway. Patterson was pretty firm that she was here to get my input precisely because I was not a suspect. I think Shively believed her." She smiled at Ellen and Trevor. "How did the apartment viewing go?"

Trevor raised his brows. With a dismissive wave of her hand, Ellen said, "The building wasn't a mansion, but a nondescript commercial building on the edge of the district. Though the interior was attractive, the location was not. It was quite unsuitable."

"Too bad." Christy glanced at her watch. "I have to go pick up Noelle and Mary Petrofsky. I think I'll get my tote and take Stormy. Frank was upset by Shively. It will do him good to focus on Noelle." She glanced from Ellen to Trevor. "Do you want to come along?"

"Not today," Ellen said. "You and Frank need time together with Noelle."

Christy nodded. "Yeah, we do."

Though Christy was facing an uncertain future as a result of the dogmatic and suspicious Joan Shively, everyday life went on. That meant keeping her worries to herself. Noelle knew Shively was a problem, but she didn't understand the full ramifications of the danger the woman represented. And if Christy had her way she never would.

So here she was, on Saturday morning, shopping for her Thanksgiving dinner, which she was holding the next day. The Armstrongs and McCullaghs had been invited, along with Mary Petrofsky, who was sleeping over tonight and would stay for dinner. The Petrofskys celebrated Thanksgiving on the Monday, which was the actual holiday in Canada, but like many others, Christy's family and the Jamiesons chose to have their Thanksgiving feast on Sunday. The basket of her grocery cart already had the biggest turkey she could find that would fit into her oven, plus sausage meat for stuffing.

Noelle and Mary Petrofsky had come with her, so she was making a game of finding all of the items on her extra long list. Quinn had also joined the expedition, aware, Christy believed, of how deeply worried she was by Shively's threat. He was trying his best to keep her grounded.

And he was doing a fine job, she thought, with an inner smile.

She halted her grocery cart in front of the cat food display and scrutinized the offerings with the goal of replenishing Stormy's cupboard with some special items. Beside her Quinn studied them as well. Christy imagined his purpose was rather different from hers.

She found the brand she wanted, then reached for a can of salmon supreme dinner, which she dropped into the basket of the cart.

Quinn picked up another can of cat food, his expression innocent. "How about this one? Liver and giblets. Yum."

Christy laughed. "Put it in. Liver and giblets is one of Stormy's favorites."

Quinn made a face but added the cat food to the other items in the cart.

With Stormy's cat food replenished, Christy headed the cart down the aisle. At the far end Noelle and Mary Petrofsky were examining the toilet paper offerings, tasked with deciding which brand offered the best price per package. Christy stopped at cleaning products and added a bottle of laundry detergent to her collection, then paused there as Noelle and Mary came toward her, each holding one end on an enormous package of toilet paper. "Okay ladies," Christy said, "why did you pick this brand?"

"It's more expensive," Mary said. "And it's not the one on sale." She nibbled her bottom lip, her expression worried. "But each of the rolls in the package are bigger."

They had more squares per roll than the rolls in the on-sale brand, she meant. Christy nodded, waiting for more.

"And it's two-ply, where the one on sale is only one ply," Noelle added triumphantly, because she and Christy had had this conversation before. Two ply beat one ply, more squares per roll meant better value. She knew she and Mary had picked the best deal, though not the obvious one.

"Good work. Throw it in the cart."

"Let me help," Quinn said. Together he and the two girls maneuvered the huge package onto the shelf for large items below the basket. When it was securely lodged, Noelle straightened and dusted her hands together in the gesture for a job well done. Quinn held his hand palm out for a high five. Both girls slapped it at the same time and giggled.

Christy laughed and said, "Okay, next on our list is frozen foods. I need some corn. Do you girls want to choose it for me?"

"Sure," said Noelle, who found the game of grocery shopping enormously entertaining.

Mary nodded, earnest and intense.

They set off, at the end of the aisle turning toward the frozen foods section. "Okay, what are you looking for when you decide which brand to buy?"

"Quality, price, and volume," Noelle announced.

"Right, off you go. Frozen vegetables are way down at the other end of the aisle."

The two girls scampered off. There was amusement in Quinn's voice as he said, "If Shively could see you giving a home ec course while you grocery shopped she wouldn't be so hard on you."

Christy smiled. "Don't forget teaching them how to use math in every day life. I don't think it matters what I do, though. The woman has me categorized as a self-indulgent good-time girl with too much money and too few morals. If something wicked happens she has me pegged for it. I mean, honestly! How often does someone about to be arrested serve the police officer cookies and coffee before being hauled away in handcuffs? Shively sees what she wants to see." She punctuated that gloomy statement by hauling open the door to a nearby freezer compartment with way more force than was needed.

Realizing what she was doing, she sighed as she selected a premade piecrust and carefully placed it in the cart. "Patterson and I were in the middle of trying to figure out where everyone was at the gala when Shively interrupted us. We never got back to it and I have this feeling there was something I know that she needs to know, but I can't put my finger on it."

"Do you want to go over it with me?" Quinn's mouth flicked up into a half smile. "I'm just hanging around. You haven't given me any shopping jobs so far."

That made her chuckle. "You picked out some cat food and you've been chill about loading giant turkeys and huge packages of toilet paper into my cart. Seems to me you're making yourself pretty useful."

Quinn grinned. "I was hoping the cat food would end up causing problems."

Christy laughed. "Yeah, I know. Seriously, would you mind going over that evening? Maybe talking about it again will trigger a memory, like retracing your steps when you can't find something."

"Sure," he said, but before they could get started, Noelle and Mary bounced up to the cart carrying three bags of frozen corn, which was not part of their brief.

Christy glanced at Quinn, whose brows were raised, and said, "What have you got, ladies?"

"The one kilogram bags of corn were all on sale, so we compared all the brands. These ones are Canada Fancy." Noelle held up her arms showing the bags there.

Christy nodded and infused approval into her voice when all she wanted to do was chuckle at her daughter's enthusiasm. "The best quality."

"And they are on sale for a dollar off," Mary said, very serious.

"So we brought three!" Noelle said, dumping the bags into the cart.

"Good thing we all like corn," Christy said, and Quinn laughed.

Noelle flashed him a mischievous grin.

Christy set the cart in motion. "Moving on, our next stop is the vegetable department. What vegetables go with the Thanksgiving turkey?"

"Brussels sprouts and green beans," Noelle said.

"Turnips," said Mary.

Noelle frowned at her. "Turnips?" She glanced at Christy, as if seeking explanation.

"Looks like turnips are part of the Petrofskys' Thanksgiving traditions," Christy said. "You'll find out about it on Monday. I think we'll stick to the sprouts and beans for us, though. We also need apples for pie." They discussed which were the best baking apples and when they reached the fresh fruit and vegetables department, Christy sent the girls off to choose the apples.

Christy and Quinn went back to discussing the murder as they picked out the vegetables. "Since Anton Gormley was released the police pathologist has discovered two important pieces of information. Karen Beaumont was most likely killed much earlier than anyone expected and there's evidence she fell from the terrace, then rolled down the lower staircase. So whoever killed her had to have been on the terrace when she fell."

"Or that person pushed her," Quinn said.

Christy nodded. "The key thing is to figure out when she was last seen and where. That will help Patterson pinpoint the time of her death, then she can compare that time with the alibis of all the people there that evening."

"What part of the evening were you talking about when Shively arrived?" Quinn asked.

Christy frowned at the plump, green Brussels sprouts. She rolled one between her fingers and thumb as she thought. "I'd told her about that ucky Samuel Moore singing the lead in the musical production. Beaumont was there during the performance and I saw her move out into the foyer after it was over. You and I went downstairs to the ball-room almost immediately, but I did see Beaumont talking to Moore in the foyer. I was telling Patterson we had stayed in the ballroom until after the band finished playing. She started to ask me a question when the doorbell rang."

"Do you remember the question?"

Christy dropped the bag of sprouts into the cart and closed her eyes, trying to recall it. "Something about Beaumont. Did you— That's it. Did you see Beaumont— Then the doorbell rang and she broke off."

Quinn took over the pushing of the cart and Christy trailed along beside. "It was probably something like, did you see Beaumont while you were in the ballroom, or after you went down to the ballroom. Something like that."

Christy nodded. "Yes, that's probably it." She wrinkled her nose. "You know, I didn't. See her that is. Did you?"

"Good question." It was Quinn's turn to think back. "No, I didn't."

"And she wasn't on the terrace when we got there after the Light-ening Rod performance was over."

They stopped at the green beans. Christy noticed that over in the apple department Mary was holding a plastic bag open while Noelle picked the apples. They were both talking animatedly as they exam-ined the fruit. Only one out of every two or three made it into the bag.

Christy grabbed a plastic bag and scooped a handful of green beans into it. She followed it with a second scoop, her mind on the gala evening. "If we didn't see her down in the ballroom and she wasn't on the terrace when we got there, that means she was probably dead before the Lightening Rod performance began."

"Which means everybody's alibi needs to be rechecked," Quinn said.

Wide-eyed, Christy said, "It could be anyone."

Quinn nodded. "Including Anton Gromley."

CHAPTER 16

From the cooking side of the peninsula that divided the kitchen into culinary space and dining nook, Christy looked with approval at the table and the crowd around it. She'd added a leaf, but still it was packed. Ellen sat at the head, as the senior member of the Jamieson family. Beside her on her right was Trevor, with Roy on her left. Noelle was beside Roy, and Mary Petrofsky opposite her.

Christy was at the foot of the table, with Quinn on her right, beside Noelle, and Sledge on her left. Stormy lay curled on the window seat behind the table, dozy after his portion of turkey and sausage dressing. The room was warm with oven heat and the scents of turkey and apple pie. Voices were raised in at least two conversations that intersected from time to time and became one.

There was laughter and good cheer and Christy loved it. This was what Thanksgiving had been like when she was growing up. After she'd moved to Vancouver with Frank, the Thanksgiving celebration had been careful and well-mannered, often at a hotel restaurant rather than the Jamieson mansion, so the servants could have time off to be with their families. In her first year in Vancouver she'd suggested that she cook the turkey, but that had earned her cool stares from the trustees and a disdainful thank you, but no from Ellen. Frank had been intrigued by the idea of fending for themselves, but not enough to battle the powerful authority figures in his life. So Thanksgiving became another polite social occasion in an annual schedule already filled with them.

Last year Frank had been missing and his fate unknown. Thanksgiving again had been just another day, so this was the first time she'd really had a chance to create the kind of family celebration she craved. So far it had turned out beautifully. The turkey had been cooked to perfection, stuffed with her mother's special sausage meat and rice dressing, and she'd cooked the Brussels sprouts and green beans with bacon from a recipe she'd found on the Internet. The potatoes were mashed to creamy perfection and Ellen had baked some buns that melted in the mouth. Everyone, including the two girls, had scoffed down their share.

Now they were on to apple pie, which Noelle and Mary Petrofsky had prepared this morning. Christy had put the pie into the oven to warm while they were enjoying their main course. She took it out and the fragrant scent, sweet with hints of spice, filled the room. "We have whipped cream, ice cream, and a nice extra old cheddar to go with the pie. Who wants what?"

Quinn came over to help her serve the slices. "I'll take a chunk of cheddar."

She looked over at him and winked as she slid slices of pie onto the plates she'd assembled. "Good. You get to dish out the add-ons."

He smiled back. "Dangerous decision. I tend to be generous with my add-ons."

She laughed. "Go for it."

The two girls asked for both whipped cream and ice cream, but passed on the cheese. Trevor and Roy chose the cheddar, and Sledge had all three. Ellen satisfied herself with a simple piece of pie.

Stormy stood and arched in a stretch. *The cat wants ice cream.* There was a brief silence. *He says he'll skip the pie.*

Sledge snorted and Noelle giggled, while Mary Petrofsky's eyes rounded at the thought of a cat eating people pie.

Roy said thoughtfully, "Not surprising. Apples are not a cat favorite."

Christy debated giving Stormy the ice cream, but when he sat in front of his dish, green eyes demanding, she caved. "Just a bit." She dropped a quarter of a teaspoon into his dish.

That's it?

"That's it," she said in her firmest voice, but she added a dollop of whipped cream. Stormy lapped up both, but stayed by the dish when he was finished, eyes accusing. When Christy passed carrying her own piece of apple pie topped with whipped cream, he butted her leg, but she ignored him.

Everyone said the pie was the best they'd ever tasted, making Noelle and Mary puff up with pride. With the pie consumed Noelle and Mary went off to have fun in the playroom down in the basement. Frank, still miffed at the small dessert portion with no seconds, decided to go with them, leaving the others to coffee, after dinner drinks, and conversation about the murder.

Christy opened the discussion with the realization that she'd had the previous day, shopping with Quinn. "Did any of you see Karen Beaumont after you came down to the ballroom?"

There were thoughtful expressions and some surprised looks were exchanged, but everyone shook their heads.

Christy looked at Quinn, then at the others. "It's unlikely all of us missed seeing her, mainly because she was so visible prior to that. So that means she never came downstairs."

"And if she fell from the terrace, she was probably murdered before the entertainment in the ballroom began," Trevor said. He appeared intrigued by that. "So Patterson will have to throw out all of the alibis she gathered for later in the evening."

Christy nodded. "She didn't give me a lot of detail from the coroner's report, but I gather it gave her a window, which was fairly large. To narrow it down she has to know where everybody was all evening. She may already have all the information she needs, but it would be nice to give her corroborating details."

"I'll get my folder and pens," Ellen said, rising from her chair.

When Ellen returned they quickly went through their own whereabouts. Quinn and Christy had been among the first to go down to the ballroom. There they'd found Sledge who'd been jamming with Lightening Rod. He admitted that he'd skipped the musical theater entertainment in favor of introducing himself to the band. He could confirm that all the band members were in the ballroom until the point when Anton Gormley had stormed off stage.

"So the students all have alibis," Ellen said, carefully making a note in authoritative black ink on her elegant blue parchment letterhead. "I'm glad. That young man has more than enough strikes against him. He doesn't need to be rearrested for a crime he didn't commit."

Trevor smiled at her. "Well said."

Ellen blushed.

Sledge raised his eyebrows at this exchange, but didn't comment. Trevor continued on, oblivious to his son's reaction. "Ellen and I remained in the foyer for some time before we went down to the ballroom. While we were mingling I noticed Beaumont speaking to Samuel Moore. I was surprised that he seemed to be pleased at what she was saying. She was so student-focused earlier in the evening I thought she'd be critical of his involvement in the musical."

Christy nodded. "Patterson mentioned she had statements from other witnesses that had Beaumont speaking to Moore. While you were in the foyer, did you see anyone else whom you didn't see in the ballroom?"

Trevor glanced at Ellen, who said, "There were still quite a few people in the foyer when we went down." She paused, looking inward. "We passed President Harding as we were on our way to the stairs. He was talking to that music executive..." She looked at Sledge. "What's his name?"

"Mitch Crosier?"

She nodded. "Yes. His wife winked at me when we passed." There was disapproval in her voice. Evidently, she considered winking at another guest inappropriate behavior when talking to the president of a college.

"I saw Beaumont go into the dining room before we went downstairs," Trevor said suddenly. "I remember hearing some shouts and banging, so they must still have been taking down the set."

"Yes." Ellen nodded emphatically, adding note to her document, in red ink this time. "We don't know how long she remained in the dining room as we didn't see her exit before we proceeded to the ballroom. She could have gone out onto the terrace, perhaps when the students were moving the set into the transport vehicle. The killer might have found her there, alone and vulnerable."

"Are you suggesting the killer is one of the people who was in the dining room doing the clean up?" Christy asked.

Ellen shook her head. "Not necessarily. There is access to the terrace from both the dining room and the drawing room. The killer could have come through the French doors in the drawing room."

"Don't forget the stairs at either end of the terrace that lead down to the gardens," Roy said. "The killer could have gone down to the ballroom, slipped out one of the doors into the garden, run up the stairs to the terrace, then killed Beaumont, before coming back to the ballroom."

They all thought about that for a moment.

"But if the killer arrived on the terrace too early, the people clearing the dining room would have heard something," Christy said. "That means we're looking for someone who was missing from the ballroom or who came in late."

Ellen nodded and wrote her comment down.

"What about the college staff?" Christy asked. "We know she was talking to Samuel Moore and of course we all saw him singing with the band. I noticed Craig Harding at a table in the ballroom, then later dancing with his wife, before he came over to help us waylay Moore after the SledgeHammer tribute."

Roy shifted. "I don't remember seeing Jackson Hargreaves in the foyer. I did see his wife, though. She was talking to Gillian Stankov, the CEO of the Arts Association—that's the group that runs MacLagan House."

Quinn raised his brows. "The Arts Association is an umbrella group that helps creative artists succeed. I suppose Jackson is involved with them?"

Roy nodded. "He's a member."

"You were on the board while Mom was alive, weren't you?"

After a moment's hesitation, Roy nodded. "Your mother provided legal advice on a pro bono basis, as well. Gillian wasn't the CEO when I was involved—I haven't been participating much in the last few years—so I don't know a lot about her. I'm not surprised she'd attend the At Risk gala, though."

"So Jackson Hargreaves could be a suspect," Christy said. "Did anyone see him in the ballroom?"

"I saw Gillian Stankov come in with an older woman just as the band began to play," Sledge said. "Could she have been Mrs. Hargreaves? Their table was on the opposite side of the room to ours."

Roy nodded. "Jackson showed up there sometime later. His wife ignored him at first, then it looked like they were arguing. When Samuel Moore began to sing they followed Anton Gromley out."

Writing furiously, Ellen said, "So Jackson Hargreaves is unaccounted for during the crucial time."

Roy frowned. "Jackson had good cause to be angry at Beaumont, but he's the kind of guy who puts off doing things. He's more likely to bitch to his co-workers and friends about her ultimatum than to do anything about it."

"Still," Christy said. "Pressure can make people do unexpected things."

"Yes," said Ellen. "We must keep him down as a suspect until his whereabouts can be confirmed."

"What about Declan West, the professor who was her ex-brother-in-law?" Christy asked. "Craig Harding told me that Beaumont's break with his brother was contentious and caused a lot of family problems. Though he did say there was no evidence of hostility in their working relationship."

"West is ex-army and has training in hand-to-hand combat," Roy added with considerable enthusiasm. "He could easily have thrown her over the edge of the terrace."

"He was in the bar, sitting at one of the tables with a glass of what looked like whisky in front of him, when I went to get drinks after Christy and I found a table in the ballroom. He looked like he'd been there a while," Quinn said.

"Did you see him in the ballroom later?" Christy asked

Quinn shook his head.

She looked around. "Anyone?"

They all shook their heads in denial.

"Okay then, he's another suspect who needs his whereabouts confirmed." She looked around. "Anyone else we can pinpoint?"

Roy stirred. "I saw Hal Wilkinson in the ballroom, at least later on when Moore was singing." Looking at Sledge, his eyes twinkled as he added, "He clapped like crazy at the end. I don't think he's a Sledge-Hammer fan."

Sledge shrugged. "He wasn't the only one clapping."

"Wilkinson had a grudge against Beaumont, didn't he?" Quinn asked.

Roy nodded. "She was going to cancel his course on graphic novels due to lack of interest." He shifted in his seat. "But Hal's the chair of creative writing. If he's reconfirmed in that position, he won't have to go back to teaching. It won't matter if his course is eliminated."

"Hal Wilkinson. Location to be confirmed. Motive thin," Ellen said, writing furiously.

"What about other guests?" Trevor asked. "We've talked about Mitch and Kim Crosier. Olivia Waters and Tamara were with us in the ballroom so I don't suppose they have any secrets to add. Anyone else who might have useful information?"

They tossed around a few more names, but decided most were dead ends. "A pity we don't know more about the inner workings of the college," Trevor said, shaking his head. "I think the killer is to be found among their ranks."

Ellen gathered her papers and straightened them decisively by tapping their bottoms against the table. "We have put together a substantial document for Detective Patterson. As usual, our input will make her job considerably easier." She handed the pages to Christy. "Tell her this is with my compliments."

Christy laughed. "I'll be sure to."

"What have you got for me?"

When Christy called Patterson saying she had further information on the Beaumont murder, the detective insisted they meet somewhere impersonal, so Christy suggested Burnaby Mountain Park. There was plenty of parking and not a lot of people using the park on a cloudy morning the day after the Thanksgiving holiday. They would be able to talk privately, without fear of interruption.

Christy handed Patterson an envelope containing Ellen's notes. "We put our heads together over the weekend to try to figure out where people were at various points during the gala. Ellen took detailed notes. She sends them along with her compliments."

Dressed in her usual outfit of jacket and trousers, Patterson took the envelope with her eyebrows raised. "Ellen Jamieson?"

Christy laughed. "One and the same."

"Amazing," Patterson said. She opened the envelope and drew out the pages. Her brows rose higher. "You people were busy."

"During the gala we were spread over the building," Christy said. "Each of us saw different people in different places. Our limitation is that we don't know all of the players. I'm sure there are people who worked for Karen Beaumont who were at the gala, other than those we discussed, but we don't know enough about the organization of the college to point them out."

Reading, Patterson nodded. "This will be very useful in any case." She tapped the page. "For instance, I didn't know Hargreaves wasn't with his wife throughout the evening. In his statement, he made it sound as if they were together for the whole time. He also implied he was always with a larger group of people." Her smile was not pleasant. "I'll have to have a talk with our famous novelist."

"Not so famous, according to Roy," Christy said with a grin. "Apparently, Hargreaves hasn't produced a novel in years and Beaumont was on his case to get writing."

"How hard can it be?" Patterson murmured.

"For Jackson Hargreaves? Extremely. Roy says he suffers from serious writer's block."

"Huh," Patterson said. She focused in on another name. "This guy, Declan West. Now he's interesting. He claimed he was in the bar while the band was playing, except for a visit to the washroom. The bartender confirms it."

Christy shoved her hands in the pockets of her jeans and leaned against her van. "His motive is personal, and there's a long history of hostility between him and Beaumont. He also has hand-to-hand combat training. Maybe there are holes in his story, too."

Patterson nodded thoughtfully. "There is the time he spent in the washroom. He says he didn't see anyone there, so he has no alibi for five, ten minutes tops. He could have run up to the main floor, out onto the terrace to meet with Beaumont and to push her off. As you say, he's got the physical training to be able to overpower her without any trouble." She nodded. "Yeah, I think I'll have another talk with Declan West."

She came to the last name they'd identified. "Hal Wilkinson. Why is his name on the list?"

"Beaumont was planning to get rid of his course on writing graphic novels. Roy talked to him and said he and Jackson Hargreaves were both complaining about the changes she was making to curriculum. Roy knows him by sight, but none of the rest of us do, so it was hard to pinpoint where he was, but we thought he was worth taking a look at."

Patterson nodded and went back to the document. When she was finished she slipped the sheets back into the envelope. "This will help me narrow down the possible time of death." She hesitated, made a decision and said, "I already knew that Beaumont left the foyer after talking to Samuel Moore and went into the dining room where they were still taking down the musical theater set. According to Monique McGrath, the professor in charge, Beaumont apologized to all the students on behalf of Moore for his involvement in the production. Then she took Korby Usher aside. He was the student who should have had the lead role, but who was reduced to playing a secondary part. Usher was, apparently, rude and McGrath was embarrassed. She thinks Beaumont was embarrassed, too, though she didn't show it. She went out to the terrace for, as she said, 'a breath of air.' She didn't come back in, but McGrath didn't think anything of it."

"Do you suspect the student?" Christy asked.

Patterson shook her head. "I did wonder at first. The kid was another of the At Risk students. He had a temper like Anton Gormley, and he apparently told Beaumont she should have stopped Moore from singing when the production started, even if doing so embarrassed Moore and the college. Unlike Gormley, he didn't stomp off after talking to her. He stayed in the dining room, and worked on the takedown until it was done. When they were loading the set into the college van, McGrath took him aside and chewed him out. The kid took umbrage and that's when he left."

"He could have doubled back."

"Could have, but didn't. A couple of friends went with him. They alibi each other."

Christy pointed to the envelope. "Talking about At Risk students stomping off, Anton Gormley is out too. Sledge slipped away before the musical theater production. He went down to the ballroom and jammed with the kids in Lightening Rod. He says Gormley was there the whole time." Christy hesitated, then after a moment said, "Why did you arrest Gormley in the first place?"

"Karen Beaumont was a well-known figure in the local film industry and apparently she was also highly respected. After she joined PGC she kept in contact with her former colleagues and used her contacts to promote her programs. Top brass had a lot of calls from those same people wanting justice for her." Patterson shrugged. "The word came down to find her killer and quickly."

"My," Christy said, impressed by the pressure put on Patterson and her team. She'd had no idea Karen Beaumont's death would cause so much behind the scenes intervention. Though, perhaps the media frenzy should have given her a clue.

Patterson's mouth turned up in a small, humorless smile. "Yeah, well. On the surface Gormley looked good for the killing. The kid had a temper, and when we questioned him he ranted on about Moore and how he wanted an apology from him and Beaumont was the only one who could force him to give it, so he went to look for her. He claimed he never found her, but at that point we didn't believe him. We assumed he connected with her, but that she refused to publically embarrass Moore, so he took out his temper on her and killed her. He fit a profile." Her mouth hardened grimly. "Arresting him was a mistake and it backfired on us."

"So you're being cautious now."

Patterson smiled that small smile again. "As we should have been from the beginning." She held up the envelope. "Thanks for this. It's appreciated."

Christy smiled. "Of course."

Patterson hesitated, then she said, "Karen Beaumont's memorial service is tomorrow."

Christy raised her brows. "I wasn't intending to go to it."

Patterson grinned. Evidently, they both remembered Fred Jarvis's service when Stormy the Cat had caused a sensation in the middle of the proceedings by licking away the grieving widow's tears. "No. I have to though, and I expect the media will be out in force. As I mentioned, Beaumont was a major player in the local entertainment industry and..." She shrugged. "She's being buried with her killer still at large. They're bound to play that up. I thought you might want to be prepared."

Christy sighed. "To be back on suspect list, you mean?"

Patterson nodded. "It could happen."

"Yeah, it could. Okay, thanks Detective. I'll keep that in mind."

CHAPTER 17

Quinn didn't jump when his father bustled into his office and said, "Time you started joining some organizations."

He was well aware of Roy's approach. It was Tuesday morning, the day after the Thanksgiving holiday and he was supposed to be working. But he wasn't.

He pushed his wheeled executive chair back from his desk and looked up at his father thoughtfully. Roy was dressed in a clean pair of jeans and a relatively unwrinkled checked shirt and his hair was brushed and tied neatly at his nape. He was plotting something. "What do you have in mind?"

"The Arts Association. You're a book author now. You should become a member." Roy added a sharp chin jerk at the end of this statement. A silent exclamation point that said the decision was made and all that remained to do was implement it.

Quinn swiveled the chair slowly back and forth while he scrutinized his father. Nothing was ever simple with Roy Armstrong. "You want to find out what the CEO of the association knows about the murder."

Roy grinned. "Probably nothing much, but it's worth talking to her." He sobered. "I'm worried about Christy. Not only has she got a lot riding on the Foundation's involvement with PGC, but I'm afraid she's going to get burned by this Shively woman."

Which pretty much encapsulated why Quinn was sitting at his computer staring at the screen and doing none of the work he was supposed to be doing. His second book, this one on the death of Vince Nunez in Sledge's front yard, was due to his editor in a month and his manuscript needed revisions and polishing before he turned it in. "We don't have to pretend I want to join the organization. I could simply interview her."

His father considered that, then shook his head. "More friendly my way. She'll open up more."

"Maybe. Maybe not. You don't know the woman. She might be the kind who loves the idea of talking to the press."

Roy shrugged. "Possibly." He waved his hand in a dismissive way. "However we decide to handle it, we have an appointment with her in forty-five minutes. We can decide our *modus operandi*—" he said the words with theatrical relish "—in the car."

Thoroughly annoyed at his father because it gave him a vent for a lot of emotions he was having a hard time handling, Quinn contemplated refusing to go along. What if he'd been deep in the kind of writing fugues his father enjoyed? Sure, he didn't write that way, he was more of a create for a couple of hours, then work on other parts of the project, like research, kind of writer. But he could have been in the middle of an intensive two-hour session when his father sauntered into his office. He wasn't, but still.

His father was looking at him calmly, amusement in his eyes as if he knew Quinn had been doing nothing worthwhile and had absolutely no reason to refuse to go to the appointment.

"Dad." He gestured to his computer. "I was working."

Roy's brows shot up and he fixed an innocent expression on his face. "It's forty-five minutes there, and another forty-five back. I doubt we'll spend more than a half an hour with Stankov. That's three hours out of your day, tops."

Quinn grimaced.

"And maybe doing something for Christy will help you concentrate so you can get some of that work you're supposed to be doing, done."

Quinn shut his laptop with a snap. He hated it when his father did that—unerringly put his finger on what was bothering him. "All right. Let's go."

Once they were in the car and on the way, he said, "We play this straight. We're there to find out what we can about the gala. That's it. No phony story about me joining the organization."

"Why don't we play it by ear?" Roy backed the car out of the carport and aimed it up the street, gunning it, because the kids were all in school and there was no action in the area. "I'll soften Stankov up by talking about my past credits with the organization. Maybe I'll tell her I want to get more involved again."

"Do you?" His father turned out of the complex onto the main street and speeded up. Quinn decided he was probably worried about rubbing Ms. Stankov the wrong way by being late for the interview.

Watching the road as they roared along, heading for the intersection that would take them to the highway, Roy said cheerfully, "No. I've done my time. But it's a good organization. I don't mind participating when necessary."

If he didn't agree to the pretense that he wanted to become involved with the association, there was no telling what his father might blurt out to Gillian Stankov. "How about this. As a long time member of the organization you want me to join, but I'm not sure it's for me. Let Ms. Stankov tell me all about the Arts Association and its mission. I'll be interested, but non-committal, particularly given the organization's involvement in Karen Beaumont's murder."

They made it onto the highway in one piece, and Roy put his foot down hard on the accelerator. It was a good thing it was the middle of the day and traffic was flowing freely. His father passed one semi-trailer, then another, before he said, almost reluctantly, "Might work."

Encouraged, Quinn said, "We could go in even more openly. You introduce me, tell Ms. Stankov I'm working on an article about Beaumont's murder and that I'd like to ask her a few questions."

Roy didn't reply. He passed another semi as if it was standing still, then took the Hastings Street exit. "That's not as much fun," he said once they'd integrated into traffic on that major artery.

The complaint was a concession. Quinn had the feeling he was on the edge of getting his father to agree to let him handle the interview the way he wanted to. "She's more likely to open up if she knows what she's facing."

"The opposite could happen." Roy swerved around a delivery van double-parked in front of a storefront. The car he'd cut off honked. Roy grunted. But he slowed down and paid more attention to the vehicles around him.

Quinn laughed. "I guess you have to trust my reporting skills to get the job done."

His father grinned. "I guess I do."

They made it to the high-rise on West Hastings that housed the Arts Association without an accident and with bare minutes to spare. The office was twenty floors up, and when they stepped out of the elevator, the first thing Quinn saw was the corporate logo of a major forest company mounted on the wall facing the elevator doors. Below it was a huge reception desk, with a decorative blonde working it. She seemed surprised when Roy announced they were there to see Gillian Stankov.

"Gillian? Really?" The blonde pointed across the hall to the opposite side of the building. "The Arts Association is down there. Most of the artists who come by usually go right to her office. They don't bother taking the official route through me."

Her phone rang and she smiled as she picked it up, then wiggled her fingers in a good-bye gesture as she talked to the person on the other end. Quinn and Roy made their way back past the elevators to the far side of the building.

"The office was in North Van when I was on the board." Roy looked around. "Then the forest company offered to provide them with space in some give back to the community initiative. A pretty sweet deal. Free space downtown isn't easy to come by."

They found the office easily, as someone had screwed a brass plaque inscribed with flowing, almost illegible script onto the dark wood door. Roy grasped the handle and pushed it open. Quinn followed him inside.

Quinn had vague memories of the Arts Association from the time when his father had sat on the board. He'd been younger then, living on his own and often overseas reporting in one world hotspot or another, but he had the impression the organization was a small operation and the CEO comprised pretty much the whole professional staff. Now he was surprised to find that Gillian Stankov didn't just have an office, she had a suite. The room behind the door was spacious and airy and housed a young woman sitting at a reception desk much like the one opposite the elevators, except smaller. Behind the woman, he could see a corridor with at least three doorways on either side, plus an open one at the very end.

The young woman looked up and smiled as the door whispered closed behind them. "Mr. Armstrong! I'm so happy to meet you. I love your books." Roy smiled and looked bashful. She continued on. "Gillian's expecting you. She's down the hall in her office." She pointed, but didn't get up to guide them. Evidently, she didn't see her role to be that of a receptionist, even though she was sitting in the front office.

Quinn and his father headed down the hallway to the office at the end.

Gillian Stankov was a blonde woman of indeterminate age. Her hair was medium length, cut in a stylish, but business-like bob. She wore a white blouse with ruffles at the wrists and flowing sleeves. When she stood to greet them, Quinn saw that the feminine blouse topped hip hugging blue jeans.

She held out her hand. "Mr. Armstrong, thank you for coming by today. My predecessor spoke highly of you."

As Roy shook her hand, he introduced Quinn. Gillian then shook his hand too and they all sat down, Gillian behind her desk and Roy and Quinn in visitor chairs that were surprisingly comfortable.

"My son's an investigative reporter," Roy said. "His book, *Finding Frank Jamieson*, comes out in a few weeks."

"Yes," Gillian said. "I've heard about it." She smiled at Quinn. "I'm looking forward to digging into it. I read all of your articles on the case and I think it's a fascinating story." She smiled in an encouraging way. "Of course, a book is a much larger endeavor than articles are. A more *artistic* form, as it were."

Roy shot him a told-you-so look and Quinn had to stifle a laugh. His father had been right about Gillian Stankov. She was selling her organization. "It certainly takes longer to write and get to press than an article does," he said in reply.

Gillian nodded. "How true. You're lucky to have Roy Armstrong as a mentor." She shot Roy a look. "He has so much experience with the business side of publishing."

His father beamed at that. Quinn resisted the urge to shake his head. He wasn't going to hear the end of this for a while. "The benefit of a book is that I can develop the work I do initially, adding more details and contextualizing it. At the same time I can continue to dig into new stories."

Her eyes widened and she looked intrigued. "Are you working on something at the moment?"

He smiled at her. "Karen Beaumont's murder."

For a moment she froze. In surprise? Because she had a guilty conscience?

Then she smiled and said, "Of course. I should have realized. You were at the gala, weren't you? I think I saw you there with Christy Jamieson." There was a gleam in her eyes. She thought she was on to some juicy gossip.

"I was there," he said, neither confirming nor denying who he was with. He wasn't going to give this woman personal details she'd use as currency to puff herself up in the artistic community she assisted. "I believe Karen Beaumont was killed not long after most of the guests went down to the ballroom. Do you remember seeing her between the time the musical ended and the band started playing in the ballroom?"

For a moment he thought he'd been too blunt, that Stankov would refuse to provide him with input. She stared at him without blinking, silent and surprisingly still. Then she spoke.

"After the musical theater performance I was in the foyer along with everyone else. Karen came out and cornered Samuel near the front door—"

"She cornered him?" Roy sounded surprised.

Gillian nodded. "She chewed him out pretty good, I think. He kept a smile on his face, but that's what he does when someone says something to him he doesn't like."

"You know him well?"

Gillian's lips pursed. "He's our president this year. I have to work fairly closely with him."

She broke off. Quinn had the sense that she had more to say but was reluctant to let it out. He smiled at her in his friendliest, most nonthreatening way and made a guess based on Moore's behavior at the gala. "He likes to dive in where he's not needed, does he?"

She snorted. "Hardly. He never does anything that won't be noticed. He likes the importance of being president, but he doesn't like the work associated with the job."

Well, that was interesting. Quinn raised his brows and let Gillian decide whether or not she wanted to unload further.

She pursed her lips, shot a quick glance at his father, then shrugged. "Samuel Moore likes to be the center of attention. No, more than that. He believes he's entitled to be the center of attention. He doesn't take criticism well, but that doesn't mean he has a hissy fit and shouts. More, he pretends it doesn't matter."

"Which is why you think Beaumont was chewing him out, when most of the other people I've talked to seem to think she was praising him."

Gillian shrugged. "She might have been. I don't know for sure. Anyway, when she was finished talking to Samuel, she made her way back into the dining room, to check on the takedown, I suppose."

"Did you see her expression when she left Moore?" Quinn asked.

Gillian shook her head. "No. I was talking to Phyllis Hargreaves at that point and I saw Karen go into the dining room out of the corner of my eye."

"Did you see her come out of the dining room?"

Again Gillian shook her head. "No. Phyllis and I went down to the ballroom together not long after." She hesitated, glanced at Roy, then seemed to come to a decision. "I wanted to get Phyllis away from the foyer before Jackson came down from the second floor."

Roy's eyebrows rose. "What was he doing on the second floor?"

Good question. The second floor had not been part of the space made available to the gala participants.

Gillian hesitated again, then she said, "Jackson rents space up there to work. He says he has trouble concentrating at home and he can't write at the college. I assume he went up to his office for some quiet." She brightened. "Or maybe he just wanted to use the washroom up there because it was less busy."

Sure, Quinn thought. "Do you know how long he was there?"

Gillian answered quickly. "Not at all. I saw him go up while Karen was talking to Samuel. Phyllis came by looking for him—that's what we were talking about—where he was. I persuaded Phyllis to come down to the ballroom with me before he came back down."

Persuading Phyllis indicated Gillian thought there was a good reason to get her out of the way before her husband returned to the main level. That made the washroom use idea unlikely. "When did you next see him?"

"While the band was playing. He came in about halfway through their set. He and Phyllis started to talk, then they left the ballroom. I guess they didn't want to interrupt the band." She smiled at Quinn. "I'm afraid that's about all I can tell you. Have I been of help?"

Quinn assured her she had and she smiled in what he could only call a seductive way.

"If you use my information, you will spell my name correctly, won't you? Gillian with a G not a J. And please do mention that the Arts Association manages MacLagan House. The publicity will be excellent for our events program."

Taken aback, Quinn said, "Right. G not J." He didn't promise the free advertising. He couldn't.

She beamed at him. "You've got it." She stood, holding out her hand. "Gentlemen, such a pleasure. Roy, I hope we'll see more of you. Quinn, please consider joining us. There's a great deal we can do for fledgling authors."

They both said something polite, then escaped. In the elevator, heading down to the ground floor, Quinn muttered, "Fledgling author, my eye."

His father laughed.

CHAPTER 18

On Wednesday evening Christy switched on the six o'clock news then crossed her fingers, hoping Karen Beaumont's memorial service wouldn't be included in the broadcast. She had checked the Internet that afternoon and apart from the usual notices, hadn't found any references. With any luck, the traditional news sources would be as uninterested as social media.

The memorial service wasn't the lead story, which described a late-breaking accident on Highway 1, the main artery into town, that had seen two people sent to hospital and rush-hour traffic snarled in both directions, but it was the second. Christy almost groaned when the image of chaos on the highway shifted to one of the exterior of a church and mourners emerging with bowed heads or sad expressions.

The reporter was a senior staffer, and people listened when he made statements in his deep authoritative bass voice. That he had been assigned to cover this event indicated how important the station thought it was.

He opened by describing the service—touching and deeply

moving—then the people who had come to grieve for Karen Beaumont.

So far so good, Christy thought. The mourners had been a who's who of the local film industry, so zeroing in on them wasn't unexpected. She swallowed nervously and hoped that the newsreader back at the station would cut the feed once all the famous names had been cited.

Unfortunately, that didn't happen. Having described the actual event, the reporter then launched into a condemnation of the police for their inability to find Beaumont's killer. In a back and forth with the newsreader, he named prominent individuals who had attended the gala, including Christy, and closed with a broad hint that the police hadn't made an arrest due to a reluctance to look too closely at these wealthy and influential people.

The station went to commercial and Christy clicked off the television. In the kitchen, the timer went off, telling her the casserole she'd made for dinner was ready. She stood up trying to shake off a feeling of impending doom, but she couldn't. She was quite certain that having her name again associated with Karen Beaumont's death could only lead to trouble.

The next day she discovered her family felt the same way. She'd been down to the Jamieson Trust offices, meeting with Isabelle Pascoe, the office manager, on planning initiatives, and reviewing applications sent to the Jamieson Foundation. She'd had to focus, which had been a relief, forcing her mind away from the Beaumont funeral and its potential implications for her. She returned to Burnaby just in time to drop her purse in the house before she walked over to the school to pick up Noelle. That was when she realized she wasn't the only one who thought the publicity from Beaumont's funeral could lead to problems.

Quinn was sitting on her front steps, waiting for her. He smiled as she emerged from the van and came up her front walk.

She joined him. It felt a bit odd to sit on the steps wearing a skirt suit made of a luxurious silk wool blend and designed by a famous name, but that smile of Quinn's was like a siren call and somehow made it okay. "I was going drop my purse, then go pick up Noelle."

"I assumed you were."

There was something in his voice that alerted her. She studied his face. "That's why you're here. You've come to give me support in case Shively is at the school."

"Or has been there," Quinn said. He stood. "We'd better get going. We have to stop by my place and pick up my dad, as well as Ellen and Trevor."

Unmoving, Christy looked at him in amazement. "Everyone is coming?"

Quinn nodded as he sent a text message to alert the others to be ready, then expelled a long suffering sigh. "Even the cat."

At that Christy chuckled and stood up. "Good heavens. I hope Ellen has told Frank to mind his manners."

Quinn waited while she unlocked the door and dropped her purse inside the house and changed from heels into flats. She slipped her house key in a pocket, then came down to meet him at the bottom of the steps.

He took her hand and they set off. "My father's been giving Frank tips on non-violent civil disobedience."

"Oh dear," Christy said, "I'm not sure if that is good or bad."

"According to Ellen, he's promised to behave. I think the tips are more my father having fun than a real assumption that civil disobedience will be necessary."

"When Patterson warned me about the memorial service, I hoped nothing would come of it, but..." She shook her head. "This murder needs to be solved."

Ellen, Trevor, and Roy were already outside waiting for them as they passed the Armstrong house. Ellen had Stormy safely tucked into his tote and all Christy could see was his head. His green eyes fixed on hers. *I promise to be polite and act like a proper cat.*

"Is that a good thing or a bad one?" Christy wondered aloud.

Trevor laughed and Stormy's head disappeared into the tote.

Quinn observed this with raised brows. "You've offended the cat."

Christy sighed. "Not intentionally."

They arrived at the school as the bell rang, announcing the end of the day. The door to Noelle's classroom burst open and children flew out in a muddle of excited energy. Christy saw Lindsay and Erin, two girls Noelle was cautiously developing a friendship with, and Devon, the boy who had a crush on her, in the mix, but Noelle wasn't among them.

Premonition shivered through her and put all her senses on alert. "Shively's here," she said as the flood of children eased into a trickle.

They went into the classroom. Mrs. Weaver, the teacher, smiled at Christy. "Mrs. Jamieson, Mrs. Kaplan asked you to come down to her office."

Mrs. Kaplan was the school principal. Christy nodded.

Mrs. Weaver observed Christy's band of supporters thoughtfully, but said, "Noelle is welcome to stay here until you are finished."

Christy looked at Noelle. She was sitting straight in her seat, her face expressionless. Jamieson manners, Christy thought. Mrs. Weaver was a more easy-going person than Mrs. Morton, Noelle's teacher last year, but she still represented authority and Noelle recognized that a crisis was upon them. "What do you say, kiddo? Want to stay here or come with Mom?"

Stormy's head popped over the top of the tote. *Come with us. I'll look after you.*

A smile split Noelle's face as she jumped to her feet. "I'm coming with you, Mom."

While she piled her homework into her backpack Christy thanked Mrs. Weaver, then they set out for the principal's office. Christy said to Noelle, "Did Ms. Shively come to your classroom today?"

Noelle nodded. "But she just came to the door, she didn't come inside. She talked to Mrs. Weaver, and they both looked at me, then she went away."

"When was that, kiddo?"

"A few minutes before the end of school. After she was gone, Mrs. Weaver had a phone call and she told me I had to stay at my desk until you came to pick me up, because she wanted to speak to you."

"That was probably the principal telling Mrs. Weaver to send me to her office. Ms. Shively is almost certainly with her right now and that's why Mrs. Kaplan wants to see me," Christy said.

"I believe that to be quite likely," Ellen said, her tone disapproving.

It's okay. We've got your back!

Noelle giggled.

Christy sighed and said, "I suppose it's a good thing I'm still wearing my Jamieson Trust clothes. I'll make a good impression."

At the office, the school secretary looked askance at their little group as they all trooped past her desk and into the principal's office. Since Shively was indeed with the principal, there wasn't much room once they were all inside.

"Good afternoon, Mrs. Kaplan." Christy introduced everyone, then said, "You wanted to speak to me?"

Before Mrs. Kaplan could reply, Shively said, "I see you've brought your usual entourage." Her tone was not friendly.

The principal, whose dark hair was cut in an asymmetrical style, and who was wearing a suit almost as nice as Christy's, raised her eyebrows. "Welcome, Mrs. Jamieson and...others. Ms. Shively came to me with concerns this afternoon and I thought it appropriate to bring them forward to you."

CAT IN THE LIMELIGHT

Shively, who was dressed in her usual polyester pantsuit and faux silk shell blouse, sniffed. "I wanted to see the child in her classroom. It is easier to assess the situation with the parent away. The child can speak freely then. When the classroom teacher refused to allow me access I moved over her head."

Noelle put up her chin. "I love my mommy. I'm happy at home and she makes me do my homework."

Well said, kiddo!

Mrs. Kaplan laughed at Noelle's homework statement, then she said, hesitating delicately, "Ms. Shively is concerned you may be involved in a rather...unpleasant situation, Mrs. Jamieson."

"Karen Beaumont's murder," Christy said.

Trevor cleared his throat. "Mrs. Jamieson is only involved peripherally. She's not a suspect and has not been questioned by the police in any way, other than to provide background information."

"She has not been questioned because of her name and the Jamieson fortune," Shively said. She looked Christy up and down, her expression scornful.

"Good to know you watch TV," Roy said. "Unfortunately, it's not always a reliable source of information."

Shively glared at him.

Christy shifted uneasily, deciding ruefully that her expensive suit might not have been such a great idea. She was disturbed by the fervor she heard in Shively's voice and the contempt she saw in her expression. She glanced at Trevor who was regarding Shively in a thoughtful way. Christy hoped that meant he figured he could use the woman's outburst against her.

She turned to the principal, "I know Ms. Shively has a tough job and that she does her best, but I am concerned she's jumped to the wrong conclusion. Detective Patterson, who is the police officer in charge of the case, will confirm what Trevor said. Like many other people, I was at the gala in support of At Risk students where Karen Beaumont was killed, but that was my only involvement."

"I understand your position, Mrs. Jamieson, but when Child Services asks us to monitor a child's well-being we are required to do so." Mrs. Kaplan's expression was apologetic. "I asked you here this afternoon to remind you of this and to assure you that Noelle's school days will not be interrupted by classroom visits. However, I will be speaking to her teacher and ensuring she is aware of the situation."

This was a concession, of sorts. When Shively had first been on the case last year, she'd gone directly to Noelle's class and had enlisted the support of her teacher, Mrs. Morton. It looked like this time the principal had intervened. Little though she liked either option, Christy had to accept this as a form of support. So she smiled at the principal and said, "I understand, Mrs. Kaplan. Is there anything else we need to discuss?"

The principal shook her head, but she looked at the childcare worker. "Ms. Shively?"

Shively narrowed her eyes and looked directly at Christy. "I want you to know I am not afraid to investigate you, Mrs. Jamieson. I won't back down because you're rich and influential."

"I never thought you would," Christy said, smiling. "Other than my supposed involvement in the murder, have you found anything you are concerned about?"

Shively glared, then reluctantly shook her head. "No, but I'm watching."

"Then we'll head home. Noelle has homework to do before dinner. Good-bye to you both." Christy kept her tone pleasant, but she was feeling anything but.

"You handled that well," Ellen said quietly as they descended the stairs that led from the front entrance of the school to the street.

"I kept my cool, but only just," Christy said ruefully. "Joan Shively will not give in easily." She looked past Ellen to the others. "This investigation has gone on too long. We need to solve this murder, now. When we get home, let's discuss how to figure out this problem."

"You will, Mom," Noelle said. She had her hand in Christy's and had taken over the cat's tote from Ellen. It was slung over her opposite shoulder.

The cat's head popped through the opening. *We have faith in you.*

Noelle looked up at Christy, then nodded decisively in agreement.

Christy's heart clenched with emotion. She wouldn't let Joan Shively separate her from her daughter or force Noelle into the child welfare system. It was unthinkable. "Thank you, sweetheart." She squeezed Noelle's hand, then bent to give her a quick kiss on the top of her head.

"Mom!" she said, indignant at this public act of parental affection, but she was smiling as she made the protest.

Christy laughed. "Sorry, kiddo. Tell me about your day and what you've got for homework."

The rest of the walk home was filled with the doings of Noelle's, and then everyone else's, day. Once home, Noelle settled at the kitchen table to do her homework, while the rest sat in the living room to discuss what to do about the murder.

Edgy and needing to act, Christy began. "When I spoke to Patterson on Tuesday she didn't have a main suspect. I gave her our information on the movements of Jackson Hargreaves and Declan West, but I think we need to dig deeper. Somebody must have seen something that will help pinpoint who pushed Beaumont off the terrace." She looked around the others. "Who do we know we can talk to who might have information?"

Roy sighed. "I can tackle Jackson Hargreaves again. He does have time that isn't accounted for."

"Patterson may have already questioned him," Quinn said.

"She might have, but who's to say that Jackson will be truthful with her this time?"

"Who's to say he'd be truthful with you?" Quinn asked.

Roy's eyes lit up. "I'll take Frank. Having a conversation with a cat may tip him over the edge."

Stormy, who was sitting on the sofa beside Ellen, fixed wide green eyes on Roy. *Road trip?*

Roy nodded.

Awesome.

"There were many more members of PGC staff and faculty at the gala than we've spoken to," Ellen said. "We need to talk to those people."

Christy nodded. "Good idea. I'll contact Craig Harding and set up a meeting. What about Mitch and Kim Crosier? I don't see either of them for the murder, but they may have witnessed something."

I'll talk to Kim. She likes the cat.

Christy nodded. For Quinn's sake, she said, "So Frank will question Kim. Someone will have to take him to her. That person can be the one to talk to Mitch. Who wants to do it?"

"I'm grilling Jackson Hargreaves," Roy said, looking virtuous. He'd been the one to question Mitch Crosier when they were investigating Vince Nunez's death and Mitch had seen it as an opportunity to add Roy to his growing empire of media stars. It had taken Roy weeks to get disentangled.

Quinn said, "What's the excuse to get access? None of us knows Crosier particularly well and he's a busy executive."

Trevor cleared his throat. "I'll volunteer Sledge. Crosier's company distributes SledgeHammer's music. Sledge can cook up some excuse to get a meeting."

"Excellent idea," Roy said, nodding.

"Sledge will not thank you," Quinn said. "He's been dodging Crosier all summer. He may have to deal with issues he's trying to avoid."

Christy frowned. "What issues?"

Quinn shrugged. "The future of SledgeHammer."

SledgeHammer is splitting up?

"Oh, poor Sledge," Christy murmured. She looked around the group. "Perhaps one or other of us should take the interview on."

But Trevor shook his head. "He's got to face it eventually. He can't keep putting the conversation off forever."

Quinn said, "We should also talk to Olivia Waters. She and Tamara were schmoozing in the foyer, then came down to the ballroom just before the music began. Like the Crosiers, I doubt they were the killers, but they may have seen something useful."

Christy swallowed. "I thought Tamara went home to Toronto before Thanksgiving."

"She did. Olivia went as well."

"Good heavens, why?" Ellen asked.

"To try to build a rapport with Tamara's adoptive parents, I guess," Quinn said. He grimaced. "I think she's trying to make up for not supporting Tamara when she was accused of Fred Jarvis' murder."

"It will take more than making nice with Tamara's adoptive parents to sort that out," Roy said, his tone cynical.

Quinn nodded. "I'll make a call and see what they say about the gala."

"Speaking of not putting conversations off, Trevor, is there anything you can do about this Shively woman?" Ellen asked. "I don't want her harassing my family in this nasty way any longer."

Trevor nodded. "I'll talk to Mallory Tait at the office about strategies. Sometimes it's better to let these things simply die off—as was happening before the Beaumont murder. However, in this case she might advise taking legal action." When Christy looked stricken, he added hastily, "But that's pure speculation. I'll need to discuss it with her first."

Christy drew a deep breath. "Okay. It's Thursday afternoon. I'm not sure how much we'll be able to get done before the weekend, but I'd like to get moving as quickly as possible."

Quinn, who was sitting on the couch beside Christy's chair, leaned over and took her hand. "We'll get this done."

The cat stared at him narrow-eyed. *You bet.*

CHAPTER 19

When she called Craig Harding early Friday morning, Christy didn't expect to secure a meeting with him until the next week. She'd told herself that Monday would be a success, but later in the week more likely.

She was surprised, therefore, when his secretary came back on the line after what must have been a quick discussion with her boss, and told her he could fit her in at twelve-thirty in his office at PGC's Point Grey campus.

She accepted, of course, but it didn't give her much time to change from the jeans and sweater she she'd worn to walk Noelle to school into what she thought of as her professional woman armor—the tailored suit with the pencil skirt she'd worn yesterday—before she began the cross town drive to PGC.

She walked into the president's suite at precisely twelve-thirty and was shown into Craig's office. She knew exactly what she wanted from this meeting and she hoped Craig would respond positively to her request that he assemble all of his personnel who had been at the gala for her to interview. After all, it was also in his best interest to have

Karen Beaumont's murder solved. Odds were, though, that he'd balk at the idea, and that was precisely what happened.

"You want to interview every PGC employee who was at the gala?" He shook his head. "Mrs. Jamieson—"

"Christy," she said, smiling, hoping to distract him and give him a moment longer to consider her proposal. Her ploy didn't work.

"Christy," he said, acknowledging her request with a smile. "The police have interviewed my people. Twice. There's nothing more they can add and I don't want them harassed."

"I understand your reservations, Craig, but the police are no closer to solving this murder than they were three weeks ago."

"What makes you think you interviewing my staff will draw out information the police don't already have?"

Christy drew a deep breath and did her best to be resolute and calm. Harding had hit on the key flaw in her argument—that an amateur would discover what the professionals could not. "The police start at the end and work back. Sometimes, that helps find the pattern. Sometimes, it only confuses things. I want to start at the beginning, before Karen was murdered. Where was she from the time the musical theater performance ended and when people lost track of her? Where was everyone else? Who was where they shouldn't have been? Who wasn't where they should have been? I think the pattern will be clearer if we begin at the beginning."

"I have faith in the police," he said, shaking his head. "If, as you say, all of this is just gathering information and looking for patterns, Detective Patterson will sort it all out and find the killer, even if she comes at the problem from the wrong direction."

"I have great respect for Detective Patterson. I'll fill her in on anything I learn."

"Then why not let her do her job and find it herself?"

Christy could feel his resistance growing with every sentence. She clenched her hands where they rested in her lap, striving for control.

"Because the media wants the killer found and they're naming people who were at the gala as suspects. You know that, Craig. I'm sure you've seen the same news reports I have." She was proud that she managed to keep her voice steady and hadn't allowed the desperation she was feeling to turn it shrill.

He nodded grimly. "I am aware, and I'm sorry. You aren't the first of our donors to contact me and complain about this. But, Christy, I can't undercut the police."

"How would having your people talk to me undercut the police?" He looked uncomfortable at that. She leaned forward, pushing her small advantage. "The media hasn't targeted you as one of those who should be considered a suspect, but every time they name one of your donors, and link that person's name to your college, they damage your brand. Who will want to be involved with PGC or the At Risk program as long as it's tied into an unsolved murder?"

"The murder will be solved."

"Will it?"

Craig raised his eyebrows at that and said curtly, "Yes, it will."

"When?" The look he gave in response told her he understood what she was getting at, but she pushed harder, just the same. "Every day the murder goes unsolved, people wonder who the killer was. It's easy for conspiracy theories to grab hold and then..." She shrugged. "Suddenly, it isn't necessarily one of the wealthy and prominent who is the killer, but you or one of your staff. When you hire Karen's replacement, are you considering anyone from within the college?"

"We are," he said uneasily, "but—"

"I assume you'll put out a press release? Provide a bio of the new dean? Let the community know that he or she is being promoted from within the organization? If the murder is unsolved, don't you think at least one enterprising reporter will check the gala guest list? And if that reporter finds the new dean's name on it? It would be easy to suggest that stepping into the job Karen's death left vacant was a solid motive for murder."

"Nonsense." His reply followed a frown and a brisk headshake.

"Is it?" Christy said. "It's no more unlikely than the media suggesting the police aren't investigating certain people because of their position in life."

He shook his head again.

Christy looked down at her hands, now clasped in her lap, then back up at him. "A year ago the media speculated I had embezzled from my husband's trust fund. Months later, I proved he'd been murdered and discovered who killed him. The rumors died down, but the attention I'm receiving because I happened to be in the same building as Karen Beaumont when she was killed proves those rumors never really ended. I know what it's like to live under a cloud of suspicion. Do you want that for your faculty and staff?"

"Of course not."

"Then let me talk to them."

But he shook his head. He was a stubborn man.

She didn't have a lot of arguments left. With a sigh she said, "Craig, my daughter is nine years old. She and her friends are old enough to know what murder means and they're also old enough to be influenced by gossip. My daughter loves me, but she has to defend me because a lot of people believe that if it's on the news then it's true." Seeing he was listening intently, she reached out to his humanity. "Do you have any children?"

"Two step-children," he said.

"Then think of how your kids would feel if your wife, their mom, was suspected of murder." He'd stiffened. She'd hit a nerve, and pressed on. "Wouldn't you do whatever you could to clear her?"

He stared at her unmoving. Christy let the silence hang while he considered.

It seemed to take an eternity before he said, "I'll set up meetings, but it will be next week."

Relief swept through Christy. She wanted to droop with the force of it. Instead she nodded, briskly. "Let me know the time and place." She stood, extending her hand. "Thank you, Craig."

He didn't look happy at the decision he'd made, but he took her hand and nodded. "I'll be in touch."

A few minutes later Christy emerged from the PGC building out into the parking lot. Her four-inch heels clicked a steady rhythm as she walked across the asphalt surface at an unhurried, confident pace. At the van, she dug through her purse for her keys, then unlocked the car. Every move was calculated to remind herself she'd achieved her goal, even though for most of the interview the result had teetered in the balance.

The car unlocked, Christy pulled open the door, and stepped up into the driver's seat. She drew the door closed, then carefully and precisely put the key in the ignition. Before she turned it, though, she put both hands on the wheel and drew a deep, steadying breath. And then another, and another.

After a minute, reaction to her narrow victory eased and she steadied. It might have been a close run thing, but she'd won her point. She deserved a treat. She nibbled her bottom lip, then grinned to herself. Pulling out her phone, she texted Quinn.

ARE YOU FREE TONIGHT?

He responded almost immediately. YES. WHAT TIME AND WHERE?

MY PLACE ABOUT NINE-THIRTY?

SEE YOU THEN.

Christy dropped her phone back into her purse. Ellen was out tonight with Trevor, so once Noelle was in bed she had the house to herself. An evening spent with Quinn seemed like a pretty good way to enjoy it.

She and Noelle made dinner together and baked cookies afterward. After an hour of TV that included cookies and milk, Noelle headed up to get ready for bed and read until lights out at nine. Stormy followed her up. They were both sound asleep by the time Quinn knocked on her door at nine-thirty.

"Hi," she said, as she opened it for him.

He stepped inside, put his hands around her waist to draw her close, then he kissed her. Christy was glad she'd paired jeans with a gauzy shirt that felt feminine and flirty, because it seemed just right for an evening with a man who began it with a kiss. She put her hands around his neck and kissed him back.

"Umm," she murmured when he drew away. "That was lovely. Come cuddle with me on the sofa. I've had a stressful day." She took his hand and led him up the stairs.

"Tell me about it," he said as they settled on the couch.

Christy had placed an open bottle of wine on the coffee table, along with two glasses and as she poured, she described the meeting with Craig Harding. "His agreement was reluctant, but he acted quickly. By the time I got home I had an e-mail from him saying that he had arranged to get everyone together at ten on Monday." She handed him a glass, took a sip from her own. "I'll need support for this. Are you free Monday?"

His smile was tender and not a little pleased. "Of course."

"I thought I'd take Ellen as well. She can write everything down for Patterson."

He nodded. "We should tape it too."

"Good idea."

They discussed details, including what questions to ask, while they sipped their wine. Christy was curled against Quinn, his arm around her shoulders. It felt so right to have him here, in her house, talking about her day.

Talking about his. "What were you up to today?"

He drew her a little closer. "I did a video call to Olivia and Tamara in Toronto."

She looked up at him, firmly suppressing instant jealousy. Olivia and Tamara had been at the gala. Quinn had been the obvious one to interview them. That didn't mean she liked it. "Find out anything interesting?"

"Nothing. They were both in the foyer after the end of the musical and they saw Beaumont talking to Moore, but when people started to move down to the ballroom, so did they. Olivia did mention that before they went down she saw a man with a blonde wife talking to Craig Harding. Harding looked like he was pretending to be interested and the blonde seemed to be on a different planet. Sound like anyone we know?"

"Mitch and Kim Crosier?" Christy said.

Quinn nodded. "So apparently they were both still upstairs. They may have something useful to tell us."

Christy leaned forward to put her glass on the coffee table. Then she reached for Quinn's and put it on the table too. He smiled enigmatically and she grinned at him before she moved back into his embrace and lifted her head for a kiss. He drew her close and obliged.

They were in the middle of this when the doorbell rang.

"Were you expecting someone?" Quinn murmured against her lips. His voice was low and velvet smooth.

"No." The kiss continued. The doorbell rang again. Christy pulled herself away reluctantly. "I'd better get that." She went down to the door and opened it, then stared with some bemusement at Roy. "Hi," she said, opening it wider.

Roy bustled inside, then stomped up the stairs to the top, where he stopped abruptly. "This is where you are!"

As Christy came up behind Roy, she saw that Quinn was standing by the couch.

"I take it you're looking for me?" he asked.

175

Roy moved into the room. "I thought you'd be home."

"Well, I wasn't. I was here." He looked over his father's shoulder to Christy. "Shall I get another glass?"

She laughed. "I guess you'd better."

Once Quinn had returned with the glass, Christy filled it and they all settled, Christy and Quinn on the sofa, Roy on a nearby armchair. He sipped his wine and said appreciatively, "Nice vintage," before he dove right into his reason for dropping by. "I went out looking for Jackson Hargreaves today, but didn't get very far. He doesn't have classes on Fridays and no one seemed to know where he was—including his wife, Phyllis."

Quinn looked at Christy. "I assume Craig Harding will include Hargreaves in his group meeting."

She nodded. "I would expect so."

"You can come down with us to PGC on Monday, Dad, and corner Hargreaves there."

"Won't have to," Roy said enthusiastically. He seemed to take it for granted that Christy would organize the group meeting at PGC. "I ran into Gillian Stankov tonight and we had a couple of drinks together. She reminded me that Jackson hangs out at MacLagan House on Saturdays. He uses one of the offices to write." Roy drank more wine. "Or at least what he calls writing." He waved one hand in dismissal. "No matter. I'm going to go down tomorrow and catch him in the act. I'm pretty sure I can get him to come clean on where he was during the gala. If I can't, I bet Frank will be able to shock him into a confession."

"If Jackson can hear Frank," Christy said.

Roy waved his hand again. "Of course, but Frank's getting pretty good at projecting to anyone he wants to. It will work out."

"Probably will," Quinn said. "I expect you'll want to start early tomorrow." He glanced at his watch in a pointed way. "It's getting late."

Christy choked. Roy look astounded. Not surprising, since Roy considered two in the morning as early to bed.

The doorbell rang again.

Roy said, "A bit late for a social call. Are you expecting anyone?"

Christy looked at Quinn, whose brows had risen as he frowned. She had to resist the urge to giggle. "No. Let's see who it is."

It was Sledge and his expression was somewhere between a pout and a glower as he stomped inside the house and said to Christy, "My father volunteered me to interview Mitch Crosier. Mitch Crosier! I can't do that!"

"Why not?" Roy asked from the top of the stairs.

Sledge looked up, frowning. "Hello. What are you doing here?"

Roy waved his glass expansively. Wine sloshed, but didn't spill over the edge. "Talking about my assignment, what else?"

"Assignments!" Sledge took the stairs two at a time, leaving Christy to follow more slowly. As Sledge passed Roy, Quinn emerged from the kitchen with yet another glass and poured.

When Christy reached the top of the stairs he held up the bottle for her to see. "Looks like we'll need to open another."

"There's one in the kitchen. I'll get it."

Sledge settled onto the couch where Quinn and Christy had been snuggling. "I can't talk to Mitch Crosier." He guzzled down half the glass. "I've been avoiding him for months. I spent half the evening at the gala staying out of his way. He caught me before the police told us all to go home and informed me we needed to talk. He'll think I want to meet with him to discuss the future of SledgeHammer."

"Great!" Roy said enthusiastically. "That will make it much easier for you to get an interview with him."

Sledge frowned and shook his head as Christy set the second bottle on the coffee table. "You don't understand. I don't want to talk about the band's future until Hammer gets back from his travels."

"When will that be?" Quinn asked. He sounded amused.

"I don't know. That's the problem. Mitch wants answers. He says Vince's company is a placeholder and we need new representation." Sledge stared down into his glass. "He's right, but I'm not ready to make the change, not without Hammer." He drank another slug of wine, then looked at Roy. "Can't you do it? You talked to Mitch when Vince died."

Roy looked horrified. "No! It took my agent weeks to convince him my books wouldn't work in his crazy convergence empire. If I ask for an interview he'll think I've changed my mind. He'll pester me forever!"

Sledge turned a pleading gaze to Quinn. "Interviewing people like Mitch is what you're good at. Why don't you do it?"

Quinn grinned. "I had to talk to Olivia and Tamara. Sorry, bud."

"Christy?"

She shook her head. "I've got the faculty and staff at PGC to interview."

"Take Frank," Roy said. "You'll do fine."

I thought I heard—Stormy paused halfway down the staircase from the second floor. *Sledge, you're here.* He galloped down the stairs, then jumped up onto the sofa. *Did I hear my name mentioned?*

Quinn tipped his half full glass of wine to his mouth and drank it all, then he refilled it from the last of the initial bottle. "Looks like we're having a party," he said, saluting Christy.

She laughed. "I guess so."

CHAPTER 20

The next morning, Roy woke much later than he expected and with enough of a headache to know he'd overdone the wine the previous night. He got up groggily and went down to the kitchen for coffee.

Two cups and a plate of bacon and eggs later, he felt more himself and ready to face the day. Quinn was off somewhere, but he'd left the car, so Roy went over to Christy's house to collect the cat. There he found Ellen, whose return home had signaled the end of the party last evening. Noelle and Mary Petrofsky were in the basement, playing, and Christy didn't appear to be around. Was she off with Quinn somewhere?

He cast his mind back to the conversation last night for a clue, but could find none. He'd realized too late that he'd barged into an evening meant to be private between Christy and Quinn, but by then Sledge had arrived and there was no point in his leaving. So he'd stayed and they'd all had a good time bringing Sledge up to date on murder details. It wasn't as much fun listening to him complain about his career crisis and why he couldn't talk to Mitch Crosier, but that couldn't be helped.

The cat grumbled when he asked Ellen for the leash and halter, but neither he nor Ellen paid any attention. As he and the cat set out, she wished them both good luck with Jackson Hargreaves. He acknowledged that with a cheerful salute. Now that they were on their way, he was looking forward to the rest of his morning. Stormy hopped onto the passenger seat and curled up while Roy stashed the halter and leash on the floorboards. No need to outfit the cat until they got to MacLagan House.

Once they were out of the development and onto a main road, the cat sat up to get a better view. *What's the plan?*

Roy considered that for a moment. "Jackson Hargreaves was missing for a significant part of the evening. We want to know why and what he was doing. Gillian Stankov saw him go up to the second floor of MacLagan House, which was closed to the gala guests. Was he on the second floor the whole time he was missing? Or did he double back and go out onto the terrace when things in the foyer quieted down."

And killed Karen Beaumont.

Roy nodded happily. "That's it exactly."

So you'll ask him.

"And he'll probably lie to me. That's where you come in. You can encourage him to come clean." Roy navigated the turn onto the highway and picked up speed.

What if I can't get through to him?

"Jackson is an artist, or at least he claims he is. He may be open to you."

What if he isn't?

Roy grinned. "That's why I brought the leash." He exited the highway onto the much slower surface roads that were the only way to reach their destination. "It's part of the stage set." He glanced at the cat who glared back at him with wide green eyes. Neither Stormy nor Frank liked the leash. "Channel your inner Siamese and pretend you're allowing your owner to walk you because you want him to."

The cat does not have an owner. He chooses to live with Christy and Noelle because they are his family.

Since Roy didn't think he'd be able pry the secret of what Jackson had been up to without the help of the cat, he added more encouragement to his attempt to get Stormy's agreement. "Even though Jackson Hargreaves likes to consider himself a deep thinker with a bohemian outlook, he's a pedestrian guy who prefers the status quo. To his mind, someone who drives from one part of town to another to walk his cat has got to be off his head."

So even if I can't talk to him, he'll underestimate you because the cat's there.

Roy nodded. "He already has a low opinion of me. You're just confirming what he already believes."

There was silence, then a reluctant, *All right.*

Roy resisted the urge to cheer. Instead, he turned the car radio on, found a rock station, and turned the sound up high. Both he and the cat rocked on until they reached MacLagan House.

The cat might have agreed to wear the halter and allow the leash, but it was more in theory than in practice. Stormy squirmed and fought while Roy was trying to fasten the buckle on the halter. It wasn't until he was finally able to slip the tab into the latch and they both heard the decisive click that the cat surrendered to the indignity. Picking up Stormy, Roy tucked the cat under his arm and carried him inside. It was faster that way. If he let the cat walk from the parking lot to Jackson's office, they wouldn't get there until tomorrow.

In the foyer, he discovered the house was the location for a wedding later in the day. The events crew were busy setting up the main floor and the ballroom level. A few paused to stare at Roy, wandering along carrying a cat wearing a halter and leash, but most simply glanced his way, then moved around him. Roy went up the grand staircase to the second floor. Once there, he put Stormy on the hardwood surface and they set off to find Jackson Hargreaves' office.

Last night, Gillian Stankov had given Roy the office number, but even if she hadn't, he would have easily guessed which one it was, because the door was the only one on the floor that was firmly closed. In other rooms he could see artists at work over canvasses or sketch books, some musicians tinkering on instruments, then adding musical notes onto blank sheet music paper, others practicing difficult passages. There were also writers happily banging away on their keyboards in the midst of the second floor's busy action.

None of the occupants of the offices paid any attention to him as he slowly proceeded down the hallway, even though he had a cat on a leash who didn't appear to understand all of the rules of leash walking. Stormy was either pulling at the leash as he went forward, or stopping abruptly for no apparent reason, other than he wanted to at that moment.

When they reached Jackson's closed door, Roy looked down at the cat. "This is it. Remember your inner Siamese. Maximum snark to throw him off balance."

Siamese are not the only snarky cats.

Reflecting that there was truth in that statement, Roy opened the door without knocking and went inside. The room was small, little more than a large closet. Perhaps it had once been a closet, because it didn't have a window. It was fitted out with a desk big enough to hold a laptop and a lamp. A simple secretary's chair, with a mesh back and seat, and two arms was set before the desk. Beside it was a high backed armless chair with a hard wooden seat, presumably for any idiot, like Roy, who happened to stop by for a visit.

Jackson Hargreaves was sitting hunched forward in the desk chair staring at his open laptop. On the screen was a blank white page.

Roy wondered how long Hargreaves had been staring at that

demoralizing, terrifying emptiness. From the expression on the man's face, he suspected it had been quite some time. Feeling a rush of sympathy, he unhooked the leash, leaving the halter on the cat, and sat down on the wooden chair, which was surprisingly comfortable.

Stormy, with no sympathy whatsoever, leapt onto the desk, then padded over to the laptop and lay down on the keyboard. The cursor came alive on the screen, leaping around erratically, though no characters made it onto the page. He observed Jackson with cold green eyes. *Going nowhere fast?*

Jackson stared in astonishment at the cat, then turned to Roy. His frustrated, despairing expression turned to one of relieved anger. "Roy Armstrong! What the hell are you doing here?" He seemed to suddenly remember that his door had been firmly closed before Roy entered. "What makes you think I want to talk to you anyway?" He gestured toward the laptop and Stormy. "You've...You've brought a cat!"

The cursor went mad as Stormy stood and yawned, then stuttered to a blinking stop as he sat down on a dozen keys at the same time.

Wow. Amazing observation. Can't say this guy isn't on top of his game.

As Hargreaves didn't react to this provocative statement, Roy concluded sadly that he was one of those people the cat couldn't reach. Not surprising. The man had no imagination. "You can't write anymore, can you?"

"What's it to you?" Jackson snarled. He gestured to the laptop again. "Get rid of your animal."

Stormy stared at him with wide, unblinking eyes, then, slowly, he stood. Roy had the definite sense that whatever Frank had planned, Jackson wouldn't like it.

He was right.

Moving with careful precision, Stormy stepped off the laptop keyboard. Then, again very slowly—for maximum effect, Roy assumed—he reached out a paw, placing it on the letter 'r'.

If you can't write, I can. A quick push and the letter sprang into life on the blank page.

Astonished, Roy almost missed his cue, until he noticed Stormy's tail twitch with annoyance. Recalled to his job, he said, "Your boss, Karen Beaumont, was pressuring you to produce a new novel. By Christmas, wasn't it?"

Stormy's paw hit the letter 'u.' Up on the screen it appeared beside the 'r'. Jackson's eyes flicked from the suddenly alive screen to Roy. He swallowed uneasily. "Where did you hear that?"

Roy ignored the question. He was starting to enjoy himself. "You were at the gala where she died."

The cat hit the letter 'd,' a delicate tap with his extended claw this time and it appeared beside 'ru'. Jackson's eyes grew wider. His voice wavered. "Yeah, so what?"

"So you disappeared for a significant amount of time. Did you use that time to kill her?"

Another swift tap with the extended claw and 'e' was added to the other letters, revealing the word 'rude.' The cat lifted the paw that had typed out the word and licked it with smug satisfaction.

Jackson swallowed hard. "No, I did not kill her." He took another look at the cat and the screen, then said, "Look Armstrong, what gives you the right to come in here accusing me of killing Karen Beaumont. Get out."

Stormy stood, arched his back, then set to work. More letters flashed into life on the screen. Slowly the words formed into a sentence.

hecanwriteyoucant

There was no spacing or punctuation and capitalization was beyond him, but the meaning was clear. Typing the word 'rude' hadn't been an accident. Roy reached over, used the mouse and the spacebar, and produced an easier to read sentence.

he can write you cant

After a moment of inspection, he capitalized the first word and added an apostrophe to the last one, then followed it with a period.

He can write you can't.

There should be a comma too, he thought, and added that.

He can write, you can't.

Jackson swallowed hard.

Roy was having so much fun, he almost laughed, but he managed to say in a cold voice, "Where were you then, if you weren't busy killing Karen Beaumont?"

Still staring at the screen, Jackson said, "I was here."

"Here where? Here, as in this room?"

Jackson nodded.

"You were trying to write?" Roy said incredulously. "During a gala?" This was too much. He couldn't believe it. Even an idiot like Jackson Hargreaves wouldn't pull a stunt like that.

Color reddened Jackson's cheeks. "One of my students wanted to see my study. I brought her up to show her."

Frowning, Roy scrutinized him. Jackson Hargreaves had been one of those creative writing masters students—or was it Ph.D?—who went straight from their writing assignments to a publishing contract. He'd been twenty-eight or nine when his first novel was published and the literary world went mad for him. His second novel, another writing assignment Roy suspected, followed the year after. Eagerly anticipated, it had received lukewarm reviews, though initial sales were good. That had been at least ten years ago, so he was still a youngish man, though to Roy's eyes, he wasn't aging well. The skin around his eyes was puffy and his cheeks were sagging into jowls. He sported a definite paunch around his middle, too.

Roy tried to see him as a student might. On the night of the gala he'd worn his tux well and in the soft lighting he looked almost dashing. It was possible a naive undergrad who loved his first great opus would accept his invitation to see the place where he worked. Where he created his masterpieces.

Except Roy didn't believe that was what Hargreaves had in mind. Neither, apparently, did Frank.

Show her? That's a laugh.

Roy had to agree. "You brought her up here to have sex."

Jackson's features went from embarrassed red to frightened white. "No, I didn't."

He'd have to deny it or he'd lose his job. Roy was willing to bet that if he asked Craig Harding if a professor was allowed to have sex with one of his students, the answer would be a resounding 'no!' and the fallout would include unemployment for Jackson Hargreaves. "Does this student have a name?"

Hargreaves glared at him. "None of your business."

Stormy stretched and began to type again. Hargreaves stared at the cat, and the screen with a kind of sick fascination. Roy straightened out the spacing and a short sentence emerged.

tell us

Hargreaves' expression turned mulish. "No."

Roy shrugged and looked at the cat. "Come on, Stormy, let's go. We have enough to get Detective Patterson to charge him with murder and for Craig Harding to fire him for cause." They didn't, but he was betting Jackson wouldn't call his bluff. He clicked the leash back onto the loop at the top of the harness then turned as if to go.

After a moment's struggle, Hargreaves said, "If I give you her name will you keep it quiet?"

"Will she corroborate your story?"

He swallowed, then nodded. "She should."

"Patterson was going to talk to you this week. Did you tell her about this girl and your creepy old man offer?" Roy asked.

Again Jackson hesitated.

The cat got back to work, his extended claw clicking emphatically

186

on the keyboard. The letters 's,' 't,' and 'u' appeared on the screen. The meaning was clear and Jackson reddened again. "No, I didn't. If the cops knew they'd tell the college and I'd lose my job."

So it was possible Patterson still considered Jackson a suspect, perhaps even a key suspect because of that lost three quarters of an hour when he'd been missing. That meant she was wasting her time and not looking for the right person.

The cat added the letters 'p,' 'i,' 'd' and the word 'stupid' appeared.

"The cat's right," Roy said. "You need to tell Detective Patterson where you were and who you were with. At the moment, you're her prime suspect. She could arrest you for Beaumont's murder any time."

"What? But—I didn't do it!" Jackson was sputtering now and he looked appalled.

"You tell her, or I will," Roy said.

Jackson shook his head. "No. Really, it's impossible—I won't—"

Roy stood. "Forget what I said. I'll tell her anyway and she can follow up with you." He tugged at the leash. "Come on, cat. Our work is done here."

Stormy hopped off the desk and trotted across the room, as regal and pleased with himself as any true Siamese.

At the door Roy paused. "It will look better for you if you tell her yourself. I'd recommend calling her right now, but I'll give you till Monday before I contact her myself." He pulled a card out of his wallet. "Here's her number." He flicked the card, which landed in the middle of the keyboard Stormy had recently used so creatively. Jackson stared at it dumbly.

Roy and the cat sauntered down the hall toward the grand staircase that descended to the foyer below, the cat happily twinning in front of and around him as they went.

I do good work.

"You sure do," Roy said fervently.

CHAPTER 21

The party on Friday night broke up when Trevor brought Ellen home and Sledge grumpily accused his father of trying to manage his life. Christy figured there was an opportunity for a good, no-holds-barred father-son battle, but Trevor hadn't risen to that challenge. Instead, he'd said goodnight to Ellen and departed, leaving his son glowering at the closed door. Sledge had left soon after, followed by Roy and Quinn.

Christy and Ellen sat up a while longer and it was then that Ellen suggested that Christy invite Quinn to lunch the next day, while Ellen stayed home to look after Noelle. Being Ellen, she didn't make any reference to Christy's interrupted romantic evening with Quinn, but she clearly understood. Touched, Christy retreated to her room where she called Quinn and made the arrangements.

So now they were sitting in a small Greek restaurant located in a plaza not far from the Burnaby townhouse and no one, not even Ellen and Noelle, knew where they were. They were simply...out.

All alone, just the two of them. It was wonderful.

The restaurant was a popular spot, busy even at midday on a

Saturday. That was because the ambience was friendly, the food was excellent, the service efficient. Christy and Quinn had arrived at the end of the lunch rush and were given one of the few tables remaining, not far from the entrance. They each ordered a glass of wine and sipped it while they studied the menu and talked about each other.

Not the murder. Each other.

Perfect.

Eventually, after lengthy conversation about favorite items, what sounded yummy, whether to go with the lunch special, the first Greek restaurant they'd ever been to, and a lot of laughter, they ordered. Christy chose calamari and Quinn a braised lamb shank. The plates arrived, heaped with Greek salad, dressed with olive oil, balsamic vinegar, and the chef's special seasonings. Christy stabbed her fork into a circle of deep fried calamari, then dipped the end into the pot of tzatziki sauce beside her plate. Her taste buds sprang to life—she was looking forward to that first burst of flavor on her tongue.

"Mrs. Jamieson?"

The voice was male and unfamiliar. She looked up. Declan West, PGC professor and one of the suspects in Karen Beaumont's murder was standing beside their table. Focused on Quinn and her food, she hadn't noticed him moving toward them. She guessed that he must have been seated at one of the tables deeper into the restaurant and now be on his way out. She glanced at Quinn, who raised his brows, then she looked back at West.

"Yes?" she said, at the same time that Quinn stood up and held out his hand. "Declan West, isn't it? I'm Quinn Armstrong. We met at the At Risk gala a few weeks ago."

West blinked a couple of times as he pulled his focus away from Christy, then he smiled and nodded. "Right. Nice to see you."

Christy said, "How are you, Mr. West?" She indicated the restaurant. "Did you enjoy your lunch?"

"Oh yes." He smiled faintly. "Like you, I had the calamari."

"They do it well here," Christy said. She didn't want to exchange small talk with West. She would much rather he said good-bye so she and Quinn could get back to having a quiet, romantic lunch. Now that he was here, though, she figured his unexpected arrival was an opportunity to grill him on where he'd been on the night of the gala.

She was wracking her brain for a way to introduce her questions without scaring him off, when he indicated an empty chair at their table. "Would you mind if I sat down?"

Now that was a surprise. She glanced at Quinn. He was watching West intently, but he turned to her and gave a faint nod. "No, of course not," she said.

He was a big, muscular man, and Christy could easily believe he worked out regularly, keeping his hand-to-hand combat skills honed and ready, no doubt. As he pulled out the chair and settled into it, his movements were fluid and economical. Controlled. He didn't seem like a man who would lose his cool at a gala and kill the ex-sister-in-law he'd worked with for five, non-violent years.

"I'm glad I saw you today," he said. "I heard a nasty rumor at the college that the Jamieson Foundation will be withdrawing its support from the At Risk program and I wanted to ask you not to do it."

This was so unexpected that Christy dropped her fork onto her plate and sat back in her chair to study him. His expression was serious, like his voice, but also worried. He cared about the program Karen Beaumont had developed. "I'm not sure what you're talking about, Mr. West. Do you have any specifics?"

He hesitated. "There's been talk about the Foundation, that it only exists to rehabilitate the Jamieson name so you'll never allow it to be associated with the At Risk program, not after Anton was arrested for Karen's murder."

"The Jamieson Foundation was developed to give back to the community. It has nothing to do with the family's reputation," Christy said. She kept her tone crisp, but anger bubbled beneath the surface.

Seated again, Quinn said sharply, "Who told you that?"

"More than one person." West grimaced. "Everyone at the college is on edge and worried about the future. The fallout from Karen's murder, I guess."

"Karen Beaumont was your sister-in-law, wasn't she?" Quinn asked. He didn't sound mollified, but at least the undercurrent of anger that had edged his previous question was under control.

"Ex sister-in-law. Karen and my brother were married for ten years. Their careers both took off and they discovered that they had more time for everyone else in their lives than they did for each other. They divorced five years ago."

"Divorce is tough," Christy said. "On the individuals, and on their families too."

For a moment West didn't respond, then he seemed to come to a decision and nodded. "They split long before the divorce was final. They both lawyered up and they fought over everything. The house, Karen's pension, my brother's business, her salary. We all took sides, the lawyers made a fortune, and Karen took my brother for half of what he was worth." He shrugged. "In the end, her lawyers were better than his."

"You must have hated working with Karen as your dean," Christy said.

It was a statement, but West was shaking his head. "We didn't interact much. I'm a prof in the Theater Arts department, so I report to Gibson Jessup, who's the chair. He has to deal with Karen, I don't." He heard what he'd said and shook his head. "I didn't—interact with her, I mean. And when our paths did cross, we both kept it professional."

Quinn raised his brows skeptically and West colored. "It's true. Look, I didn't interrupt your lunch to talk about my family's problems. I care about the At Risk kids. I think the program is fantastic and I want to see it grow. What can I do to convince you not to pull your funding, Mrs. Jamieson?"

Declan West was an annoying man. He'd interrupted her lunch with Quinn and he'd insulted the Jamieson name, without apparently realizing he was doing so, but he'd put himself into a position Christy could use. She almost grinned at the opportunity that had fallen into her lap. Instead, she assumed her Jamieson princess persona and said coolly, "The police now believe Karen was killed after the musical theater performance and before Lightening Rod began to play. You can tell me where you were at that time."

His eyes brightened. "Sure, no problem. I was with the rest of the crowd in the dining room while the kids did *West Side Story*. When it finished, I stayed for a few minutes to commiserate with Monique McGrath. She was fuming because Sam Moore had taken over the lead roll from one of her students. She's not a fan of Sam's, you know."

"I didn't," Christy murmured. She picked up her fork, which still had the calamari ring attached. Normally, she wouldn't eat when someone dropped by her table, but with Declan West she felt it was okay.

He didn't appear to notice when she popped the food into her mouth. He just kept talking. "Yeah. Monique was chair of music before Sam and when he decided he wanted the job he undercut her with the music faculty." He shrugged. "Anyway, when Monique and I finished talking and I went out into the foyer, it was packed, with most of the crowd milling around chatting. Those kind of evenings make me edgy, so I thought I'd go down to the bar and get a drink. As I made my way to the stairs I noticed Karen and Sam talking over in one corner." His mouth rose up in a grin. "Man, she was ticked at him."

"Ticked?" Quinn said. He'd gone back to his meal too and had a forkful of Greek salad halfway to his mouth. "You mean angry?"

West nodded.

Christy exchanged a look with Quinn. "Most people we've talked

CAT IN THE LIMELIGHT

to said they thought Beaumont was praising Moore, because he was smiling."

Screwing up his face in a thoughtful way, West shook his head. "You're right that Sam was smiling, but Karen's body language said she was angry." His smile faded. "That made me really happy. I know that sounds terrible, because she was killed that night, but although Karen and I were polite, I didn't like her much. Having someone like Sam cause her problems was fine with me."

He broke off. Christy ate her calamari and let him decide when he wanted to continue.

Finally, he drew a deep breath and resumed. "I went down to the bar and ordered a drink—and then another. The bartender and I chatted until he got busy with the rest of the crowd buying drinks before the band started. I finished my drink and was going to order another, but by that time the bar was packed, so I used the bathroom, then went upstairs to help Monique with the take-down. There wasn't much left to do, so I carried some stuff out to the van then went back downstairs. I heard Gibson Jessup introduce the band, so I ducked into the bar, which was pretty much empty by that time. I ordered another couple of drinks while the band played. When Sam Moore started to sing SledgeHammer songs, I went upstairs to get away."

"You sound as if you don't like Samuel Moore," Christy said. She dipped another piece of calamari into the sauce and ate it as West lifted his hands in a careless way.

"Sam's Sam. He's full of himself and likes everyone to know he's got a professionally trained voice. He thinks that opera-style is the only way to sing. I happen to prefer Sledge's style. I thought Anton Gormley did a way better tribute to SledgeHammer than Sam did."

"So you went upstairs," Quinn prompted.

West nodded. "Yeah. I'd thought I'd go out onto the terrace, look at the city, and get some fresh air, you know? But when I reached the French doors in the drawing room I saw Jackson Hargreaves and his wife out near the stairs down to the garden. They were in the middle of an argument I didn't want to overhear." He shook his head. "Man, that guy has problems. Anyway, I turned around and backtracked out to the foyer." His eyes lit with amusement. "I saw you guys wander into the dining room. I thought I'd warn you about the Hargreaves' fight, but you were pretty into each other, so I went on my way."

"Will the bartender vouch for you?" Quinn asked.

"He should. We were talking about theater productions and stage-craft. I teach physical acting—body language, of course, but also staging fights and that kind of thing. He wanted to know how I got into it, and I told him about my time in the army. Then we got into where I'd served and he was pretty interested in hearing about my tours in Afghanistan. While the band was playing he didn't get a lot of business and we were both pretty bored. Talking helped to pass the time."

Christy dug into her salad. "There was a period, while the bar was busy, that you were on your own. Is there anyone who can corroborate where you were?"

He wrinkled his forehead as he thought back. Then he shook his head and shrugged. "Someone probably saw me, but there was no one else in the bathroom when I was there. People were milling around in the lounge area between the bar and the ballroom, so I suppose someone must have seen me go into the bathroom then come back out, but I can't put a name to anyone." His tone sounded dubious. Then he snapped his fingers. "Wait. Lana Drabble was there when I came out."

"Who is Lana Drabble?" Christy asked after she swallowed green pepper and feta cheese from her salad.

"She's a prof in the music department, a voice coach. She was at the end of the line waiting to buy a drink. We said hello before I went upstairs to talk to Monique." He looked from Christy to Quinn, then back to Christy. "So that's my story. I didn't kill Karen and I'm sorry someone did. I didn't like her much, but she got things done around PGC. The At Risk program was her initiative and it's a good one. I want to see it continue."

Christy put down her fork and fixed West with a stern expression. "If you haven't already told this to Detective Patterson, then you must contact her as soon as possible." She reached for her purse where she found one of Patterson's cards. She handed it to West. "Here's her number."

West held up his hand and shook his head. "We talked yesterday and I told her what I just told you. I don't have anything new to add."

"Good," Christy said. "Thank you, Mr. West, for dropping by."

He pushed his chair back, but hovered uncertainly. "The At Risk program?"

"I haven't pulled the funding, Mr. West. Nor do I intend to."

A smile broke over his face and he sighed with relief as he stood up. "Thank you. You won't regret it."

"I hope not," Christy said, Jamieson princess cool.

Later that day, after she and Quinn had finally finished their lunches, they found Ellen out on the townhouse's front porch. Roy was sitting on the edge of the planter box where Christy's flowers were drooping with the shorter days and cooler weather. Ellen had her leather binder open on her lap and she was writing furiously while Roy talked. Christy parked the van and she and Quinn joined the other two. "You have news?" she said to Roy, who nodded.

He caught them up on his meeting with Jackson Hargreaves, laughing as he described Frank's involvement. "After Frank finished with him, he was so shook up, I believed him. I don't think he was anywhere near the terrace when Beaumont was killed."

"Declan West seems to be out too," Christy said. She outlined what West had told them. "He might have gone out onto the terrace through the drawing room after he dropped his load at the PGC van. It's unlikely anyone would have noticed him, but Quinn and I think the timing is too tight for him to have waited for everyone to have cleared out of the dining room, then killed Beaumont, before racing back down to the bar to hear Gibson Jessup introduce Lightening Rod."

Ellen tapped the end of her pen on her paper. "So we've washed out our two best suspects. She looked from Christy to Quinn to Roy. "Let's hope our meetings Monday prove more fruitful."

CHAPTER 22

C raig Harding rose when Christy and her little band of supporters were ushered into his office. He frowned at them in an astonished way and said, "My faculty are going to think you're here to do job interviews."

It wasn't a bad assessment, as they were all dressed in professional business attire, except for Roy who was in his usual jeans and a checked shirt. Christy blushed a little, but she shot back tartly, "Perhaps we are." His eyes widened at that, which gave her some satisfaction, and he gestured for them all to sit down.

Originally, her plan had been to bring Ellen, who would take notes, and Quinn for his interview skills. Roy got involved when she and Quinn imparted their information to Ellen and Roy had been telling her his bit about Jackson Hargreaves. Then on Sunday, as she brooded about Declan West's comment that there was a rumor going round the college about her reasons for starting the Jamieson Foundation, she decided to ask Trevor to join them as well. Now, before they began, she wanted to address that rumor with Craig Harding and hopefully bury it forever.

Harding gestured to a conversation nook beside the windows that made up one wall of his office, indicating they make themselves comfortable in the padded club chairs while they worked out the details of the morning's interviews. Christy sat with her back to the spectacular views of downtown Vancouver and the North Shore mountains. Having the light behind her would give her a bit of an advantage—she hoped. She waited until they were all settled, then said, "I have been told there is a rumor going around your college that casts aspersions on the Jamieson Foundation and our reasons for funding the At Risk Students program." He stiffened and she nodded. "I would like the person who initiated that slur found and straightened out."

"What exactly was the aspersion?" Harding said uneasily.

"That the Jamieson Foundation was formed to whitewash the Jamieson name and since it is only funding the At Risk program to make us look good, our funding will be pulled even if none of the At Risk students are involved." His lips tightened. She clasped her hands in her lap and continued on keeping her gaze firmly on his face. "Neither of those statements is true. The foundation was created to give back to the community and we still believe in the At Risk program and will continue to support it."

"As I am aware, and do appreciate," Harding said. His mouth was a thin line, but Christy didn't think his anger was aimed at her.

"Looks like you have a saboteur in your organization," Trevor said.

"Possibly," Harding said. His eyes were watchful, his features expressionless. He wasn't about to toss one of his administrators under the bus, so Ellen did it for him.

"I believe you should look to Samuel Moore as your source. He has issues with the Jamieson family and I know him to be vindictive."

Harding studied her, but gave no indication of his thoughts. "I will look into the matter and if Samuel had anything to do with starting the rumor, I'll ensure he knows it's wrong and must not continue."

Ellen gave him a steely-eyed look and a stiff nod.

Christy said, "Thank you, I'd appreciate that. Now, can you tell us about who we will be interviewing and how the interviews will be arranged?"

Still looking unhappy, Harding nodded. "Ten of my faculty were at the gala. I've broken the interviews into two groups based on the schedules of those involved. Our first meeting will be with Lana Drabble, Lewis Barber, Gibson Jessup, and Yves Peltier. The second includes Paige Moran, Monique McGrath, Hal Wilkinson and..." He hesitated. "Samuel Moore. Per your e-mail yesterday, I scratched both Jackson Hargreaves and Declan West." He scanned their faces. "May I ask why you're not interested in meeting with those two individuals?"

"Quinn and I ran into Declan West on Saturday and chatted. I think we found out all he had to tell us," Christy said. "Roy knows Jackson Hargreaves through a professional association they both belong to. They also spoke on Saturday."

Harding nodded. "All right. I've asked the first group to be at the conference room at ten o'clock. You can meet with them one at a time or we can do a round table with all of them at once. The choice is yours."

Christy looked from Quinn to Ellen, then at Roy and Trevor. Each gave her a nod. The decision was hers. "Let's try the roundtable process. We're not here to accuse anyone, we're looking for information. Discussing the evening together may help to trigger memories, or it will expose inconsistencies."

Harding nodded. "In that case, I'll give you a quick rundown on the background of the individuals in the first group before we begin." He rose, going over to his desk where he picked up a stack of printed papers.

As he handed her a copy, Christy saw it was a list of the eight professors and a their position in the college's hierarchy. He added information verbally. "Lana Drabble is a professor of voice in the music department. She's been with the college for seven years and sings with one of the city's best choirs. Lewis Barber is also part of the music department. He coordinates the instrument training program. He's been incredibly supportive of the At Risk students and developed the rock music component for the program."

"The instrumental program focuses on classical training?" Quinn asked.

Harding nodded. "The current chair, Samuel Moore, believes the rigors of classical training enable students to function in a symphony orchestra or a rock group."

"Interesting philosophy," Roy said. "I guess that's why he did such a good job singing SledgeHammer songs at the gala."

Harding shot him a quick, skeptical look. Roy returned it with one of innocent candor. The PGC president went back to his introductions. "Yves Peltier teaches guitar. He worked closely with Lewis designing the instruction plan for the At Risk students." Harding paused and smiled faintly. "Although he's a talented guitarist and quite comfortable in the classical mode, I think he prefers teaching the students rock and pop." He indicated the sheet of paper, pointing to the last name in the first group. "The final person is Gibson Jessup, chair of theater arts. He was the master of ceremonies for the evening, so his whereabouts are well documented. I'm not sure how much he'll be able to tell you."

"I believe I met Gibson at the reception after Quinn's talk," Christy said. "He seemed to be an observant man. I'm sure he'll be able to add information."

"Good," Harding said. He glanced at his watch. "We'd best make our way to the conference room."

The conference room was down the hall from the executive offices. Like the president's office, the outside wall was mainly glass and it was obvious the architect had designed the space to take advantage of the view. For a moment, Christy allowed herself to soak in the cloudless blue sky, the sun glinting off the water of English Bay, and the cluster towers that was downtown Vancouver shining against the looming backdrop of the North Shore mountains.

A minute later she turned away to study the room. A large rectangular table dominated the center of the spacious area. It seated at least a dozen people on either side. Was it better for her and the others to gather at the end, or to take one side of the table, leaving the PGC professors to face them on the other side, she wondered? And if they spread themselves out along one side, which side would be the more effective in providing them the dominant position?

Not sure, she moved deeper into the room as the others followed her in. Suddenly, the overhead lights came on, startling her.

Harding noticed her reaction and said with a small smile, "The lights are programmed. They come on when people enter the room. There's an automatic shut off, but as long as there's movement they remain on."

The huge bank of windows allowed so much light in that she hadn't noticed the overheads were off. She turned to Harding. "Is there a way we can shut off the lights, so they aren't on during the interviews?"

He frowned. "Yes, but why?"

She gestured to the others. "My team and I will sit along the far side of the table, with our backs to the windows. We'll have your staff sit opposite us."

"You want your faces in shadow and theirs in the light from the windows," he said slowly. "You're putting them at a disadvantage."

Christy smiled.

"It also means they'll be looking at the view, which is a more welcoming backdrop, and less intimidating than having a blank wall behind us," Quinn said. The approval in his voice added to Christy's confidence and brightened her smile.

"Well," said Harding. "Where do you want me?"

"At the head of the table," Christy said immediately. "I'd like them to see you as they come in, and for you to make eye contact with each of them."

At that, one side of Harding's mouth shifted up into a half smile. "I was wrong. This isn't a job interview. This is a tribunal."

"And so it should be," Ellen said briskly. "This unfortunate situation has gone on far too long. It is time we tidied it up."

Harding raised his brows at her choice of words.

She ignored him. "I think you should sit in the middle, Christy, with Trevor on your right and Quinn on your left. I'll be on Quinn's other side, closest to the door."

"What about me?" Roy asked.

Christy tried to imagine how she would feel if she walked into this room and saw the five of them arranged on one side of the long table. Christy, in the center, the presiding judge, Trevor the legal expert on one side, Quinn the professional interviewer on the other. Beside him, Ellen quietly writing down the words they spoke. And Roy?

She smiled at him. "You're our wild card, Roy. You're between Trevor and Craig and your job is unnerve anyone who seems to be hiding something."

His eyes lit up. "Awesome."

They settled into their places and Craig switched off the overhead lights.

Lana Drabble was the first to arrive. She was a large woman who sported a worried frown. She cast an apprehensive look at Christy's group as she paused at the end of the table, hovering uncertainly. "Hi, Craig. Am I late? I'm sorry I'm late. I didn't mean to be."

"You're fine, Lana," he said in a soothing voice. "In fact, you're the first to arrive, so I'd say you're early. Why don't you sit over here?" He gestured to the empty side of the table.

She nodded, then cautiously moved to a chair opposite Ellen. As she reached to pull it out, Ellen shot her a haughty look designed to intimidate. Lana gulped and found a seat further down the table, opposite Trevor.

After Harding introduced everyone, she said on a rush, "I don't know why I'm here. I don't think there's anything I can tell you."

"We hope talking about the evening will help us pinpoint where everyone was and what they were doing," Christy said. She had her hands clasped in front of her on the tabletop, aiming for a judicial, but not threatening appearance.

Lana shook her head. "I don't know…"

The arrival of a second instructor had her drifting silent. Yves Peltier, the guitar prof, was medium height, with flowing dark hair casually styled and swirling to his shoulders. He sat down beside Lana, opposite Christy. As the introductions were made, he shot Christy a wide smile that was just shy of flirtatious. Christy blinked. She hadn't expected this.

Lana said, "They want to talk to us, Yves. They think we know something about who killed Karen."

Peltier turned the smile on Lana, but he shrugged in a dismissive way. "Maybe we do."

Lana's shoulders twitched and her frown deepened. "I didn't hurt Karen and I don't know who did!"

"Then there's nothing for you to worry about, is there?" Peltier said. He sounded bored. Evidently, the practiced smile was more automatic than purposeful.

Gibson Jessup bustled in at that point and forestalled anything Lana might have responded. He looked around the room, smiling when he saw Christy, Roy, and Quinn. "Hello. Nice to see you again," he said affably. Christy introduced Ellen and Trevor. He nodded as he sat opposite Quinn, then asked, "What's this all about?"

The final person, who must be Lewis Barber, rushed into the room, glancing at his watch. "Right on time," he said. "Not a minute early, not a minute late. Morning, Craig." He looked pointedly at

Christy and the others. Harding introduced them. He nodded and pulled out the chair beside Jessup. Like Lana he said, "I don't know anything."

Ellen shot him her disapproving look, but unlike Lana he didn't budge. Trevor said, "Why don't you sit beside Ms. Drabble, Mr. Barber?"

When he hesitated, frowning and evidently trying to figure out why he was being positioned further up the table, Harding said, "If you would, Lewis." He slowly pushed the chair back against the table, then reluctantly went to his assigned seat.

When he was settled, Christy smiled at them all. "Thank you for coming this morning. What I'm going to ask you to do is to tell us where you were on the evening of the gala, from the time when the musical event broke up to the end of Lightening Rod's set. We'd also like to know who you remember seeing, where they were and when you saw them. I'll begin and you can chime in with your own personal details." She looked at each of them and received grudging nods in return.

"I was with Quinn during the musical entertainment. We had seats near the rear, but it still took us a while to exit the room. When we reached the foyer, I saw Karen Beaumont talking to Samuel Moore. As we made our way through the crowd to the staircase, I saw you, Craig, talking to Mitch Crosier."

"And his wife, Kim," Harding said following her lead and joining in. "As I recollect, she slipped away while Mitch Crosier was telling me about his latest business model."

"Cross platform entertainment?" Roy asked.

Harding raised his brows and nodded. "Yes. How did you know?"

Roy grinned. "He's given me the same talk."

"Do you know where Kim went?" Christy asked.

"Is she a pretty blonde?" Barber asked. When Christy nodded, he said, "She came into the dining room while we were taking down the set. She talked to the students. Seemed particularly interested in Korby Usher. He was the student who was supposed to sing the lead roll until Sam took over."

Quinn glanced at Christy. "How long did she stay?" he asked.

"Quite a while. She even tried to help with the clearance until Monique put her foot down and chased her away. I'm not sure where she went after that."

"How long were you in the dining room, Mr. Barber?" Christy asked.

"Till we finished the clean up. Then I went downstairs, got a drink, and went into the ballroom. The band was about to start."

"I followed Karen into the dining room after she finished talking to Samuel. I wanted to talk to her about how the evening had turned out, but she didn't have time for me," Yves said. He nodded at Barber. "You were there, Lew. Sure, she praised Usher, she had to! After all, he should've been the star of the evening, but I knew she'd done nothing to Samuel. She didn't even chew him out."

"You were angry," Quinn said.

"Yeah, I was." Peltier shrugged, apparently to minimize the anger he'd admitted to.

What was it, Christy wondered, about guitarists? Did they all come with specially equipped with flirtatious natures and built-in cool?

"I left Karen giving her pep talk to the rest of the students and went downstairs. I got a drink and I saw Declan West at the bar. We shot the breeze for awhile, then I went to the ballroom to watch the band."

Being at the end of the row, Jessup leaned forward so he could see the faces of the other PGC staff. He was smiling. "I, of course, was the master of ceremonies for the evening. Once the musical entertainment was over, I made my way down to the ballroom where I conferred with the band—made sure there were no changes from the plans we'd made earlier, checked that everything was on time, that sort of thing. Then I used the washroom. I was going out when Declan West went in. I saw you, Lana, before I went back into the ballroom. You were going into the ladies. I said hello, remember?"

She flushed, as if talking about the bathroom made her uncomfortable. Then she nodded in an agitated way. "Yes, I do. You waved as you went back into the ballroom. A little while later I saw Samuel and said hello to him."

"When was that, Lana?" Christy asked.

She swallowed and frowned. "After I finished in the washroom, when I was on my way to the ballroom. I think he was coming out of the bathroom. It was before the band started to play." She looked around eagerly. "He has such a lovely voice, doesn't he? I thought the way he handled the SledgeHammer songs was magnificent. So much better than how the group does them."

"Not my preference," Roy said suddenly. He was leaning back in his chair, watching Lana with a disapproving expression.

Christy wondered if he saw something she didn't, or if he was truly just stating his preference.

Lana straightened, surprised. She frowned as she shot Roy a sideways look, evidently uncertain how to respond.

Christy supposed it wasn't unexpected that a voice teacher would prefer Moore's operatic style to Sledge's rough-edged sexy, but she wondered if there was more to Lana's gushing approval than that. "What did Samuel say when you spoke to him?"

She seemed relieved to be able to focus on Christy. "We said hello. I went into the ballroom and lost track of him."

Ellen, who had been writing furiously, paused to study her, then she wrote more notes.

"Did any of you see Karen Beaumont on the lower floor, in the ballroom or the lounge, perhaps?" Trevor asked.

They all looked at each other, then shook their heads.

"I last saw her in the dining room," Peltier said. Lewis Barber nodded in agreement.

"I saw her go into the dining room, but I didn't see her leave it," Harding said. "I assumed she must have gone out onto the terrace, then used the stairs to the garden to get down to the lower level. I was surprised when she didn't come into the ballroom."

Lana sniffed. "I didn't notice her and I didn't care where she was. I didn't have a lot of respect for her as an administrator. Imagine, appointing Celene Warden as her associate dean! The woman ran the publishing program before she was promoted. She wasn't even part of the music and drama community."

"Who do you think Karen should have made Associate Dean?" Harding asked.

"Why, Samuel Moore, of course. He's a fabulous chair and he knows everybody in the business."

Jessup moved uneasily in his seat and Barber said cautiously, "Sam tends to be rather traditional in his approach to music—"

"Well, of course!" Lana said, looking shocked. "He understands the need for discipline and excellence."

Barber said, "I think Karen was moving into a more pop and rock focus. There are only so many positions in symphonies and operatic companies. Musicians these days need to be versatile. That's what Karen was going for."

Yves Peltier nodded. "Totally agree. I think she was pushing in the right direction, too."

"Well," Lana said indignantly, "I don't agree. Karen was wrong."

"Perhaps you'd like to have that discussion with the new dean when he or she is hired," Harding said. "Right now, is there anything else any of you can tell us about that evening?"

They looked each other again and heads were shaken.

"Thank you very much for participating," Christy said. "We appreciate your help."

One by one the four PGC staff members nodded, murmured good-bye and filed out.

When they were gone, Harding said, "Has this helped?"

Ellen was reading over her notes, a little frown on her forehead.

"Do you see something, Ellen?" Christy asked.

"I'm not sure," she said slowly. "I want to put my notes in order, and then maybe it will become clear."

Harding glanced at his watch. "You have an hour before the next group arrives. You are welcome to stay here and work. I have a meeting, but my assistant will help you if you need anything." With that he nodded, rose to his feet, and headed out.

Christy thought he looked relieved.

CHAPTER 23

S ledge guided the Lamborghini through the entrance to the underground parking at the West Georgia office tower where Mitch Crosier's offices for his entertainment empire were lodged.

The Lambo wasn't a really a practical car to get around in—his little Ford subcompact would have been a better choice in Vancouver's congested downtown—but when he drove the Lambo he was Sledge of SledgeHammer and he needed to remember that today as he visited the one man in his musical world who could make him feel the way his father had when he was a misbehaving teenager.

He was Sledge of SledgeHammer, damn it, rock hero, guitar god. He needed to remember that.

Man, I love this car.

Now that dim artificial lighting had replaced the brilliant blue sky, and the walls of the parking lot were closed around them, the cat had curled on the seat beside him. Until then he'd been standing on his hind legs, front paws on the dashboard, gaze glued to the street scene around them. Sledge figured that the Lambo probably meant a lot to Frank too, reminding him that he was Frank Jamieson, the Jamieson heir, the Jamieson bad boy whose good looks, charm, and silver spoon had doomed him to an early death.

He found a parking spot and cut the engine. "This needs to be quick and targeted."

Mitch can't hear me.

"I know. He thinks I'm here to talk to him about the future of SledgeHammer." He glanced down at the cat, and found Stormy watching him with bright inquisitive eyes. "He's going to want answers and I don't have much to give him."

Why didn't we wait until tonight and visit him at home?

Sledge opened the door, pleased as always the way the scissor doors opened upwards instead of the traditional out. That buoyed him and reminded him, again, that he was Sledge of SledgeHammer, a power in his world.

Take that Mitch Crosier.

The cat followed him across the seat and hopped out. He closed the door and locked the car. Together they stood for a moment, studying the vehicle.

He heard a heartfelt a mental sigh. *Man, it's gorgeous.*

Sledge nodded. The cat was right. He turned for the exit and the elevator that would take them up to Crosier's twentieth floor suite.

Sledge of SledgeHammer. Remember that.

He carried the cat in the elevator—Frank said Stormy was scared by the technology and didn't like the sounds rumbling around the tiny box or the smells of the many humans who crowded into it when the elevator paused on the main floor. So he held the cat snuggly in his arms and stroked him as they ascended—and enjoyed the consternation of the office drones who cast him scandalized sideways looks and edged as far away from him as possible.

Though he didn't see any cameras taking videos or grabbing pictures, he'd bet this stunt would be all over the internet before he got to Mitch's office.

Sledge of SledgeHammer carried his cat around with him in crowded elevators. Who knew? The world would be agog.

Fine with him.

By the time the elevator doors opened on Mitch's floor, he'd regained his swagger.

Mitch's company had the whole floor, so Sledge stepped out into the reception area. A four-foot high desk stretched across a good portion of the space. On the wall behind, the company's name and logo was six feet high and nine wide. When you exited the elevator you immediately knew where you were and if you'd stepped off at the wrong floor, you'd be able to hop back in without annoying anyone with your unneeded presence.

Sledge put Stormy down and wished he could slink back on to the elevator like some unwanted intruder. Since he couldn't, he sauntered over to the reception desk and smiled at the highly polished young woman who sat there. She smiled back, a spider drawing unwitting star wannabes into the Crosier World cross platform entertainment web.

"I have an appointment with Mitch." He didn't bother to introduce himself. If the babe didn't know who he was, she wasn't worth the money Crosier was paying her.

Her smile didn't dim. "I'll tell him you're here."

Pick the cat up. I want to see.

Sledge stared at the woman who was murmuring into a headpiece, and wondered what she'd do if he plunked the cat onto the raised top of her reception desk. Freak? Take it all in stride? Raise her brows in disdain?

It looked like he was about to find out.

By the time he bent to pick up Stormy she'd finished her call and as he straightened he found she was eying him quizzically. Her eyes widened as he put the cat on the desk. Then she sneezed. Once, then again.

Horrified, he grabbed Stormy, who was stretching luxuriously as he looked around the area from his elevated position. "You're allergic?"

Hey!

She nodded. He put Stormy on the floor and rubbed the top of the desk with his sleeve to eliminate all evidence of the cat's existence.

She bestowed an approving smile on him as she stood. "Come with me. Mitch will see you soon."

He followed her across the plush carpet, then down a corridor and the cat followed him.

That was rude.

He resisted the urge to reply. He was already flustered enough. He didn't want this poised, polished woman hearing him talking to himself.

Mitch's office was its own solar system inside the Crosier World galaxy of offices. The interconnected suite was guarded by a secretary and she was as polished and poised as the receptionist. She sat at a huge walnut desk, remarkably old-fashioned for Mitch's modern occupation. But then, the whole room was a throwback, with dark wood paneling on the walls and hand-knotted carpets in jewel tones on the floor. On the gleaming dark surface of the desk there was a computer, a single piece of paper— something the woman was apparently working on—a telephone console, a lamp, an in-out box and nothing else, not even a pen or a paper clip.

The receptionist hovered in the doorway as he strolled into the office, trying hard to remember he was Sledge of SledgeHammer. She murmured his name and that he was here to see Mitch. The woman at the desk didn't even look away from her computer as she said, "His assistant will see you in a moment. Please take a seat."

Her message came through loud and clear. Rock heroes were a dime a dozen at Crosier World. Remember your place and be good.

The door shut quietly behind the receptionist. He didn't bother to try to soften up Mitch's secretary with his flirtatious desk perch and practiced smile. This one wouldn't buy into it. She'd been around for years, and he'd already tried. All that would happen was that she would look down her nose at him and request that he remove himself from her desk. He knew. It had happened before. He wasn't going to obey her command to sit down, though, so he sauntered over to one of the wood paneled walls where SledgeHammer's latest platinum album hung.

It was a reminder. He was Sledge of SledgeHammer. Remember that.

I only heard that album a few times.

The album had come out last spring, not long before Frank Jamieson disappeared and Sledge heard wistfulness in the voice. "It wasn't my favorite."

Which one is?

He grinned. "Our first. It was raw and loud and not as polished as the ones we did later, but it was us, alive and caring and real." He pointed to the albums displayed on the wall. "You won't find it here. It didn't do really well, but it got us started and proved that we had something the audience wanted."

I remember that album and the tour that went with it. Fantastic.

"Thanks, man." He turned around to find that the secretary, who had never paid a second's worth of attention to him on any of his many visits here, was staring at him with a pronounced frown on her face. He swallowed and wondered why his crewnecked silk sweater felt like it was strangling him. Resisting the urge to pull at the neckline, he grinned and winked at the secretary. She turned back to her computer and he breathed a sigh of relief.

Mitch's executive assistant, yet another poised and polished woman, a notch older than the secretary, opened the door and invited him into her inner sanctum. "Mitch has allotted you fifteen minutes.

He will be discussing—what is that disgusting animal doing here? Karina, where did this creature come from?"

The secretary swiveled her chair. She pointed to Sledge. "He brought it."

I'm not an it. I'm a he.

"The beast will have to go."

No way.

Sledge didn't say anything as he waited for them to figure out that if the cat went, so did he. For the first time that morning he was enjoying himself.

The two women looked at each other. The assistant cleared her throat. "Reception?"

"Shannon's allergic."

"Mitch knows the cat. He'll be fine," Sledge said. "Shall we go in?" Taking charge, he strode over to the final door that led to the inner sanctum and opened it. Stormy dashed past him, tail high, intent on getting through it first. The executive assistant made a little sound of protest, then hustled behind.

Mitch's office was at least the size of the other two combined, and perhaps more. A wall of windows behind his desk showed a view of the North Shore Mountains and the cities of North and West Vancouver crawling up their massive slopes. White fluffy clouds floated above the tops of Grouse and Seymour mountains and hovered over the city of North Vancouver, but to the west he saw heavy grey storm clouds coming in off the water and he suspected that his house in West Van, perched on the shoulders of Cyprus Mountain, would soon be engulfed in rain.

Mitch's desk was dominated by a computer, which was set up in the middle of the surface so Mitch could hide behind the big screen if he wanted to avoid eye contact. Now he looked over it and frowned, as if he wasn't expecting this interruption. "Sledge." The frown deepened, became more real. "You brought your cat."

Sledge grinned. "You remember Stormy the Cat, don't you, Mitch?"

Stormy leapt up onto the desk, then walked around the big screen and butted Mitch's hand, which hovered over the keyboard. *How's Kimmy?*

Crosier absently scratched him behind the ears. "This is Armstrong's cat."

I am not! Nobody—

"Not really. Nobody owns him."

Mitch tickled Stormy under the chin and he started to purr. "Nice cat. Kim liked him. She asks if I've seen him, sometimes." His frown turned to bemusement. "She says we should get a cat."

It wouldn't be me.

Mitch's mind, which always travelled in Mitch-centric ways, found the inevitable direction. His expression brightened. "If the cat's a stray, I could take it home. It would make Kim happy—"

Stormy went from a purr to batting Mitch's hand away, claws out. *No way!*

Sledge almost laughed. "The cat's chosen Christy Jamieson and her kid, Noelle, as his people. He just visits with the rest of us."

Remember that, music mogul, and we'll get along just fine.

Mitch sighed and looked wistfully at Stormy. "When are you and Hammer going to ditch that second rate replacement for Vince and get a proper manager?"

Sledge sat down in a chair on the other side of Mitch's desk. "Hammer was traumatized by Vince's death and the way his brother was treated. He needed time away."

"He's had it." Mitch stroked Stormy's back. The cat crouched on the desk and let him do it.

"Some of it," Sledge agreed. "He'll be back when he's ready."

"Your fans won't wait forever," Mitch said. Stormy started to purr.

"They'll wait until the new year when Hammer says he'll be back in Vancouver. Until then, I'm not bothering him with business stuff."

Mitch eyed him. "Will you be ready to get back to work then?"

In other words, would he have a collection of songs available and ready to be recorded? The answer to that was easy. He grinned. "We'll have an album that will rock your socks off."

Stormy rolled on his side to give Mitch access to his belly. *We've been writing songs together. They're great.*

Mitch obliged, his fingers working absently. Stormy purred louder. "SledgeHammer needs promo." He waved his hand and Stormy's eyes popped open as he stopped purring. He meowed and Mitch looked guilty and began rubbing again. "Not this negative stuff about the woman's death at the gala, but something positive."

"I may be going to Hollywood."

Mitch's eyes gleamed. "Movie?"

Sledge shook his head. "Replacement sub-in for a judge on one of the network singing competitions."

Mitch stared thoughtfully at Sledge while he considered that. "Could work. You're good-looking and you have a way about you in front of the camera." He narrowed his eyes. "You'd have to be nice to the contestants, especially the wimps. Give them caring advice. Sound like you mean it. People like that." He nodded to himself, apparently pleased by this sage advice. "Play it right and you have thirteen weeks of positive media attention." His eyes glazed as he considered details. "Social media posts. Lots of pics with you and the contestants. Funny, but not mean, situations. Rueful, you're having fun, but you're a little surprised that everyone likes you so much."

Crosier would go on like this for the rest of their fifteen minutes if he let him. "Great ideas, but like you said, we need to get the negative stuff from the gala out of the way."

Mitch blinked, caught off guard by the change in subject. "Right." He nodded.

"We need to know where everyone was that evening after the end of the musical."

"Are you trying to solve this thing?" Mitch asked incredulously.

Sledge opened his eyes wide. "Someone has to."

"Like the cops."

"Or me. So where were you?"

Mitch shook his head, then shrugged, playing along. "Kim and I came out of the dining room into the foyer. We talked to a few people. I was chatting with Craig Harding about opportunities for his students when Kim went off to look at the building's architecture." He'd given up stroking Stormy and the cat had sat up and was now industriously cleaning a front paw. Mitch waved his hand. "She loves interior design, you know. All that kind of stuff. Harding and I went down to the ballroom together. She followed us a while later."

"Did she say anything?"

Mitch frowned. "About what?"

"About Karen Beaumont? Or anything she'd seen?"

"No."

"When did you last see Karen Beaumont?"

"She was talking to one of the PGC administrators. The guy who sang." He shook his head. "Nice voice. No market, though."

Sledge didn't care about markets for Samuel Moore's musical talents. "That was it? You didn't see Beaumont again?"

Mitch shook his head.

The cat jumped down from the desk. *We're done here. Time to go.*

Sledge nodded, relieved. The interview had gone more smoothly than he expected.

CHAPTER 24

"Who's in our next group?" Trevor asked as the door shut behind Craig Harding.

Ellen inspected her notes. "Paige Moran, who is..." She moved papers around. "She's the coordinator of music writing. There's also Monique McGrath, the woman who seems to have been in charge of the musical; Samuel Moore, who, as the chair of music, is their boss; and Roy's friend, Harold Wilkinson. He's the chair of creative writing."

"Hal isn't a bad guy," Roy said, leaning forward and resting his elbows on the table. "The stuff he writes is a combination of visual and words, and sometimes it can be pretty strange. Unlike Jackson Hargreaves, he's been writing and publishing steadily while he teaches. He loves the graphic novel form, and he was upset that Beaumont was thinking of cancelling his course."

"His term as chair is almost over. He can reapply for the position, but if he doesn't get it, he has to go back to being a professor," Quinn said.

"And if his course was cancelled, he'd have to teach the basics, like

Jackson Hargreaves." Roy sat back, his expression thoughtful. "I know he wasn't happy about that."

"And if he refused to teach the basics, would he be out of a job?" Trevor asked.

Roy nodded. "From the way he and Jackson were talking when I saw them at Quinn's reception, that seems to be the case."

Trevor pursed his lips and rubbed his hand across his chin. "Not liking your job is a thin motive for murder."

"And who's to say the person hired to replace Beaumont as dean won't do exactly the same thing she had planned," Quinn said.

"Roy saw him in the ballroom before the band started, and clapping for Samuel Moore at the end, but nobody noticed him in between, so we'd better confirm where he was," Christy said.

The others nodded.

"I think among all of the people we're seeing today, Monique McGrath is the key," Ellen said. "Unless someone saw Karen later, the last time anyone noticed her was when she walked out of the dining room onto the terrace. After that she seems to vanish." She tapped her papers. "Since she died from the fall from the terrace and then down the stairs, it must have happened after the dining room was emptied, or one of the people clearing out the room would have heard voices, or a scuffle, or a cry as she fell."

"And so far no one admits hearing anything," Christy said.

Ellen nodded. "If she fell after Lightening Rod began to play it's unlikely anyone in the ballroom would have heard a cry. And with the rooms on the main floor empty, there was no one to hear people talking on the terrace, even if they were arguing or shouting at each other."

"Jackson Hargreaves was in the ballroom, arguing with his wife, about halfway through the performance," Quinn said. "They went up to the terrace to finish their fight in private, but they didn't see Karen Beaumont there. That means she must already have been dead."

"Let's focus on Monique McGrath, then," Christy said.

The door opened and Harding's assistant entered. She was carrying a coffee urn and was followed by another woman holding a tray with cups and a plate of pastries. "We thought you'd like some refreshments," she said as they set the items down in the center of the table. "The sweet rolls were made by students in our baking program at the Yaletown campus. We do hope you enjoy them. Craig will be back in a few minutes. I'm sure the others won't be far behind."

Roy's eyes gleamed. As the two women left the room he reached for a fruit stuffed Danish. "This is great. I didn't have breakfast."

They did enjoy the pastries and while they ate the case was forgotten. They were just finishing off when Craig Harding and Samuel Moore walked into the conference room together. Moore was saying earnestly, "Celene is trying very hard, but her inexperience in the entertainment industry is showing. She doesn't understand the importance of connections and professional respect. She needs to—"

He broke off as Harding nodded and said, "I think we should discuss this later, Samuel." He smiled and indicated the group. "I don't think you know everybody." He introduced each of them.

"Of course I know Christy Jamieson and Quinn Armstrong," Moore said. He held out his hand to each of them, beaming with apparent pleasure. "And Roy Armstrong. I love your books."

He showed no interest in Trevor, but when he would have done the same to Ellen, she forestalled him. "It has been many years, Samuel, but I think you will remember me."

He stared at her unblinking for a few moments, his face expressionless, then he smiled broadly. "I do. Frank spoke of you often."

Ellen raised her brows. "I had no idea teenaged boys were so interested in the previous generation. I expect he was complaining about me."

Samuel laughed. "No, of course not. He was always very complimentary."

Christy shifted in her seat. She knew this was a complete fabrication and she wondered why he'd said it. She glanced at Ellen. Her gaze was fixed on Samuel, and her expression was cool. When she said, "Kind of you to say so," her tone was dry and that aloof expression didn't change. Christy wondered what she was thinking.

Samuel ran a hand through his thick, dark hair. A lock fell over his forehead, accentuating his deep-set brown eyes and perfect cheekbones. He looked around, those dark eyes bright and apparently unconcerned by Ellen's unspoken hostility. "Craig tells me you're here to try to discover who killed Karen Beaumont."

Christy smiled at him. "We're here to find out where everyone was after the musical performance ended."

Moore returned the smile, showing gleaming white teeth. "I went downstairs get a drink."

"Is there anyone who can confirm your whereabouts?" Christy asked.

He shrugged. "The bartender, I suppose." He snapped his fingers. "Oh, and Lana Drabble. I saw her as I was coming out of the washroom a while later."

Since this fit with what Lana Drabble had told them, Christy said, "We know that earlier in the evening you spoke to Karen Beaumont in the foyer. Can you tell us what that was about?"

He smiled. "She was complimenting me for my performance." The smile dimmed. "Karen was always incredibly supportive of me. With her practical experience in the entertainment industry, she was such an asset to our school." He shook his head. "I miss her guidance every day. Celene...Well, Celene tries hard, but she is no Karen Beaumont, as I was telling Craig when we came in."

Ellen put her pen down and clasped her hands together over her pieces of paper. "Karen wasn't criticizing you?" she asked.

He raised his brows in surprise. "No, what would make you think that?"

"Not everyone who saw you talking to her thought she was happy with you."

He waved a hand airily. "I don't know who said that, or why, but they misinterpreted. Karen loved my work. She was never anything but positive about it."

"Did you see her again that evening?" Christy asked.

He shook his head. "No." His expression turned reflective. "How interesting. You know, now that I think about it, I was hoping she'd join me when I went to speak to Sledge, but she wasn't around." His eyes widened. "I guess she must have been dead by then. Oh, how awful!"

At that point the other witnesses began to arrive. A tall, slim woman with thin blond hair scraped back from her face in tight bun was introduced as Paige Moran, the coordinator of music writing. After the introductions over, she cast a wary glance at Moore, who was her boss, and said "Hi, Samuel."

He nodded at her, smiling affably. "Paige. I hope you'll be able to help these good people."

Paige swallowed and nodded. "I'll try, of course."

Harold Wilkinson sauntered in at that point. "Roy Armstrong! Are you part of this amateur detection gang?" He looked around, saw Quinn and said, "I can't say I'm surprised about your boy, here, since he's a reporter. But you?"

"I've got a new series coming out," Roy said. "Mystery fiction. This is research."

"Really? How's it going?"

"The first book in the series will be out for Christmas," Roy said.

Wilkinson nodded. "November launch? Or will it be December?"

The arrival of a dark-haired woman Christy recognized from the gala cut the conversation short. "Hi," she said. "I'm Monique McGrath. Terrible thing about Karen. I hope this helps you guys find her killer."

Moore said, "Don't you have a class coming up, Monique?"

She shot him a cautious glance, but nodded, and said, "In about fifteen minutes." Her brows knit in a frown when he smiled warmly at her.

He turned to Harding. "Since I've told our guests everything I can, why don't I head off? I can babysit Monique's class until she's available."

From his place at the head of the table, Harding said, "Your call, Christy."

Monique's mouth had tightened as Moore made his offer, suggesting she didn't want him interfering in her class. Christy had noticed, too, the cautious way Paige Morin had greeted him. Both women worked for him. It would be best if they didn't have to worry about speaking frankly in front of him. "Fine with me," she said.

Harding nodded agreement and Samuel Moore rose, wished them luck again and left, strolling without any hurry. Christy turned to the three remaining people and went through the patter she'd used with the first group, talking about where she and Quinn had been, then asking for input from them.

"I was with Monique helping to clear the dining room," Paige said.

Monique nodded. "The students were the core of our work crew, but we had lots of help. It didn't take long, even though we had...visitors."

"Like Karen Beaumont," Christy said, watching her closely.

Paige looked at Monique and nodded. Monique's mouth had tightened again, and she too nodded. "Karen came in to talk to Korby Usher, the boy who was supposed to sing the lead roll."

"How did she seem?" Quinn asked.

"How do you think?" Monique snapped. "The gala was supposed to be a showcase for the At Risk students. Instead, a department chair takes over the premier roll in the musical. How does that showcase the students?" She shook her head. "Mitch Crosier was there that night.

This was a huge opportunity for the kids, and Samuel screwed it up for them. Karen was upset."

Quinn raised his brows. "We were told that she complimented him when they spoke in the foyer."

"I doubt it," Monique said.

"People who saw them talking said he was smiling. That doesn't sound like she was criticizing him."

Paige's face screwed up into a frown. "Samuel loves to perform. Maybe Karen was being tactful and he misunderstood?"

"Or maybe she wasn't criticizing him at all," Hal said. "Look, Karen Beaumont liked Sam Moore. We all do. She thought he had a terrific voice. I remember her excitement when she hired him. Samuel Moore, who could have been an operatic star if his family hadn't been loaded and haughty with it. What an asset to the college!" He shook his head. "She wasn't about to criticize him for showing off his talents."

"What did Karen do after she spoke to the student?" Christy asked.

Monique shrugged. "She said she needed some air and went out onto the terrace."

"I didn't see her again after that," Paige said.

Monique said, "I didn't either."

"What did you do after the dining room was cleared?"

"I went downstairs," Paige said. "I met Lana Drabble in the bathroom and we talked a little. Then I went into the ballroom."

"Did you see Karen again that evening?"

She shook her head.

"Monique?"

"I supervised the loading of the van and made sure the kids knew they had to take it back to the college that night. Then I went down to the ballroom."

"When was that?"

"I got there just after Lightening Rod began to play."

"At any point, did you hear anything unusual or see anyone you didn't think should be where they were?" Quinn asked.

"I didn't see anyone around, but..." She looked away as she hesitated. Then she looked back at Quinn. "After I saw the van off, and I came back inside, I looked into the dining room to make sure we hadn't missed anything. The room was empty, but I thought I heard voices on the terrace."

"Did you catch what was being said?"

She shook her head. "Gibson Jessup had just introduced the band and there was clapping. It was difficult to make out the words. When the band started to play, their music drowned out everything else. I wasn't interested in listening in on a private conversation anyway, so I continued on my way to the ballroom."

Though he nodded, Quinn dug deeper. "So you don't know who the people were?"

Again, she hesitated. "Though I couldn't make out the words, I'm pretty sure it was a man and a woman talking. Because Karen had gone out to the terrace earlier and I hadn't seen her come back inside, I assumed she was talking to Declan West."

"Declan West?" Christy said sharply. "Why?"

"The woman's voice sounded angry. If it was Karen's, then I figured the man was Declan." Monique shrugged. "They have a history."

"Did you see anyone when you reached the lower level?" Christy asked.

"Not until I went into the ballroom, which was packed. I had to stand at the back."

"How about you, Hal?" Roy asked. "See or hear anything interesting?"

"I went downstairs with everyone else and found a table," Hal said. "Then I got a drink—with everyone else, I might add—and sat down to enjoy the show. I didn't notice anything special until Jackson showed up and had a fight with his wife."

"When was that?"

He thought back. "About midway through the set, I suppose."

Monique glanced at her watch. "Is that everything? It was kind of Samuel to offer to babysit my class, but I'd like to get going. I don't want impose on him. I'm sure he has other things he should be doing."

Christy nodded. "I think so." She looked around the table. "Thank you all. You've been most helpful."

CHAPTER 25

To reach the Crosier home, Sledge had to drive his impractical power car through the congestion of downtown, across a bridge, then through the busy areas of Kitsilano, Shaughnessy, and Kerrisdale. It was a long traffic-filled drive. He didn't know how Mitch managed the commute every day.

Well, that wasn't precisely true. He did know. Mitch had a luxury car and a driver who handled the traffic while he worked from the back seat. But still, it was a long way from home to work. That said, when they reached the Crosier estate in the quiet oasis south of Marine Drive, he understood the draw of the big house, the manicured lawns and gardens, the gate that provided privacy and made the whole place a sanctuary. To top it off, this was where Kim, the domestic goddess, held sway. It would be a good place to come home to at the end of a tiring day.

He held the cat in his arms as he rang the doorbell. Frank had told him he and Kim were on the same wavelength. He figured she'd be more interested in talking to the cat than him, so he shelved his ego and put the cat front and center.

Kim Crosier herself opened the door. Sledge knew there was a security person somewhere because a male voice had responded when he buzzed and then opened the gates for him. He suspected there was also a housekeeper in the background doing the cleaning, but Kim apparently did the cooking, if her apron and the flour on her nose were any indication. Her expression was polite, but not particularly welcoming—until she saw the cat. Then pleasure leapt into her eyes and her whole body seemed to come alive.

"Hi," he said. "I think Mitch called to let you know I was coming over."

She dragged her gaze away from Stormy and frowned at him. He wasn't sure if she knew who he was, so he added, "Sledge? Of Sledge-Hammer? I need to talk to you about the At Risk Gala a few weeks ago."

She blinked and opened the door wider. Gesturing, she said, "Come on in."

"Thanks." Once inside, he put Stormy on the ground.

The cat twined around Kim's ankles, then he looked up, green eyes demanding. *Pick me up.*

Kim giggled and did as asked. "Sweet kitty," she said, stroking the cat's back. To Sledge she said, "Come into the kitchen. I'm baking cinnamon rolls for Mitch's afternoon coffee break."

The kitchen was enormous, which was a good thing, because there were at least eight bowls with puffy dough inside them aligned along the counters. There were also bowls with what appeared to be a cinnamon-sugar mixture, and a stack of pans waiting to be used. He peered at one of the bowls filled with dough as Kim put the cat on the ground then went to wash her hands. "You seem to be making a lot of cinnamon buns."

"Eight dozen," she said absently. She took one of the bowls over to the central island and dumped it onto the granite surface. She pulled the dough into a square, then reached for a rolling pin which she used to flatten it into a thin sheet.

Sledge sat on one of the tall chairs on the other side of the island. The cat leapt up onto another and sat with just his eyes and nose peeping over the countertop. "Mitch sure must like cinnamon buns."

Kim laughed. "He does, but so does his staff. When I send over baking for him I like to include everyone. His secretary says this is the best job she's ever had."

Surprised, Sledge asked, "How often do you bake for Crosier World?"

She shot him a mischievous look. "Once, maybe twice a week. It depends on my schedule."

"Wow." A domestic goddess indeed.

Apparently satisfied with her rectangle, she slathered it with butter, then took one of the small bowls with the cinnamon-sugar mixture and shook it over the dough. That done, she lifted the long side of the rectangle and began to roll the dough into a log. "You wanted to talk to me about the gala."

We're trying to solve the murder.

She didn't look up from her dough rolling. "Shouldn't the police be doing that?"

"Well, yes," Sledge said. "But they're slow. Anything we can learn will help speed up the whole process."

Kim's busy hands stilled for a moment, then she finished the task, producing a perfectly rolled log. She looked from Sledge to the cat, then back to Sledge. "You can hear him too?"

Of course.

Sledge grinned. "It comes as a bit of a shock, doesn't it?"

Kim picked up a knife and began to cut the log into chunks. "Mitch can't hear him. Why can you? Why can I?"

I speak. Not everybody listens.

Kim took a minute to consider that statement as she finished slicing the log, then she nodded. "True enough. People see what they want to see and judge in a way that fits into their world." She positioned the sections into one of the pans, close together so that each piece touched the others. After covering the pan, she set it aside and began the process all over again.

"Mitch told us that after the musical entertainment ended you and he went out into the foyer to mingle."

She nodded. "We chatted with a few people, then Mitch started talking to Craig Harding about opportunities for the At Risk kids. I tuned it out." She smiled faintly. "I've heard it before."

Mitch said you went wandering. He said you were looking at the architecture for design ideas.

She had a dough rectangle again, nicely coated with butter, and was pouring cinnamon on it. "I was, but not for decorating ideas. I appreciate the craftsmanship you find in these old houses. Design elements like the ornate plaster medallions on the ceilings that were made by an artist who worked with his hands to create something beautiful, not a pre-fab, factory made replica."

"The students were still pulling down the stage and backdrop when you went into the dining room," Sledge said.

"They were about halfway through." She rubbed her forehead with her sleeve, then got to work rolling the dough rectangle into a log. "I offered to help, but that professor, what was her name? McGrath, maybe? Anyway, she thanked me and said they had plenty of help. I talked to some of the students for a bit, but it distracted them, so I decided to leave them to it." She finished the roll and began to cut. A smile tickled her lips. "I snuck past Mitch and Craig Harding as I went over to the drawing room. Mitch never noticed, but I think Craig saw me. I put my finger to my mouth to ask for his silence and he smiled, just a bit. He didn't say anything to Mitch, though, so I think he got the message."

Was there anyone in the drawing room?

"No." Another set of rolls ended up snuggled together in a pan. She set to work on the third batch of dough. "There was someone on the terrace, though."

Sledge exchanged a look with the cat. "Karen Beaumont?"

"I think so," Kim said.

"Was she alone?"

"Then," Kim said, flattening the dough into a rectangle. "I hung around in the drawing room for a while, until the foyer was empty and I guessed Mitch and Craig had gone down to the ballroom." With the rectangle now ready she reached for the butter. "I was about to go when I heard angry voices out on the terrace."

What did you do?

She paused in her construction to look at Sledge and the cat. Her expression was amused. "I went to look, of course."

"You must have seen the murderer," Sledge said.

For a moment she didn't move, then her face crumpled and she put a hand to her mouth in a gesture of consternation. "Oh, no. Are you sure?"

"The timing is right," Sledge said.

Tell us what you saw.

For the first time, Kim's hands were still as she spoke. "There was a woman and a man. The woman, Karen Beaumont—I'm pretty sure it was her, because she had such a striking gown—had her back to the balustrade. The man was larger than she was. He was standing close to her, but not in a friendly way. They were arguing, if tone of voice was any indication."

Fascinated, Sledge said, "Do you know what the argument was about?"

She nodded. "He was furious that she'd told him off in the foyer. She said he deserved it, that he knew all the entertainments at the gala were designed to showcase the students. She said he shouldn't have participated in the musical, even if he did have the best voice in the college. He said she didn't understand the arts, that she didn't have his back, and that she didn't deserve to be dean. She laughed at that, and he told her it was time to move on."

She swallowed hard. "I thought the same thing. I didn't want to be part of their bickering." Tears flooded her eyes and trickled down her cheeks. "If I'd wandered onto the terrace and made a stupid comment about the weather, she'd probably be alive today. I never thought...I could hear the band start to play and I just slipped away, then went down to the ballroom so I could dance with my husband."

The cat stood up on his hind legs and put his front paws on the edge of the countertop, careful to stay away from the bakery area. *You didn't know.*

Kim dashed the tears from her eyes. "No I didn't, but I do now." Her jaw had hardened. "Mitch's buns may be late. I need to talk to the police. Who is the detective in charge?"

"Patterson," Sledge said. "But you said the man complained Beaumont had chewed him out for taking over for one of the students. So the man with her was Samuel Moore?"

"If that was the name of the dark-haired fellow she was talking to in the foyer, then, yes, it was."

Samuel Moore? Sammy Moore the two-faced, lying bastard who is your friend until he isn't? The guy who promises much and delivers nothing? The so-called friend who stabs you in the back and tells you it's for your own good?

This was more than Sledge had ever heard the cat say all at once. He stared down at the furious green eyes and said, "You know him?"

I went to high school with him, for a while. Why didn't you tell me he was at the gala?

"I didn't know you knew him."

Well, I did.

The cat was very still now, only the tip of his tail twitching with suppressed energy.

Is Sammy one of the people Chris is interviewing today?

"I think so."

We need to get to the college. In a burst of energy the cat leapt down from the chair and bolted through the house to the front door. *What are you waiting for?*

"But—" Sledge looked helplessly at Kim. He didn't want to leave her alone to deal with the realization that she might have stopped Karen Beaumont's killer.

Kim didn't even consider the eight batches of dough waiting to be turned into succulent buns. She threw her apron onto the work surface and marched out of her kitchen. "Yes, what are we waiting for? Let's go nail this sorry excuse for a human being."

CHAPTER 26

"Well? Now what?" Craig Harding asked after Monique, Hal, and Paige left the room.

"I think we have enough information to pinpoint when the murder took place," Christy said.

She looked around the table at the others and got nods in response. "After the scene from the musical was over the audience left the dining room, including Karen. Monique, Paige, and others, stayed to help the students pack up the stage and backdrops. In the foyer, Karen was seen talking to Samuel Moore, then she returned to the dining room where she spoke to the students, particularly Korby Usher, who had been sidelined by Moore. After that, she went out onto the terrace. The work to clear the dining room continued and Kim Crosier visited for a few minutes before she crossed the foyer to the drawing room. The students and the instructors packed everything into a college van, which then departed. Monique went back into the building, took a quick look around the dining room to make sure they hadn't missed anything, and heard two people arguing on the terrace. She pinpointed the time as being when Gibson Jessup introduced Lightening Rod and the band began to play." She looked around the room. "The question is, who were those two people?"

"Monique thought they were Karen Beaumont and Declan West because the male voice sounded angry," Roy said. "But Declan West puts himself down in the lower level, at the bar, and later in the washroom, around that time. Gibson Jessup confirms that."

"Yves Peltier is out," Trevor said. "He puts himself in the bar with Declan West. That can be confirmed by West or by the bartender."

Roy leaned forward. "Hal Wilkinson says he was in the ballroom and bar about the same time as everyone else. There's anonymity in a crowd, but there may be enough people who know him who saw him standing in line to buy a drink or finding his table in the ballroom."

"I can do that," Harding said. "I saw him come into the ballroom a few minutes before Gibson made his introductions. He was holding a glass in his hand. He sat at a table with Phyllis Hargreaves. When Jackson came down, he and Phyllis started fighting. Hal looked relieved when the Hargreaves left."

"So that eliminates Hal," Roy said. He shrugged. "I'm not surprised. Takes a lot to kill someone. Worrying about your favorite course being cancelled doesn't read as a motive for murder."

Harding frowned. "What course was that?"

Roy raised his brows. "The one Hal taught before he became a chair."

"The graphic novels course?"

Roy nodded.

Sounding surprised, Harding said, "That course isn't being cancelled. Karen was going to work with Hal to revamp the whole curriculum for the creative writing program. She intended to suggest the graphic novels course be rewritten, then delivered as an optional course, but no decisions had been made."

Roy shrugged. "Maybe someone should tell Hal that. He seems to think the course is going to be chopped, no exceptions."

"Gossip and speculation," Harding said. There was annoyance in his voice.

"Has there been a lot of that recently?" Quinn asked.

Christy looked at him. He was staring intently at Harding, as if willing him to consider the question deeply. She sensed he had found a link, one he thought was important. She too turned to scrutinize the president.

For his part, Harding was staring right back at Quinn, but his eyes were narrowed and his brows lowered as if he was deep in thought. Slowly he nodded. "Yeah, there has been. Karen was embraced by the School of Entertainment Arts when she first came onboard. There was a lot of positivity and her chairs all claimed to love working for her. About two years later people started grousing. I was the VPA—vice president academic—at that time and I remember being surprised by some of the complaints. The worst was that she didn't understand the creative arts. Ridiculous! She was starting to make modifications to the school about that time—she'd developed the publishing program and it had just begun to accept students. I put the complaints down to people being unsettled by change."

"But the complaints continued," Quinn said.

Harding nodded. "They never stopped. Karen was tough. She said they were tame compared to some of the stuff leveled against her when she was in the film business. But it amounted to a whispering campaign and no matter how I tried to track it down I couldn't find the source."

"Someone wanted her job," Quinn said.

Harding stared at him for a moment, then nodded. "Yeah. Yeah, you're probably right. Do you think this is tied into her murder?"

"I do."

"Spill," Roy said to his son. "Don't keep us in suspense."

A small smile lifted the corner of Quinn's mouth. "I'll start from the beginning. After the dining room cleared, Karen went out to the foyer where she was seen talking to Samuel Moore. They were standing near the front door, in a corner of the room. Moore's back was to the wall, so he was looking toward the crowd. Karen was standing facing the wall, meaning that those who noticed them talking only saw her from behind. Moore was smiling, but her expression was obscured. I think that's important."

"Why?" Harding asked.

"Because assumptions were made. Most people thought Karen was praising Moore for his lovely singing voice, but a few didn't. What if those few were right? What if he was smiling so people didn't know he was being royally chewed out? That would mean Karen kept her back to the room because she didn't want donors like Christy to see there was a problem."

"So why dress him down at the gala?" Roy asked. "Why not wait until the next day and haul him over the carpet in her office?"

"I can answer that," Harding said. "Because she wanted to make sure he knew that what he'd done was not acceptable. Karen didn't wait around. She made a decision and she acted. I have to admit that at the time I was surprised Samuel seemed so cheerful about their conversation. I knew she was annoyed and I expected her to reprimand him."

Trevor rubbed his chin. His gaze was far away. He must have been visualizing the action that night, linking the interpretations with what he'd seen and experienced. "Interesting theory. Fits with what comes next, I think."

Quinn nodded. "When she finishes with Moore, she goes into the dining room to talk to the students, but basically to apologize to Korby Usher for having his opportunity stolen from him. Then she goes out onto the terrace to give herself a few minutes of privacy to fume, then calm down. While she's out there alone, Moore finds her. They argue and she falls to her death."

"Moore!" Roy said. He was frowning impatiently. "Can't be. No one saw him go into either the dining room or the drawing room after the show."

"There are doors to the garden in the ballroom. He could have slipped out before the band started and used one of the side staircases to go up to the terrace," Harding said.

Trevor shook his head. "If he went into the ballroom, Sledge would have seen him, but he didn't."

"I think he did use one of the outside staircases, but he didn't leave the building from the ballroom. He went out the front door. Remember, people remark on seeing him talking to Karen Beaumont, but no one noticed him afterward," Quinn said. "She'd given him a dressing down in front of an audience of important people. He was angry, furious probably, but he couldn't allow anyone to see, so he slipped out the open door into the darkness."

Roy nodded. He had a dreamy look in his eyes, as if he was imagining the scene in his mind. "There are a few people outside smoking, but he doesn't want to talk, so he starts walking, pretending he's exploring the grounds, getting some air. While everyone else is drifting down to the ballroom, he walks around the house and finds one of the paths that wind through the gardens. It brings him to the staircase up to the terrace. He knows he can get back into the house from the terrace so he goes up the staircase."

"And finds Karen Beaumont there," Quinn added, nodding. "She's dealing with her own residue of anger and when she sees Moore she's ready for a confrontation."

"But he has an alibi. He was down on the ballroom level at that time. Lana Drabble saw him coming out of the bathroom when Gibson Jessup was introducing the band," Christy said.

"No, she didn't." Ellen had been shuffling papers and reviewing her notes while the others discussed. Now she put both hands on the stack of fine letterhead and said with considerable authority, "She can't have seen him, because he wasn't in the washroom."

Everyone shifted in their chairs to stare at her. She stared back, nodding. "When Christy and Quinn interviewed Declan West he stated he was in the washroom, but he had no one who could vouch for his being there. Don't you think that if Samuel Moore had been in the washroom at the same time that West would have said so? Instead, he said quite specifically that he was alone in the washroom."

"We need to talk to Lana Drabble again," Trevor said.

Harding was already on his phone. "Lana, are you free? Can you come up to the conference room? Yes, right now. Good. Thanks." He hung up. "She'll be here in a minute."

While they waited, they decided Harding should be the one to question her. He was her boss and if she was lying, he had the right to find out.

Lana looked worried as entered the room. "Is there something you needed?"

"Sit down, Lana," Harding said. He indicated the chair opposite Roy, who smiled at her.

She looked warily from Roy to Harding as she pulled out the chair and sat down. She swallowed nervously.

"Some of the testimony you gave us conflicts with what others have told us about that evening." Harding didn't look or sound angry, but his expression could certainly have been described as stern.

Lana caught her upper lip between her teeth then pinched her mouth into a worried expression. "Like what?"

She's not surprised, Christy thought. She glanced at Quinn. He was watching Lana with narrowed eyes. He was thinking the same thing.

"You told us you spoke to Samuel Moore when he came out of the washroom." Harding raised his eyebrows. "But you didn't, did you? Because Samuel didn't come out of the washroom at all."

Lana relaxed. She appeared to be relieved. "But he did. I know he did."

At that, Harding frowned. "How do you know?"

"Well, he told me, of course."

"He told you? You didn't see him?"

"Well, no, not exactly. You see, I was thinking about going to the bar to get a drink before I went into the ballroom, so I was looking away from the bathrooms. I missed him completely. And then Gibson announced the band, and the PA system was so loud that I didn't hear Samuel say hello to me. It wasn't until later, just before he got up on stage for the SledgeHammer tribute, that he teased me about snubbing him. Well, I would never do that, would I? Of course not! He's my boss and such a lovely man. I just wasn't paying attention. As you can imagine, I was embarrassed. I apologized, but he was so gracious—as he always is."

"So to clarify, you did not see Samuel Moore come out of the washroom. Nor did you speak to him prior to Lightening Rod beginning. In fact, the first time you saw him was toward the end of their set."

She nodded. "Yes."

His mouth hard, the expression in his eyes one of suppressed anger, Harding turned to the others. "Anyone have anything else they want to ask?"

Quinn nodded. "Did you happen to notice where he'd come from?"

Lana glanced at him. "What do you mean?"

"He wasn't near you prior to the time he sought you out in the crowd. He must have come from somewhere."

Lana pursed her mouth and frowned thoughtfully. "I can't say specifically. People were moving around, visiting other tables, getting up to dance. In fact, when he put his hand on my shoulder to let me know he was there, I assumed he'd been sitting at another table and had come over to ask me to dance."

"But he didn't ask you to dance, did he?" Quinn asked gently.

Sadly, she shook her head.

"Where were you sitting? Maybe that will help us figure out where he came from." Christy tried for an encouraging tone that would keep Lana talking. The poor woman was clearly besotted with Moore. Reminding her that he hadn't shown any interest in her must have been painful.

Lana hesitated, then shrugged. "My table was toward the back, near the French doors that led out to the gardens." She smiled. "It wasn't very good for viewing the stage, but the room was so hot, it was a great spot, because there was a breeze, at least for part of the evening."

"The doors to the garden were open, then?" Quinn asked.

She shrugged. "I thought they were closed earlier, but I must have been mistaken."

She had nothing more to contribute. As the door closed behind her, Trevor said, "Lana Drabble is the innocent victim of a very smart man."

"You think Samuel Moore is the killer?" Harding asked.

Quinn nodded. "He lied about where he was. Trevor's right. He duped Lana and got her to cover for him. He had plenty of time to confront Karen on the terrace. Somehow during that confrontation, she fell over the edge of the balustrade, landed on the top of the garden stairs, and tumbled down them. Whether he deliberately pushed her, or the fall was an accident, I don't know. Nor do I know what exactly he did after she fell, but I believe at some point he went down from the terrace to the garden, checked her to see if she was alive or not, then went into the ballroom through the garden doors."

"I need to call Patterson," Christy said, pulling out her phone.

"Why would he kill her? Karen was one of his supporters." Harding sounded baffled.

Quinn shook his head. "I'm not sure, but I have a suspicion he's the one who is behind your whispering campaign."

"He was the one who started the rumor about the Jamieson Foundation," Ellen said. Her expression was grim.

"He wanted to be dean, but Beaumont was a lifer. She wasn't going to move on anytime soon. The only way he could get her job was to eliminate her," Roy said.

"So he started a whispering campaign against her, to force her to resign," Quinn said grimly. "When that didn't work, he killed her."

Harding sat very straight, his still, serious gaze fixed on Roy. "But I'm not going to appoint someone to the position. The job has to be posted. I can guarantee that we'll have dozens of candidates, both external and internal."

Roy leaned forward. "He's been buttering you up, trying to sound managerial, even judicial, when he talks about the division and the people in it. He was doing it when you walked into the room with him today. Remember? I heard him acting the same way at the end of the reception that followed Quinn's talk."

Christy's phone connected with Patterson's and she lost track of the conversation. "Hi. I'm at PGC's Point Grey campus. I've got important information. Can you meet me here?"

"I'm heading there now," Patterson said. "What's going on? I got a call from Kim Crosier, who says she and Sledge and your cat are on their way to the college and it's vital I meet them there."

"Sledge and Kim Crosier are coming here?" Christy said. The room stilled as everyone paused to listen. She looked at them all and shrugged as she made an I-don't-know-what-is-going-on face.

"Yup. Kim says she thinks she knows who the killer is." Patterson paused. "I don't suppose that's what you wanted to talk to me about."

"As it happens, Detective, it is. We'll meet you—" She broke off to look at Harding. "Where is Monique McGrath's classroom?"

"She's in the Student Union Theater. It's near the main entrance."

Christy repeated the information. "We'll meet you there, Detective."

CHAPTER 27

K im Crosier was a very scary person. Sledge was convinced of that as he wove the Lamborghini through congested traffic faster than was either safe or acceptable.

She was working her phone like a weapon, first calling Detective Patterson and telling her to meet them at the college, then ruthlessly tracking down Samuel Moore so they wouldn't lose time looking for him when they reached their destination. All the while, she stroked the cat, who was sitting on her lap in various positions to take advantage of her caresses and purring loudly.

Moore was apparently in the Student Union Theater, conveniently located near the doors that gave access to the main parking lot. After Sledge parked the Lambo, Kim led the way inside, uncaring of the smudge of flour on her nose. She carried the cat, who sat upright in her arms, watching everything curiously. At the theater, which they found without a problem, Sledge held the heavy door for Kim and the cat to pass through, then they were all inside.

The theater was a lovely room, not large by SledgeHammer standards—it probably sat seven hundred and fifty—but designed to be an intimate experience between the audience and the performers on the stage. The seats were arranged in a semi-circle, allowing the stage to jut into the audience. Blond wood had been used to create the stage, panel the walls and to craft the railing around the balcony. It gleamed in the dim light, providing the room with a lightness that was appealing. The entrance was to the left of the stage, rather than at the rear, so they found themselves very close to the action as they slipped into the room. They hovered just inside, taking stock, as the door slowly closed behind them.

On stage, a student was singing as they entered. Sledge saw Samuel Moore, who was standing in front of the kid, slash his hands in the air. The young man's voice faltered and died away.

"No, no, no!" Moore said. "You're flat and there's no depth to your voice." He started to sing, apparently to show the kid what he should strive to sound like.

Sledge thought the kid's voice had a quirky quality that added interest to a song that was a traditional favorite. Moore's voice might have depth and resonance, but to Sledge the student's artistry was real, while Moore's was polished, but artificial.

Standing near the two men, her hands on her hips, was an older woman. Sledge thought he'd met her before, though he couldn't place her. He assumed she was an instructor. Her lips were pursed and her forehead was knit in a tight frown. It didn't look like she approved of Moore's teaching methods. The rest of the class, about a dozen students, were seated in the audience in groups of two, three, or four.

Put me down.

Kim put the cat on the polished concrete floor. He crouched at her feet, only the tip of his tail moving.

Hey jerk!

Moore continued to sing.

Sledge squatted beside the cat and stroked his soft fur. He said in a low voice, "I don't think he can hear you."

Kim hunkered down too. "Will the kitty be able to reach him?"

Sledge glanced at the stage, then back to Kim. "I don't know. Some people seen to be immune to him." Kim raised her eyebrows. Sledge grinned. "Detective Patterson, for example."

"I'll keep that in mind," Kim said.

He will listen to me.

Although the group on the stage seemed unaware of the discussion, the students, especially those nearby, were beginning to look their way. Sledge scooped up the cat and went over to the first row of seats. He sat down, placing the cat on his lap. It would be easier to whisper into Stormy's ear from a seated position than crouching on the ground beside him. Besides, if someone else—like Patterson—came through the door behind them, they risked being slammed in the back, something he wasn't keen on.

Kim settled into the seat beside him. "What do we do now?" she asked in a low voice.

"We wait for Patterson to arrive," Sledge said.

No, we don't. I get that idiot Sammy Moore to listen to me.

"Go for it," Sledge said cheerfully. He was rather looking forward to watching Moore unravel because a voice in his head started talking to him, a voice he couldn't silence.

Moore finished the song, which sounded like a damned operatic aria to Sledge, and said to the student, "You do not have that vocal range—"

"As yet," the female instructor said.

Moore turned to her, a disdainful expression on his face. "Pardon me?"

"As yet," she said. "You don't put students down in my classroom."

Why not? It's what he does best.

Moore frowned. "We should not be having this discussion here and now. Make an appointment with my secretary and we can discuss it in my office."

Yeah, that's right. Cut her out from the crowd. Get her into a private space, then bully her into submission. Go for it, pal. It's just your style.

"I believe in transparency—which you do not," the woman said. She put her hands on her hips and widened her stance, straightening into a combative posture. "I want my students to know there's a right way and a wrong way to critique a performance and telling a talented artist like Chris that he doesn't have the vocal range is the wrong way!"

"But he doesn't have the range," Moore said. His tone was matter-of-fact and it was clear he thought the woman was making a great to-do over nothing. The student would never be best and so he wasn't worth wasting time over.

Just because your family's almost as rich as the Jamiesons doesn't mean you can use people then put them down. I'm on to you, Sammy Moore.

"He's young and he's still learning. He will have the range, eventually."

"But he doesn't now. Look, Monique, this is the first course you've taught for a good ten years. You need to work on your skills. I can arrange to get you into a basic instructor's class."

"You jerk—"

That's what I said!

Kim muffled a giggle with her hand.

Monique raged on. "My teaching skills are better than yours were before you cheated me out of the chair's position. You came into my department, you played up to me and told me what a great leader I was, then you convinced the rest of the department to vote for you when my term as chair came up for reelection."

"Honestly, Monique, you're getting paranoid."

No she's not. The cat jumped off Sledge's lap and ran for the stairs that led up to the stage. *That's what you do. You make promises you never plan to keep. You're friends with everyone, until you're not. You seek out people who can help you, until they can't. She's got you nailed, Sammy.*

Kim leaned over and said in Sledge's ear, "Do you know what happened between them in high school?"

"Not a clue," Sledge whispered back. He had a feeling there had been a lot more between Frank Jamieson and Samuel Moore than what had came out during the conversation in Kim's kitchen.

Monique shook her head. "No, I'm not. I've got you nailed, Samuel, and you know it."

Kim looked at Sledge, wide-eyed. Sledge shrugged. He didn't know if the woman's choice of words was because she could hear Frank, or simply a coincidence. Either way, it didn't look like Frank was getting through to his target, Samuel Moore.

The cat began to cross the stage, each step a slow careful stalk, his gaze fixed on his prey. Further down the row of seats Sledge and Kim were in, Sledge saw one of the students, a young woman, elbow the boy sitting beside her. She leaned close to him and whispered something in his ear. The boy nodded.

You made my teen years miserable, Sammy Moore. But you know that, don't you? And you don't care.

The girl jumped to her feet. "What did he do?" she burst out.

Everyone went silent. Except Frank.

Do you remember Bryan Greer, Sammy? The timid kid who would do anything to please you so you'd be his friend. The kid who did your math homework for you, so your grades would be good enough for you to be in the school musical?

Moore frowned. "What is going on here?"

The only problem was Bryan didn't make your homework look different than his and your teacher caught you out.

"You cheated?" the girl said. She sounded shocked.

"Oh, my," Kim whispered to Sledge, who had settled more comfortably in his seat. This was like going to an improv play that had veered off in an unexpected, but vastly entertaining, direction, and he was thoroughly enjoying himself.

"Are you talking to me?" Moore demanded, advancing across the stage in an aggressive way until he reached the edge where he looked down at the girl.

She gazed up at him without any appearance of concern. "Yeah. You cheated at math in high school."

Moore stiffened, then took a step back. "How do—I did not."

Sure he did. Only you told the teacher that you were doing Bryan's homework for him, and he was too faithful to you to disagree. You got him kicked out of the school.

The girl said, "That's horrible!"

Moore swallowed, but he said, "What are you talking about?"

We're talking about you, Samuel Moore! About grade eight, when you sold me out because I punched you in the face after Bryan was expelled and his dad grounded him for a year!

Samuel Moore touched his nose. The girl cheered.

Yeah, you can hear me now, can't you? You went to the principal and accused me of being a bully and said I used my name to intimidate the other kids. You got your pals to support you too, didn't you?

"That's not—" He broke off, swallowed again and looked around the stage, a desperate expression on his face.

Then that A-hole, Gerry Fisher, who was a friend of your dad's, supported you, not me, and I got expelled too! They sent me to boarding school, you know. Out in the middle of nowhere, on the other side of the country. A school for troubled youth that specialized in extreme outdoor activity. I hated it!

"Oh man," Sledge said.

"That wasn't my fault," Moore said.

Sure it was and now I'm finally going to take you down.

CHAPTER 28

T he heavy double doors to the theater were closed when the
Christy and the others arrived. She hesitated, wondering if it
was better to wait for Patterson here, or to go inside. Craig Harding
took the initiative and made the decision. He pushed one door wide
and secured it open.

From inside the theater a woman's voice said forcefully, "What is
with you, Samuel? This isn't about your past, it's about Christopher's
singing ability." She clapped her hands. "Let's focus here, people."

"Monique McGrath," Harding murmured. "Sounds like problems
in her class."

"I'll leave you to it, then," Moore's voice said hastily.

Running away, jerk? Typical. Can't stand the heat, can you?

Christy's eyes widened and looked at the others. "Sledge and Kim
must be inside. We should go in."

Harding frowned at her. "What makes you think that?"

Since she couldn't tell him that her late husband lived inside the
family cat, she shrugged. "Just a guess."

Samuel cleared his throat. "We'll conclude our conversation later."

No, we won't. We'll do it now. You think running away is going to stop me? Think again.

One by one, they slipped into the theater. Christy saw Sledge and Kim. She touched Quinn on the arm and nodded in their direction. Together they moved to the seats behind them. The others followed. Ellen, Trevor, and Roy found places behind Christy and Quinn. Craig Harding sat in the front row in the seat beside Kim.

The house lights were low, while the stage was bathed in light. The participants on the stage appeared to be oblivious to the watching audience. Christy leaned forward to whisper to Sledge, "How long have you been here?"

He half turned in his seat as he answered. "A while. Did you know that Frank was sent to boarding school because he punched a kid in the face?"

Christy nodded.

Sledge pointed to the stage. "That kid was Samuel Moore."

Christy stared. Sadness knotted her stomach and she had to work to keep a quaver out of her voice. "I never knew the other boy's name. Frank didn't talk about his childhood much. When he did, he was angry and bitter about it. I do know that being sent to boarding school ruined his relationship with Ellen. She was his guardian after his parents died, but instead of standing up for him, she let Gerry Fisher make the decisions. Frank resented that."

On stage, Moore was standing with his back to the door. Apparently, he wasn't aware that more people had arrived and were watching from the audience or that he was being stalked by the cat whose voice was sounding in his head. He stared at Monique McGrath, who was to his right. She was looking toward the audience where the rest of her students were seated. She too seemed unaware that more people had come into the room. Facing Moore and to Monique's right was a young man who must be Christopher, the student whose voice and singing technique was being critiqued. He had a direct view of the door, and from the expression on his face he'd seen Christy and the others slip in.

Monique McGrath said, "There's nothing to discuss, Samuel. Now I'd appreciate it if you would leave my classroom."

Moore made a move, as if to leave.

Stay.

He froze in place.

We have business to discuss.

The cat's statement seemed to cheer Moore. "What business? Math class was a long time ago. No one cares now."

"Math class? What on earth are you talking about?" Monique said impatiently. "What's got into you, Samuel?"

Murder.

Moore took a step back and ran into Stormy. The cat howled, then hissed.

Monique said, "There's a cat in the theater. Why is there a cat in the theater? What is going on?" The last was said on a rising note of frustration and impatience as she put her hands on her hips and looked around. Her gaze took in the expanded audience and caught on Craig Harding. "Craig, what are you doing—" She lifted her hands into the air and said, "Oh, this is impossible!"

"Whose murder?" said the young woman in the audience, who was still standing, enthralled by the action on stage.

"The cat just accused Moore of murder?" Quinn whispered in Christy's ear.

She nodded. "Looks like Frank plans to get Moore to confess." She frowned as she looked at Quinn. "Should we get him to wait until Patterson arrives?"

Quinn shot her a sardonic look. "Do you think we could?"

Trevor leaned forward from behind her. "If Moore confesses the people in this room can testify as to what he said. Most are disinterested parties, so his defense won't be able to claim a conspiracy against him."

Since Quinn was right, it was unlikely that they could stop Frank even if they wanted to, it was nice to know Trevor believed any confession Moore made would be admissible in court.

On the stage, the cat had retreated far enough away from Moore so he wouldn't be stepped on again if the man made another abrupt move, but Frank wasn't finished with his old nemesis yet.

The murder of Karen Beaumont. Remember her, Sammy boy? The woman you pretended to support? The one who chewed you out at the gala, after you decided to show off in front of the crowd of important donors? The one you didn't have any use for anymore?

Moore was looking around the stage now, his mouth tight, his eyes narrow. He was angry, and probably wanted the voice to stop, but he clearly didn't know where the attack was coming from, or why only he and apparently one of the students could hear the accusatory words.

The girl gasped. "Karen Beaumont? You killed the dean?"

"What are you talking about, Bethany?" After shooting the student an annoyed look, Monique McGrath shook her head. "Look, this has gone on long enough." She clapped her hands together. "Everybody, back to work. We have a scene to rehearse."

Moore took advantage of that. He headed off the stage.

Chicken.

His stride faltered, then he shook himself and went forward again.

The cat galloped after him, running between Monique's legs so she shrieked with surprise. "Someone corral that cat!"

"Easier said than done," Quinn murmured.

Sledge snorted. "We can't let Moore out of this room. I'm closest to the door. I'll tackle him if he tries to make a getaway," he said with considerable enthusiasm.

"Not necessary," Harding said. He stood, then strode to the edge of the stage. The action there, including Moore's getaway, halted.

"Monique, I'm sorry to interrupt your class, but an accusation has been put on the table and we need answers. Samuel, on the night of the gala did you have an argument with Karen Beaumont on the terrace?"

"No, of course not. What would we have to argue about?"

Sure you did. We have a witness.

"Were you on the terrace with her around the time Gibson Jessup was introducing Lightening Rod?" Harding demanded.

"No. I was in the washroom. Craig, we've been over this before. I spoke to Karen in the foyer, then I went down to the ballroom level where I used the washroom."

Liar.

"And you can prove that."

"You know I can. Craig, what is this all about?"

He was doing an excellent job of feigning innocent indignation, Christy thought, but his body was tense and his eyes wary. She caught a movement out of the corner of her eye and saw Patterson hovering in the doorway. Relief swept over her.

"Your proof is Lana Drabble's assertion that she saw you leaving the washroom, is it not?" Harding asked. He paralleled the stage to the steps and ran up them so that he and Moore were facing each other.

Moore nodded. "Exactly."

"But Lana doesn't remember seeing you. She remembers wanting a drink and wondering if she had time to get one before Lightening Rod began. She also remembers you coming up to her much later and telling her that you had said hello to her as you exited the washroom but she didn't notice you. That doesn't make her a witness and it doesn't mean you were where you said you were."

But someone else remembers seeing you on the terrace, someone who saw you hover over Karen Beaumont in a threatening way, who heard you tell her it was time for her to go. She was stopping you from getting what you wanted, wasn't she, Sammy? So you gave her a shove and over the edge she went.

"Who is talking?" Moore demanded. His voice rose on the question, and he looked around, his eyes glittering with growing panic.

Christy glanced at Patterson to see how she'd reacted to Moore's shout. The man was unraveling in front of them, but if he sounded too crazy, he'd be entitled to an insanity plea and Christy's gut was telling her that he had committed the murder with cold, clear-headed deliberation. It might have been a spontaneous act, but it wasn't an involuntary one. They'd reached a point where Frank had to stop.

Kim must have come to the same conclusion Christy had. She leapt to her feet and ran to the stage. "I am. I'm the one who saw you on the terrace with Karen Beaumont. I heard you threaten her."

Moore jumped on that. "Did you see me push her?"

Kim didn't answer.

"No, you didn't, because I didn't push her. She fell!" He stopped abruptly, as shocked by his admission as everyone else.

Except the cat wasn't buying it. *Sure she did. A convenient excuse. A lie.*

Patterson strode across to the stage and mounted the shallow flight of stairs. As she advanced on Moore, Harding stepped out of her way, allowing her to stop in front of Moore and look him in the eyes as she advised him of his rights.

He paled and shook his head, denial etched on his features.

Patterson said, "Mr. Moore, you stated that Karen Beaumont fell from the terrace. How did that happen?"

"She...I...I was on the terrace enjoying the view when she came through the French doors from dining room. She didn't see me at first, because I was at the other end. Then..." He shrugged. "When she noticed me, she came over to talk. We were chatting—it was very amicable!—then suddenly she stepped backward. I...I thought she was going to perch on top of the balustrade, but she overbalanced and, well, she fell."

"That balustrade is waist high," Kim said, her voice indignant. "What did she do? Try to hop up like a teenager planning to sit on a countertop?"

Patterson cut her a quick, quelling glance. "Mrs. Crosier, please." She raised her brows as she turned back to Moore. "But the lady has a point. The railing was designed to keep people from losing their balance and tumbling down a ten foot drop to the stairs below."

You pushed her, didn't you? You put your hand on her shoulder and you shoved her, didn't you?

"I...She had a way about her. She could be very aggressive when she wanted to be. She stepped toward me and poked her finger in my chest, like she was some kind of tough guy and I was a wimp. She told me she wasn't going anywhere. That she liked being a dean and she planned to stay in the job until she retired. She was fifty-four! I'd have to wait years!"

"That's what this was about? You wanted her job?" Harding said incredulously.

"I deserved it! I have a master's degree in music. What did she have? I don't think she even had a BA."

"She had a wealth of experience in the field. And, though she didn't advertise it, she was working on a master's in education." He shook his head, bewildered. "You killed her because you wanted her job."

"I didn't say I killed her," Moore said.

Patterson shot a sharp, quelling glance at Craig, then looked back at Moore. "What happened after she poked you in the chest and told you she had no intention of leaving the college?"

Moore shrugged. "I fended her off, of course."

"There was a struggle."

He shrugged again. "Of sorts. I had the right to defend myself."

Big, bad Sammy, afraid of a woman.

He reddened.

"How did you defend yourself?" Patterson asked, studying him.

He pulled himself together and the moment of betraying emotion was replaced with a fine theatrical display. "I wasn't afraid of her! I grabbed her arm to push it away and she stumbled backwards. I fell forward, against her, and she stepped back to the railing. She lost her balance and went over the edge." He swallowed hard. "That's the truth. That's how it happened."

"I don't think so," Patterson said. "You're taller and heavier than she was. If you landed on top of her, your body would have pinned her to the railing. She wouldn't have gone over the edge."

"She twisted away, trying to break my hold on her arm. She fell over the side."

"Did you let go of her arm?"

"No, I..."

His voice dwindled off. Into his guilty silence Patterson said, "If you were still holding on to her she wouldn't have gone over the side. Even if she did, and you lost your grip, her fall would have had less momentum. She would have been hurt, sure, but not fatally."

One lie after another. Keep trying, Sammy boy. Sooner or later you'll get it right.

"I didn't mean for her to die." The words were almost a whisper. His audience strained to hear, not willing to miss a syllable. "It was an accident."

"When did you let go of her arm?" Like Patterson's other questions, this one was matter-of-fact, not judgmental, almost as if they were having a conversation and she was merely curious.

"As she fell." Moore swallowed and his jaw worked. "She grabbed for me. I thought she was going to take us both down, so I..." He lifted his hands, palm outward. "I was protecting myself."

"You deliberately opened your hand and released her as she fell," Patterson said.

Moore nodded. "Yes, that's it. That's what happened. I had to or I would have fallen too."

"You could have saved her," Kim cried, her voice anguished. "You let her fall to her death."

"Samuel Moore, I am arresting you in the matter of the death of Karen Beaumont."

As Patterson hauled out her handcuffs, he stared at them in horror. "But this isn't right. I didn't kill her. She just died. That's all."

While Patterson snapped handcuffs on the babbling Moore, the cat sauntered over and sat in his careful way in front of him.

No one believes you, Sammy. No weaseling out of it this time. I told you I'd take you down, and I did.

Then he trotted over to the edge of the stage and leapt from there into Kim's arms.

Monique McGrath stared at her with astonishment. "That's your cat?"

CHAPTER 29

"No," Quinn said. "That's the Jamieson cat." He stood up and circled around the first row of seats to where Kim was standing just in front of the stage.

Stormy was limp in Kim's arms, his eyes slitted as he purred with pleasure at her stroking.

Quinn reached the cat. "I think I should take him now. He looks entirely too comfortable."

Kim raised her eyebrows, but when she looked down at the purring cat her mouth quirked in a rueful smile. "Maybe you should," she said and let him take Stormy into his arms.

Hey! I was enjoying that.

Christy raised her brows too. She guessed that Quinn disapproved of Frank cuddling with Kim, and that he worried how she, Christy, would feel about it, but there was no need. Still, his protectiveness gave her a warm glow that had her smiling despite the seriousness of all that had happened today.

Sledge abandoned his seat and wandered over to Kim and Quinn.

"No need to be uptight, mate. Kim and the cat were comforting each other."

"Seriously?" said Monique McGrath. She had her hands on her hips again and her expression was disapproving.

The others ignored her. Quinn sent Sledge a hard look and said, "Stormy is Christy's cat. He should be with family."

Roy decided to add himself to the fray. He joined the group, waving his phone. "Speaking of family—Kim, I called Mitch. He's on his way to pick you up." He turned to Sledge. "He said something about how he can maximize your TV exposure and he wants to discuss it with you. Know what he's talking about?"

Sledge's expression turned wary. "Mitch Crosier is on his way here?"

Monique advanced to the edge of the stage. "Mitch Crosier? The Mitch Crosier of Crosier World Music?"

Roy nodded.

"He's coming here? You're sure?"

Roy nodded again.

Monique turned decisively and marched over to Patterson. "I need my stage back. How long are you going to be?"

Patterson said coolly, "I'll be here as long as I need to be."

"Of course," said Craig Harding. "Monique—"

"Craig. Mitch Crosier! This is an opportunity for him to meet some of my most talented students, to hear them perform. We can't let this slip by!"

Is this woman crazy? Kim saw the murder. Mitch won't care about a bunch of students.

Samuel Moore chose that moment to once more take center stage. He raised his handcuffed hands to point at Kim. "She didn't see me kill Karen!"

Kim glanced at Quinn and Sledge, then she straightened and took a step forward. Her expression was militant. "What makes you think that?"

"You couldn't have. There was no one on the terrace when I pushed her—" He stopped abruptly when he realized what he'd just admitted. He paled and sucked in a deep, horrified breath.

"So it was more than just letting her fall," Patterson said, though she frowned.

As well she might. Moore's outburst was response to Frank's jibe, but Patterson couldn't hear the cat. Kim had covered it well, but Patterson had to be wondering why he suddenly started talking about the murder again. Christy hoped it could be argued that he was reacting to Kim's impassioned statement that he could have saved Karen Beaumont, but didn't. She did not want Moore to get away with an insanity plea, when he was a very sane, very cold-blooded killer.

He drew a deep breath. "I am not guilty of murder."

"Yes, he is," Kim said. She turned to Quinn and stroked Stormy. "Thank you, kitty."

"I didn't come expecting to make an arrest," Patterson said to Harding. "I've called for back up. I want to get this guy downtown, so I'll be out of your way as soon as I can."

"I'm not!" Moore said, raising his voice. "I didn't intend for any of this to happen."

"But it did," said Harding. "Samuel, surely you knew that even if Karen was no longer dean, her position would have to be advertised and you would have to apply for it. There would be no guarantee that you'd win the competition."

"I would have been the popular choice," Moore said. "People were already starting to realize she wasn't the best leader the division could have."

"People were already starting to realize...Samuel, are you the person responsible for the whispering campaign against her?" Harding asked.

Of course he was. That's his style. Make up dirt and let it fly. He's too chicken to complain to someone's face.

"What a ridiculous little man," Kim said. There was a curl to her pretty lips that could only be called a sneer.

Christy realized she was providing the vocal counterpoint to the cat's silent conversation and cheered silently. Kim was as anxious as she was to make sure Samuel Moore couldn't use an insanity plea to escape justice.

"How dare you! You don't know anything about the academic world. I should have been dean. Karen Beaumont didn't know what she was doing. She chose Celeste Winters as her associate dean, a woman who wasn't even from the artistic community. That's typical of her poor leadership."

"But I know this community," Harding said grimly. "Karen Beaumont was one of the best academic leaders I know. She will be greatly missed."

Through this exchange, Patterson was standing by Moore, but she was making no effort to hustle him away. Christy turned in her seat to whisper to Trevor, "Can Patterson use what he's saying?" She noticed Ellen surreptitiously wipe tears from her cheek and knew a family discussion would be needed. Frank had revealed a lot today, probably more than Ellen had ever imagined.

His arm still around Ellen's shoulder in a comforting hug, Trevor said, "She advised him of his rights so he knows he can ask for a lawyer at any time and that he shouldn't answer any questions without one present." He gestured to indicate the audience and those on the stage. "If it comes to a trial, his lawyer might try to have this information made inadmissible, but the detective has an incredible number of witnesses who will confirm that Moore spoke freely, without pressure to disclose. I think all of this can be used in the case against him."

Ellen sniffed and said, "Heavens, I wonder what he'll say next."

Trevor shook his head. "He shouldn't say anything at all."

What Moore might have said remained moot, because the back up Patterson had requested arrived in the form of two uniforms. They bustled into the theater, full of authority and intent.

Moore whitened.

"At last," said Monique McGrath. She made sweeping motions with her hands that had Patterson raising her brows before she turned to the uniformed officers to give them her instructions.

Quinn headed back to the seats. Kim, Sledge and his father followed him. He handed Stormy to Christy, then sat down.

"We need to talk," she muttered to the cat.

Stormy yawned. *I suppose.*

On the stage, Moore was once again sputtering protests that had absolutely no effect on the two policemen who were only interested in doing as ordered by their superior and taking him away.

As he disappeared out the door, Christy sighed. "It's finally over."

"Now maybe that awful woman, Joan Shively, will leave you alone," Ellen said. There was a thickness to her voice that confirmed Christy's earlier suspicion that she'd shed some tears.

At that, Trevor grinned. "I think we can make a strong argument that the woman is persecuting you, Christy, and to ask for your case to be closed, since it was initially opened because of a malicious tip."

About time.

She drew a deep breath. "That would be great." She turned to Ellen. "You and Frank and I need to talk. He revealed some things today...I don't think you realized how he felt at the time." Though he had told her of his years in boarding school, she hadn't understood how deeply he'd felt. Nor had he been open about why he'd ended up being sent away. He'd said casually that he'd gotten into a fight with another student, but not why. Or, indeed, how soon after his parents' death it had been.

Ellen nodded. "I trusted Gerry Fisher. I shouldn't have."

The cat glared at her. *Got that right.*

"Mind your mouth," Trevor said sharply, causing everyone to look at him.

"The cat's talking again, isn't he?" Quinn said.

Christy laughed. "Can you doubt it?"

FLEECE THE CAT

THE 9 LIVES COZY MYSTERY SERIES, BOOK SEVEN

"Mrs. Jamieson." Bonnie, the receptionist at the Jamieson Trust, sat ramrod straight, her complexion pale, her eyes wide. "The police are here. They were waiting when I arrived to open the office."

Christy Jamieson had some experience dealing with the police and it didn't include the kind of abject fear she saw in her receptionist's eyes. She frowned. "Did they say what they wanted? Or give you names?"

Bonnie gulped. "The woman was Detective Patterson. I knew her because she's been to the office before. The man said he was Detective Jones."

Christy nodded, even more confused by Bonnie's dismay. Patterson was a smart, methodical cop who tended to get her answers through thoughtful questions, not intimidation.

A man's voice, harsh and threatening, broke into the conversation. "I told you to alert me when she came in."

Bonnie's fear started to make sense. The voice must belong to Detective Jones, a man who seemed to have a very different investigative style than Patterson. Christy turned slowly to face him. "She has a

265

name and it is Mrs. Jamieson. Remember that and use it when addressing me or referring to me with my staff. I gather you are the policeman Bonnie mentioned."

Jones narrowed his eyes, but before he could speak, Patterson entered the reception area. "Good morning, Mrs. Jamieson. We would like to speak to you on a police matter."

Turning away from Jones, Christy allowed her haughty expression to relax into a smile. "Good morning, Detective Patterson. Of course I'll make time for you. If you'll join me in the conference room?"

She led the way, taking off her coat when they arrived and draping it on an unused chair. Then she sat down at the head of the long mahogany table, Patterson on her right, Jones on her left. Ignoring him, she turned to Patterson. "Now, Detective, how can I help you?"

"Do you know a Pamela Muir?" Patterson asked.

Christy raised her brows. "Yes, I do. However, there isn't much I can tell you about her."

Jones jabbed a finger at Christy, claiming her attention and making her jump. "Sure there is. She came here wanting to bust into your fancy Trust." He smiled rather nastily. "Afraid of losing your millions to some upstart, Ms. Jamieson?"

Patterson made an impatient sound that Jones ignored. Christy arched her brows and said coolly, "I assume you are referencing Ms. Muir's claim that my late husband, Frank, was the father of her son?"

Jones glared at her. Patterson said quietly, "We are. Can you tell us about it?"

Christy turned to Patterson with considerable relief. She didn't like men who thought women were there to be bullied. "Of course. She showed up here a couple of weeks ago and made her absurd claim. That was the first I had ever heard of my husband having an illegitimate son."

"You didn't believe her."

"Honestly? No, I didn't."

"Why?" Jones demanded. "Frank Jamieson had a bad reputation. There's no reason to believe the kid isn't his."

Christy wondered if he was being deliberately provocative, or if he was just a colossal jerk. "There is every reason to believe, Detective Jones. If Ms. Muir had said her son was five years old, or younger, I might have accepted her claim, but according to her, her son is thirteen, older than my daughter. My relationship with my husband deteriorated over the years, but in the beginning we were very close. I would have known. And," she added, emphasizing the word, "there is the absurdity of a woman who knows the father of her child is wealthy beyond her wildest dreams and does nothing about it." She made a small dismissive movement with her hand. "Please! If Frank was the boy's father, she would have been feasting on the Jamieson Trust from the day of his birth."

Jones narrowed her eyes at her answer.

Patterson asked, "Did you have a meeting with her last Wednesday morning?"

Christy nodded. "Yes. Pam was supposed to bring documentation proving her allegations, but she never arrived." She frowned at Patterson. "What is this all about, Detective?"

It was Jones who replied. He placed his hands on the table and half rose in his seat. Leaning forward, his face close to Christy's, he said, "Murder, Mrs. Jamieson. We're here to find Pam Muir's killer."

Available in Paperback and eBook from Your Favorite Bookstore or Online Retailer

ABOUT THE AUTHOR

The author of the 9 Lives Cozy Mystery Series, Louise Clark has been the adopted mom of a number of cats with big personalities. The feline who inspired Stormy, the cat in the 9 Lives books, dominated her household for twenty loving years. During that time he created a family pecking order that left Louise on top and her youngest child on the bottom (just below the guinea pig), regularly tried to eat all his sister's food (he was a very large cat), and learned the joys of travel through a cross continent road trip.

The 9 Lives Cozy Mystery Series—*The Cat Came Back, The Cat's Paw, Cat Got Your Tongue, Let Sleeping Cats Lie,* and *Cat Among the Fishes* —as well as the single title mystery, *A Recipe For Trouble,* are all set in her home town of Vancouver, British Columbia. For more information please sign up for her newsletter at http://eepurl.com/bomHNb. Or visit her at:

www.louiseclarkauthor.com

 facebook.com/louiseclarkauthor